OUT IN THE OPEN

First published in English in 2018
by SelfMadeHero
139–141 Pancras Road
London NW1 1UN
www.selfmadehero.com

Written by: Jesús Carrasco
Adapted by: Javi Rey
Translated from Spanish by Lawrence Schimel

Publishing Director: Emma Hayley
Sales & Marketing Manager: Sam Humphrey
Editorial & Production Manager: Guillaume Rater
Designer: Txabi Jones
UK Publicist: Paul Smith
US Publicist: Maya Bradford
With thanks to: Dan Lockwood

First published in Spanish by Editorial Planeta in 2016
© Editorial Planeta, 2016

A CIP record for this book is available from the British Library

ISBN: 978-1-910593-47-9

10 9 8 7 6 5 4 3 2 1

Printed and bound in Slovenia

OUT IN THE OPEN

Javi Rey   based on the novel by Jesús Carrasco

SELF MADE HERO

Thanks to the team at Planeta Cómic, and especially to my editor David Hernando, for his trust and support throughout the journey.

To Jesús Carrasco, for writing as he writes and, above all, for being who he is.

And to Marina, for her advice and patience.

- Javi Rey

The town was built on the bed of a broad gully down which water had flowed at some point. Now it was just a long hollow in the middle of an endless plain.

There was a time when that plain was a sea of grain. On windy spring days, the wheat undulated just like the surface of the ocean. Green and fragrant waves awaiting the summer sun. The same sun that now baked the clay, pulverising it until it turned into dust.

A strip of olive trees spread out along the north side of the old riverbed. A shortcut for soldiers back from the front. Wounded, but moving. In a march that had already lasted so long that no one could testify to any advance. They weren't witnesses of the passing of time; instead, it was time which owed its nature to them.

I

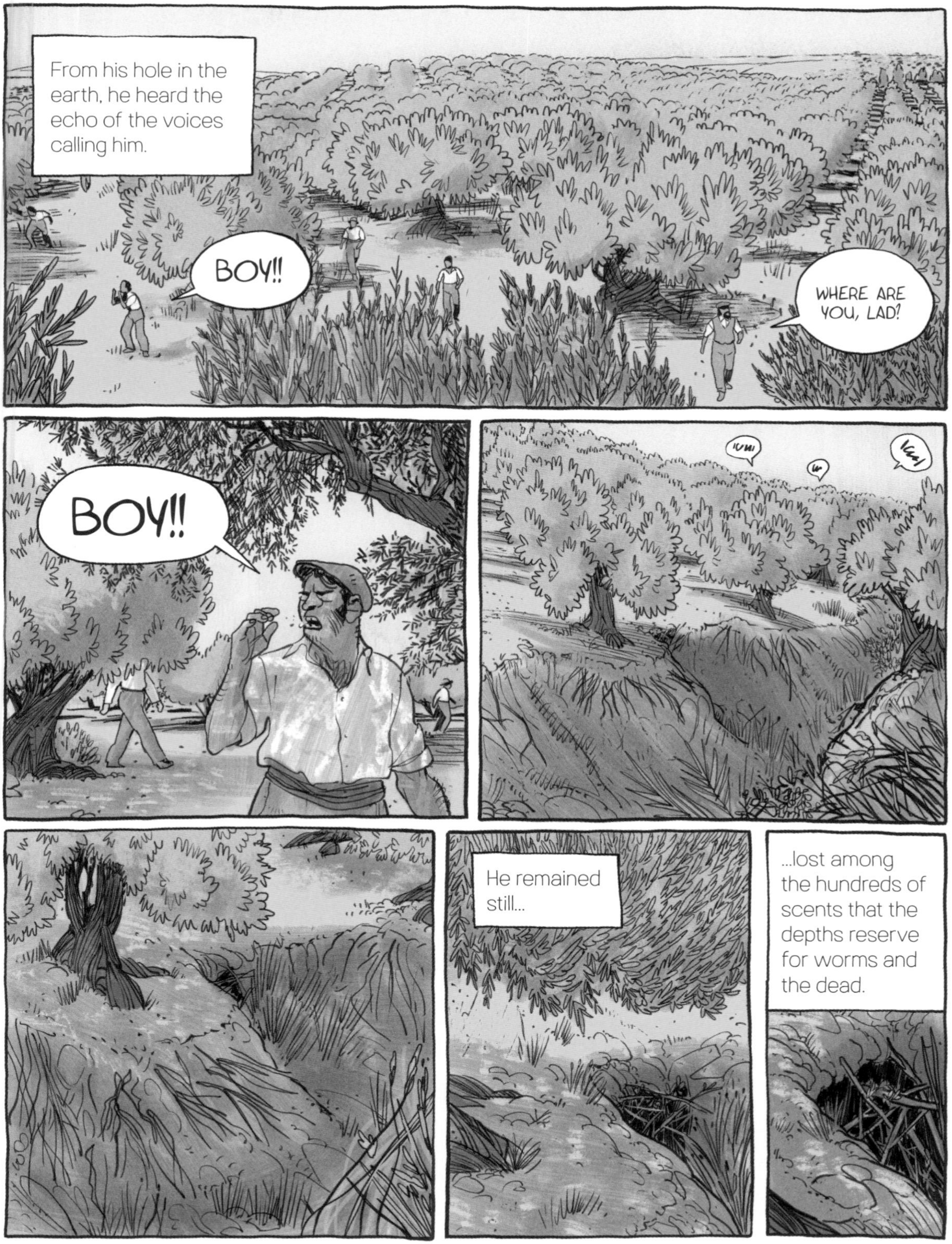
From his hole in the earth, he heard the echo of the voices calling him.
BOY!!
WHERE ARE YOU, LAD?
BOY!!
He remained still...
...lost among the hundreds of scents that the depths reserve for worms and the dead.

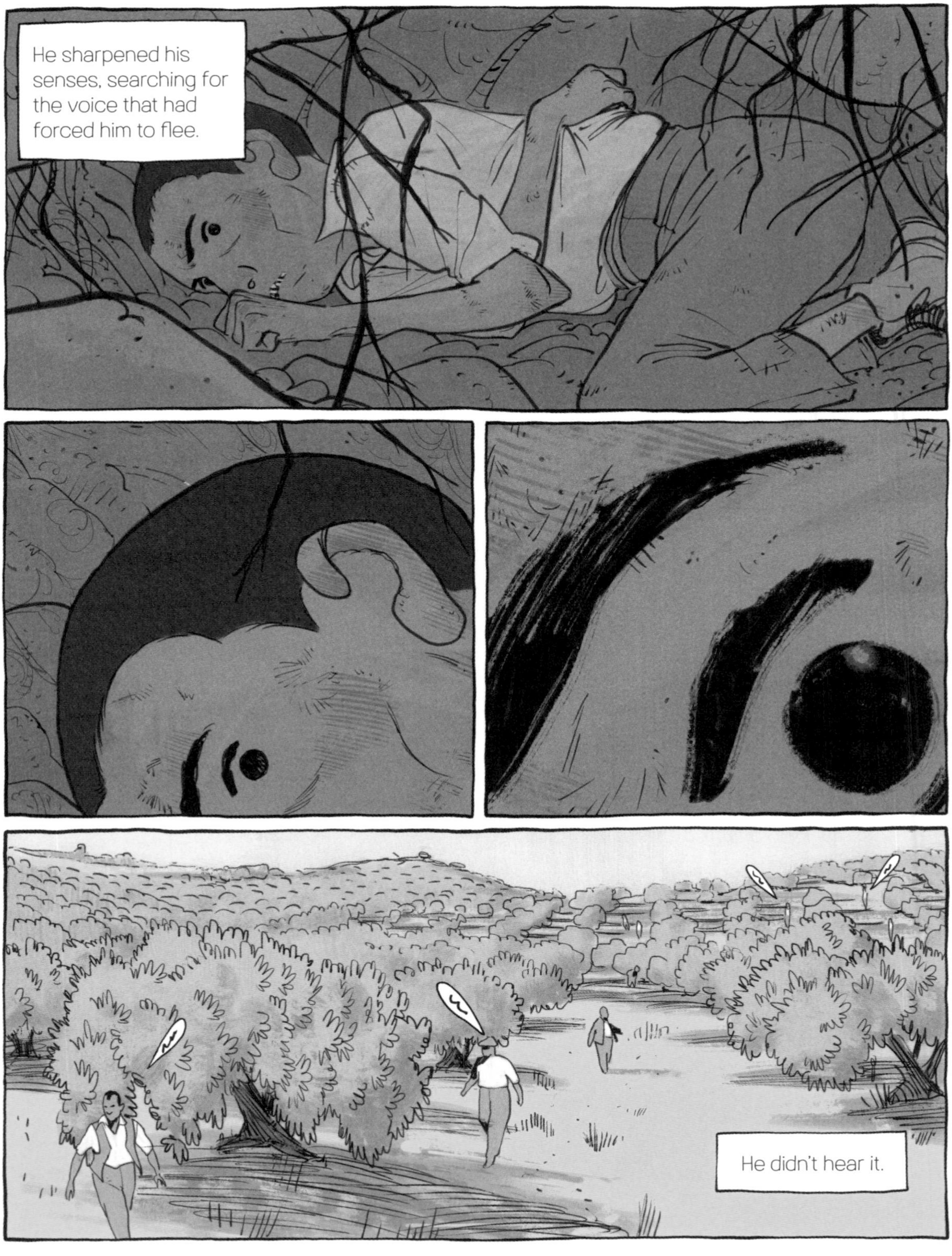
He sharpened his senses, searching for the voice that had forced him to flee.
He didn't hear it.

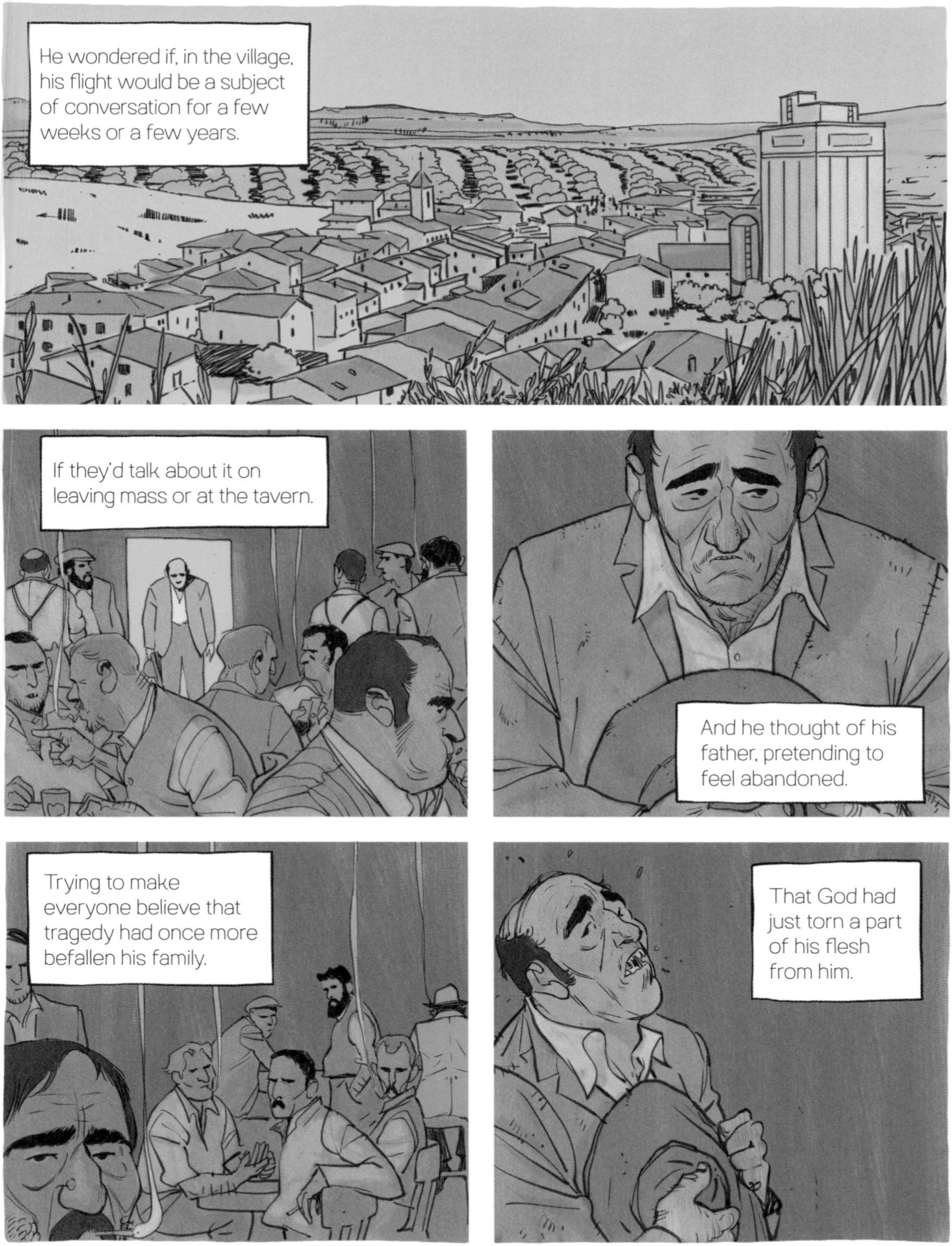
He wondered if, in the village, his flight would be a subject of conversation for a few weeks or a few years.
If they'd talk about it on leaving mass or at the tavern.
And he thought of his father, pretending to feel abandoned.
Trying to make everyone believe that tragedy had once more befallen his family.
That God had just torn a part of his flesh from him.

And the image of his father playing that role...

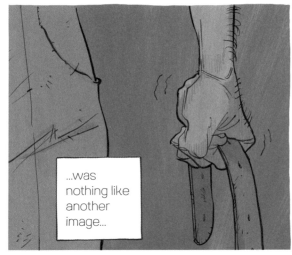

...was nothing like another image...

...he'd lived so often.

Suffered so often.

The stone walls of his home the sole witnesses.

He saw his father giving explanations to one and all.

And among them...

ROOOOOOMm

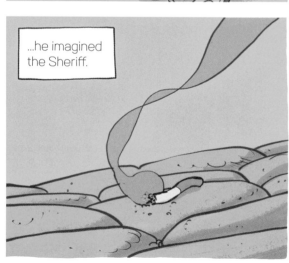

...he imagined the Sheriff.

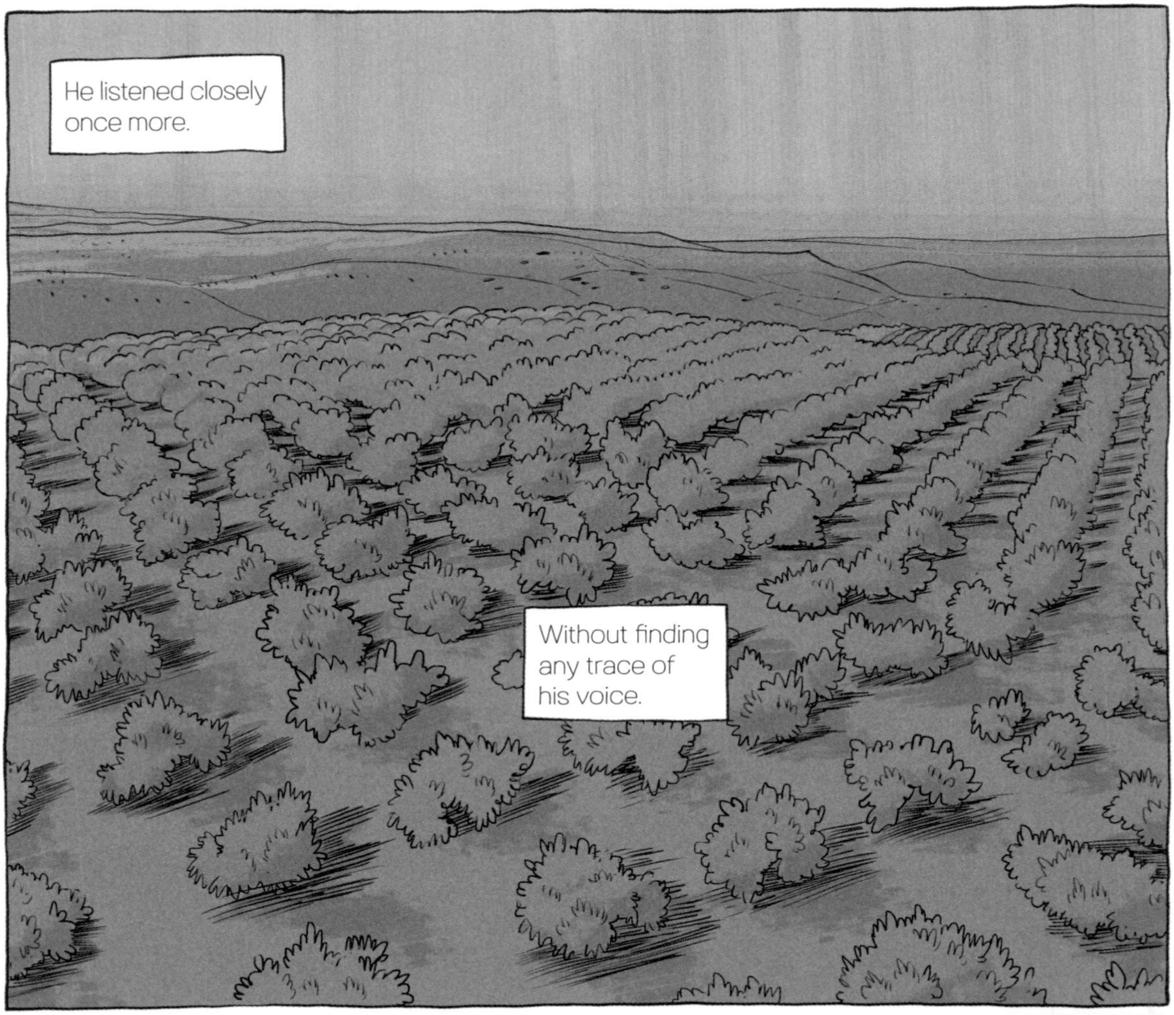
He listened closely once more.
Without finding any trace of his voice.

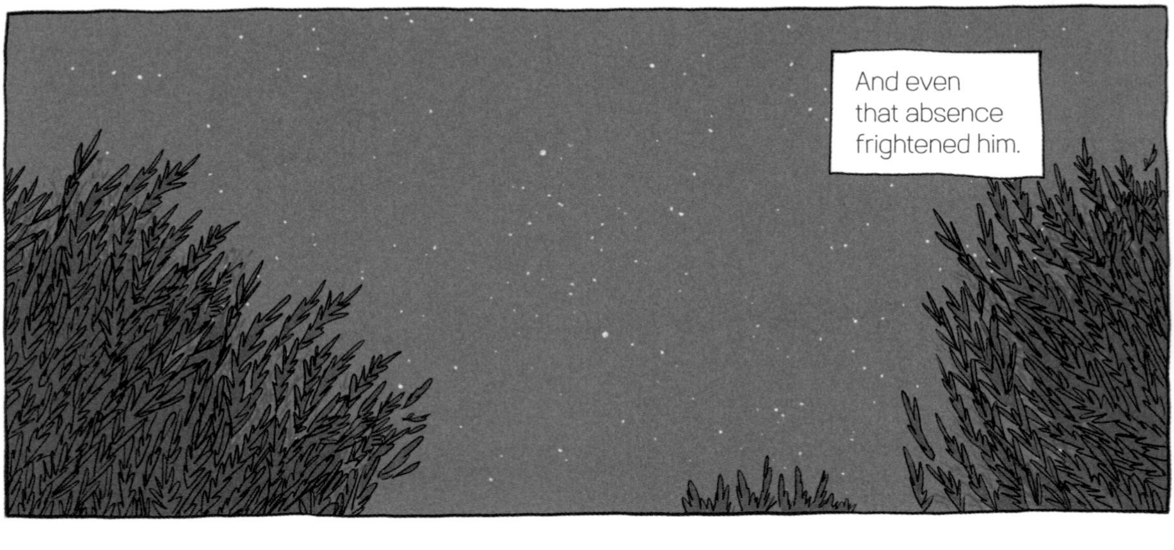
And even that absence frightened him.

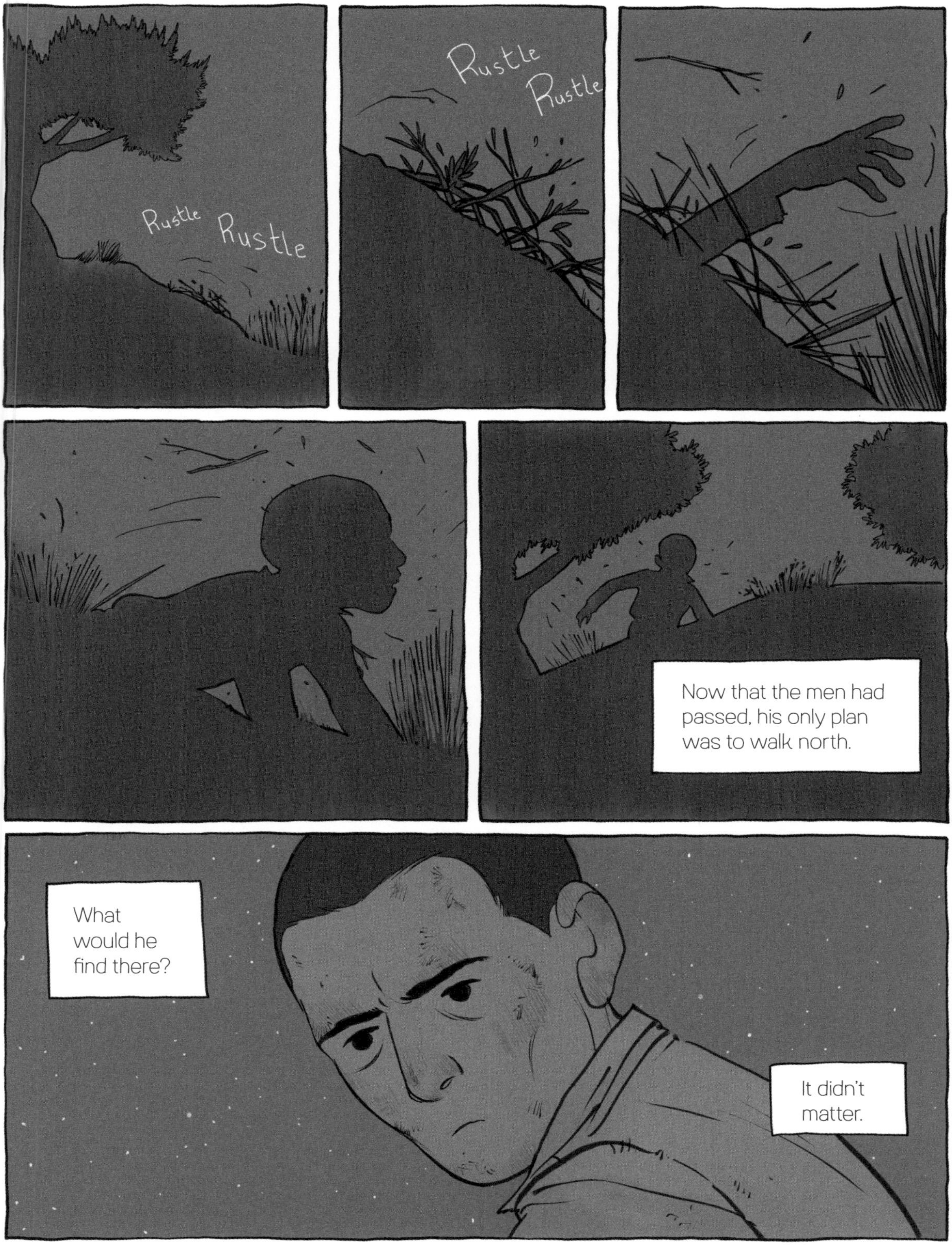
Rustle
Rustle
Rustle
Rustle
Now that the men had passed, his only plan was to walk north.
What would he find there?
It didn't matter.

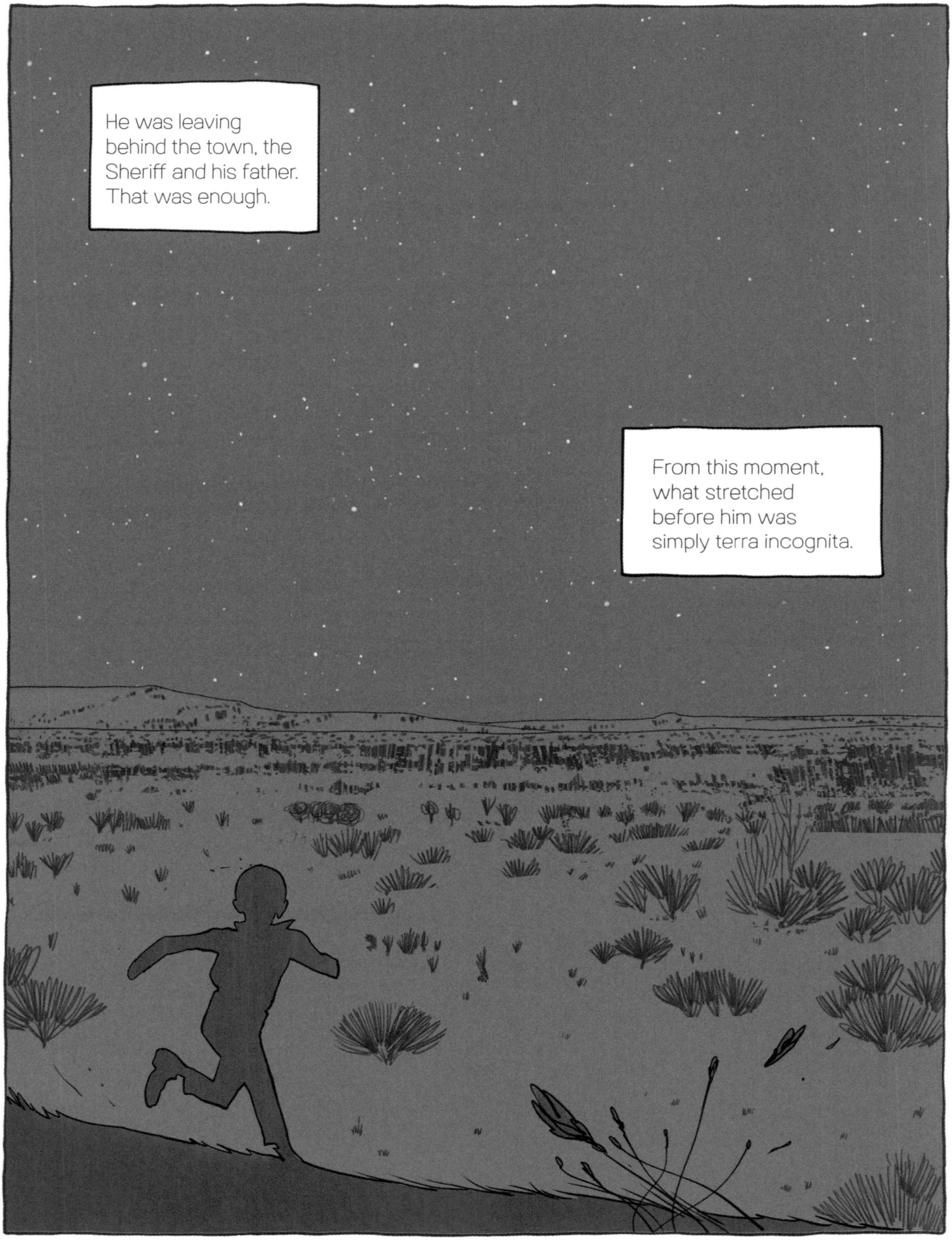
He was leaving behind the town, the Sheriff and his father. That was enough.
From this moment, what stretched before him was simply terra incognita.

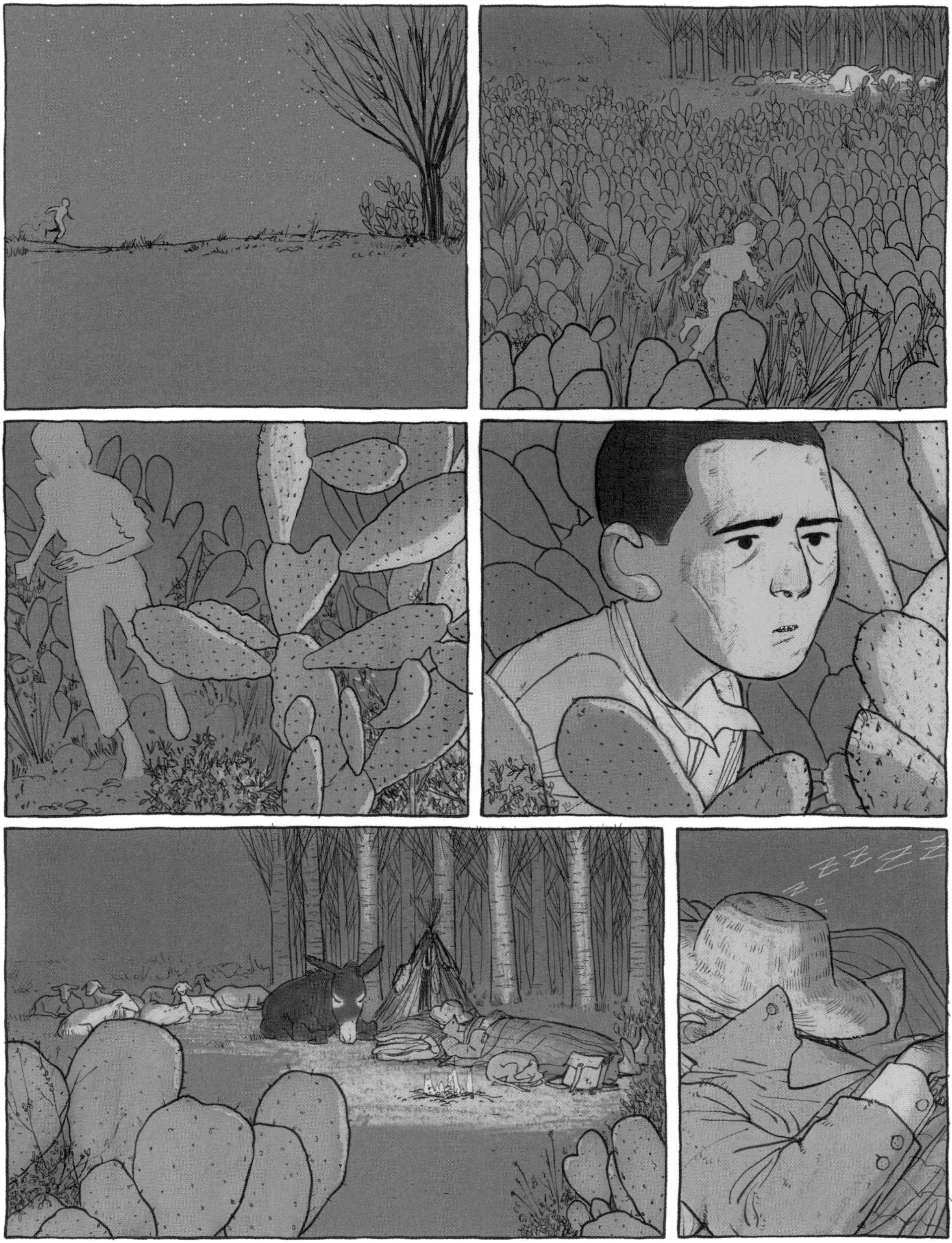
ZZZZZ

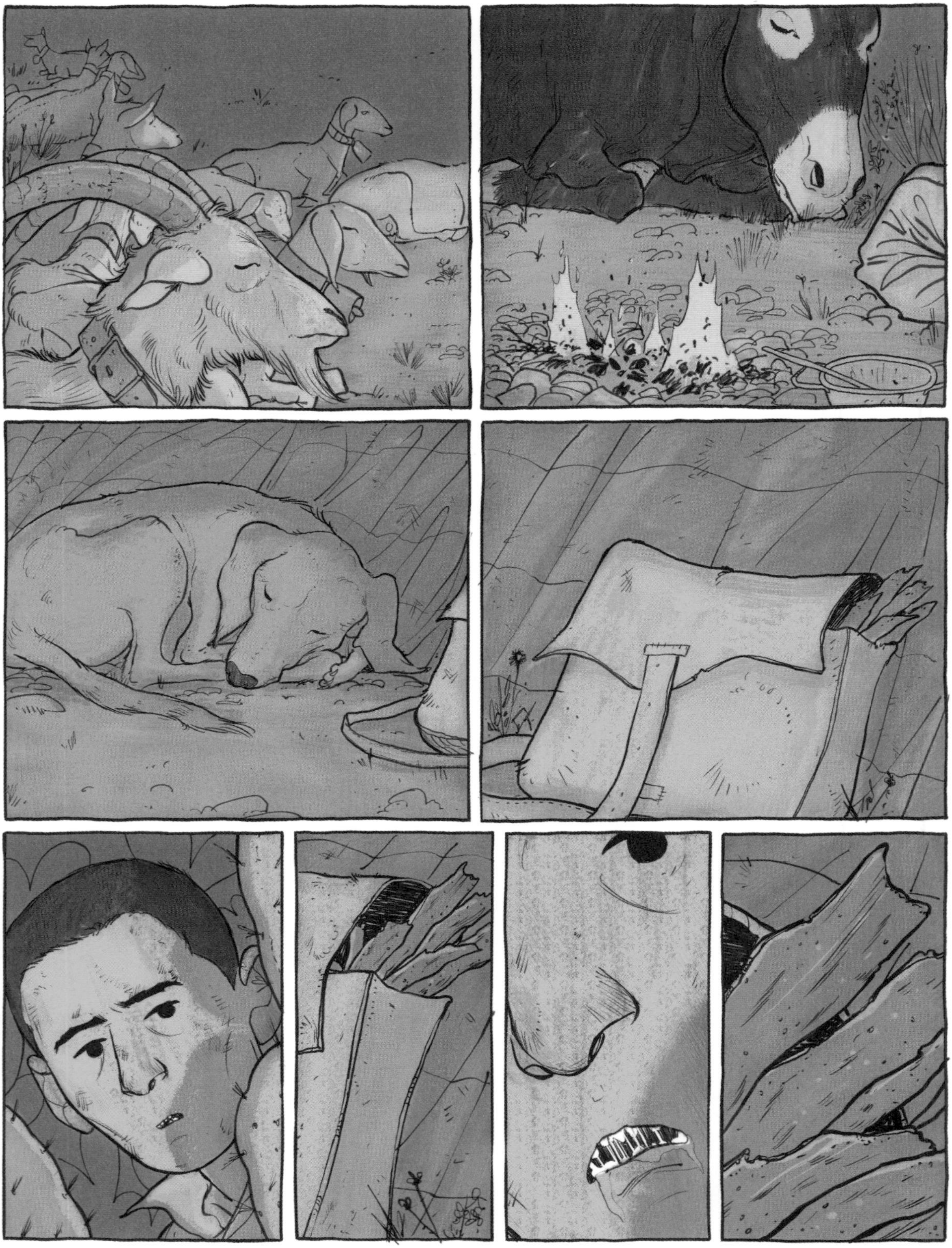

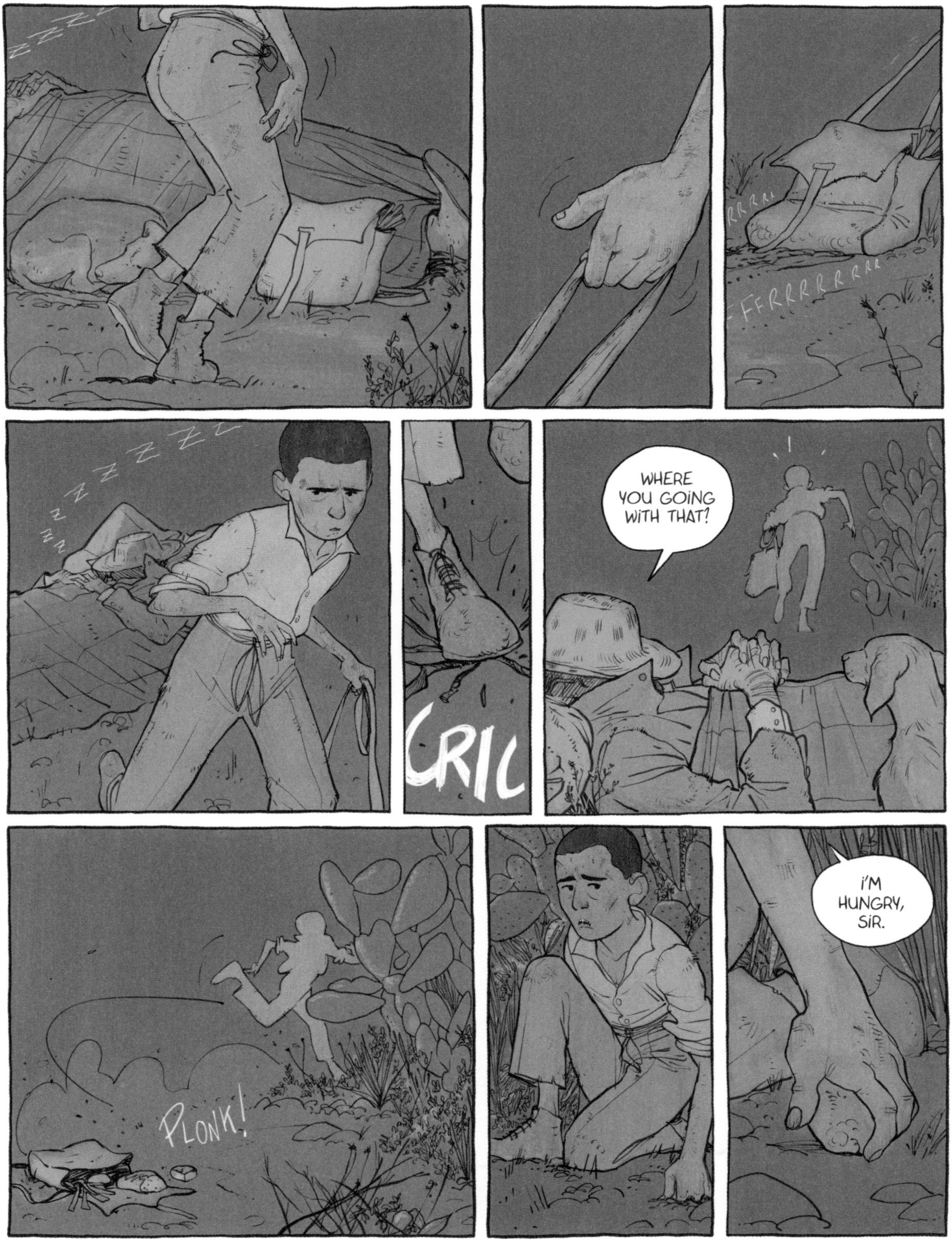
ZZZZZ
RRRRR
FFRRRRRRRR
ZZZZZZZ
CRIC
!
WHERE YOU GOING WITH THAT?
PLONK!
I'M HUNGRY, SIR.

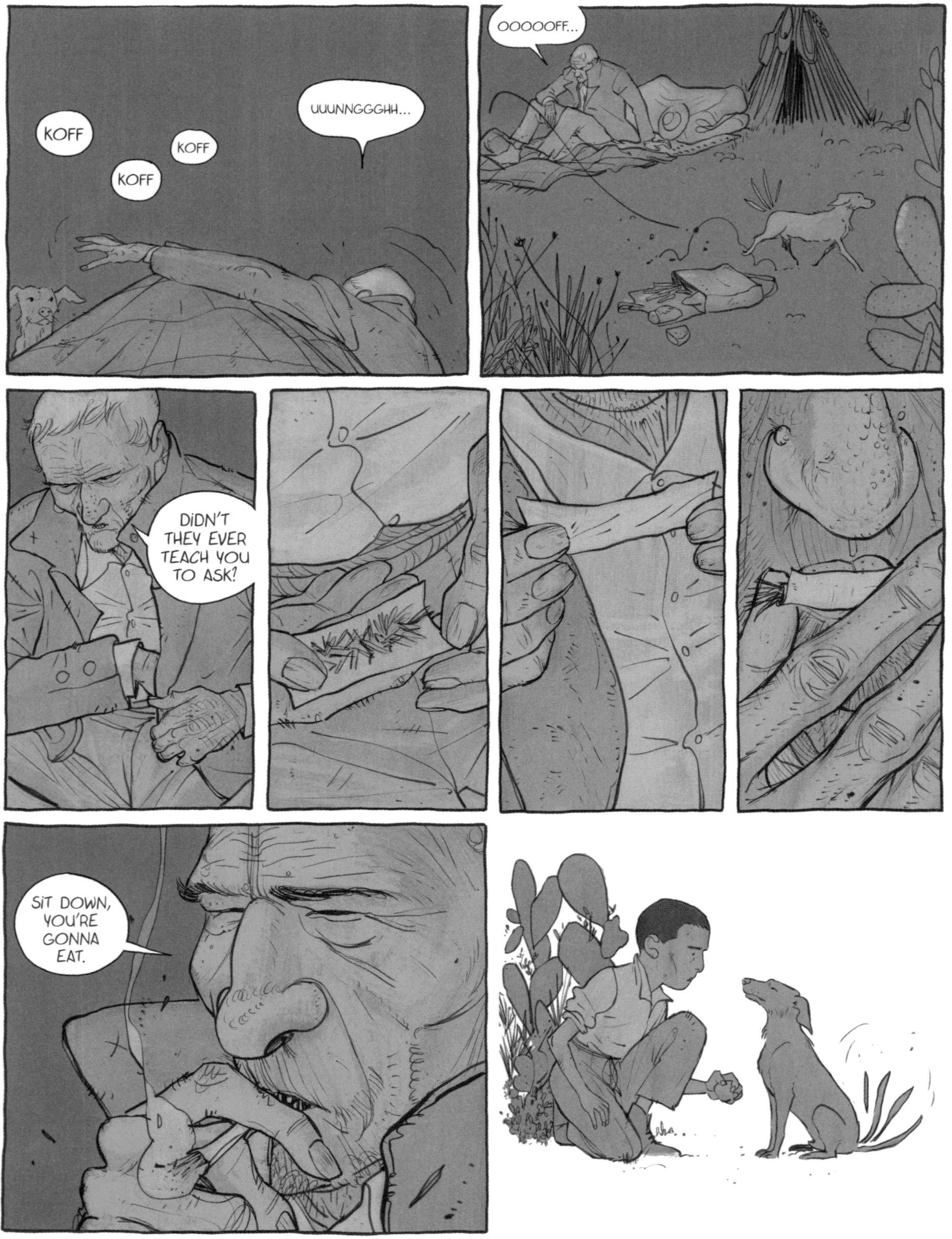
KOFF
KOFF
KOFF
UUUNNGGGHH...
OOOOOFF...
DIDN'T THEY EVER TEACH YOU TO ASK?
SIT DOWN, YOU'RE GONNA EAT.

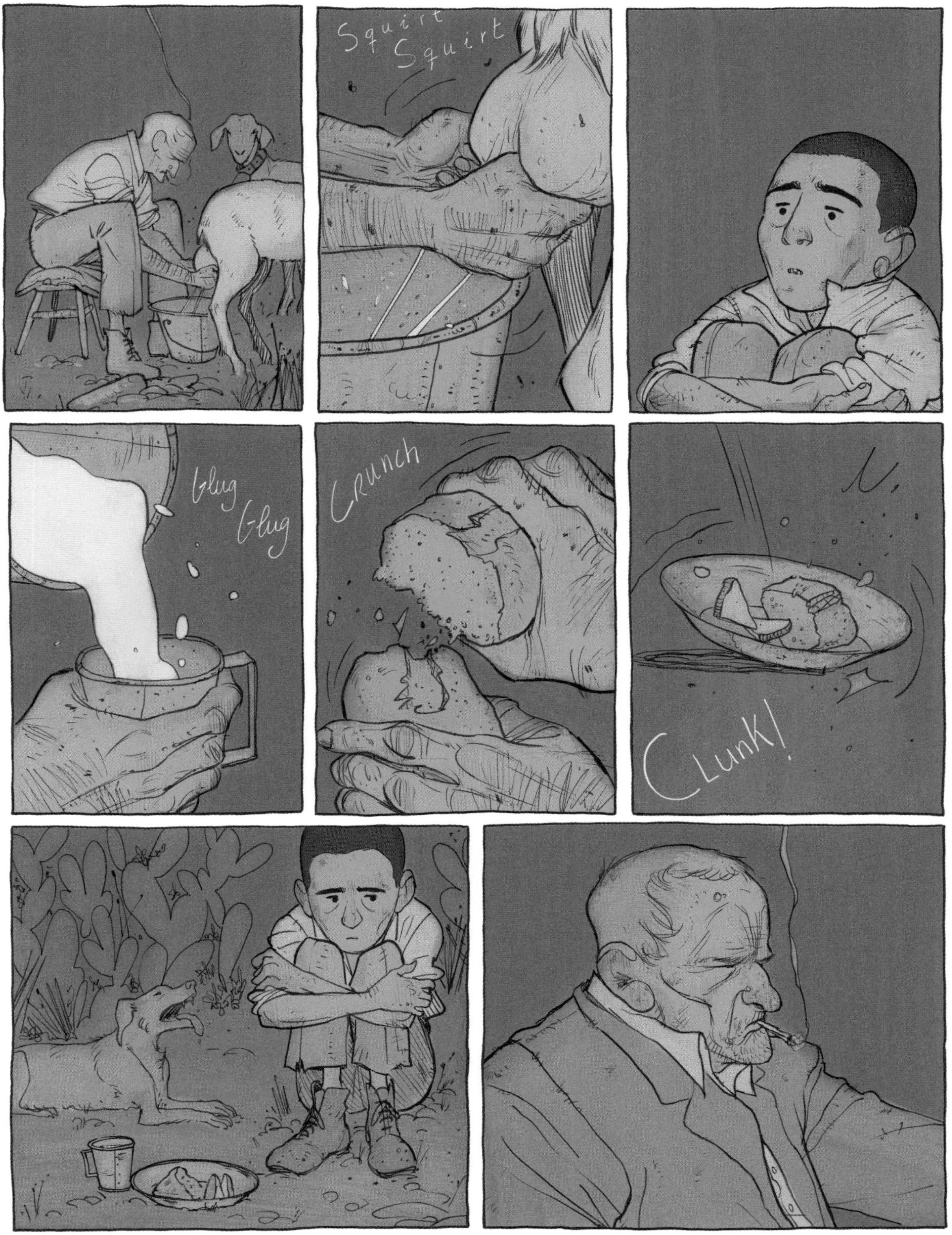
Squirt
Squirt
Glug
Glug
Crunch
Clunk!

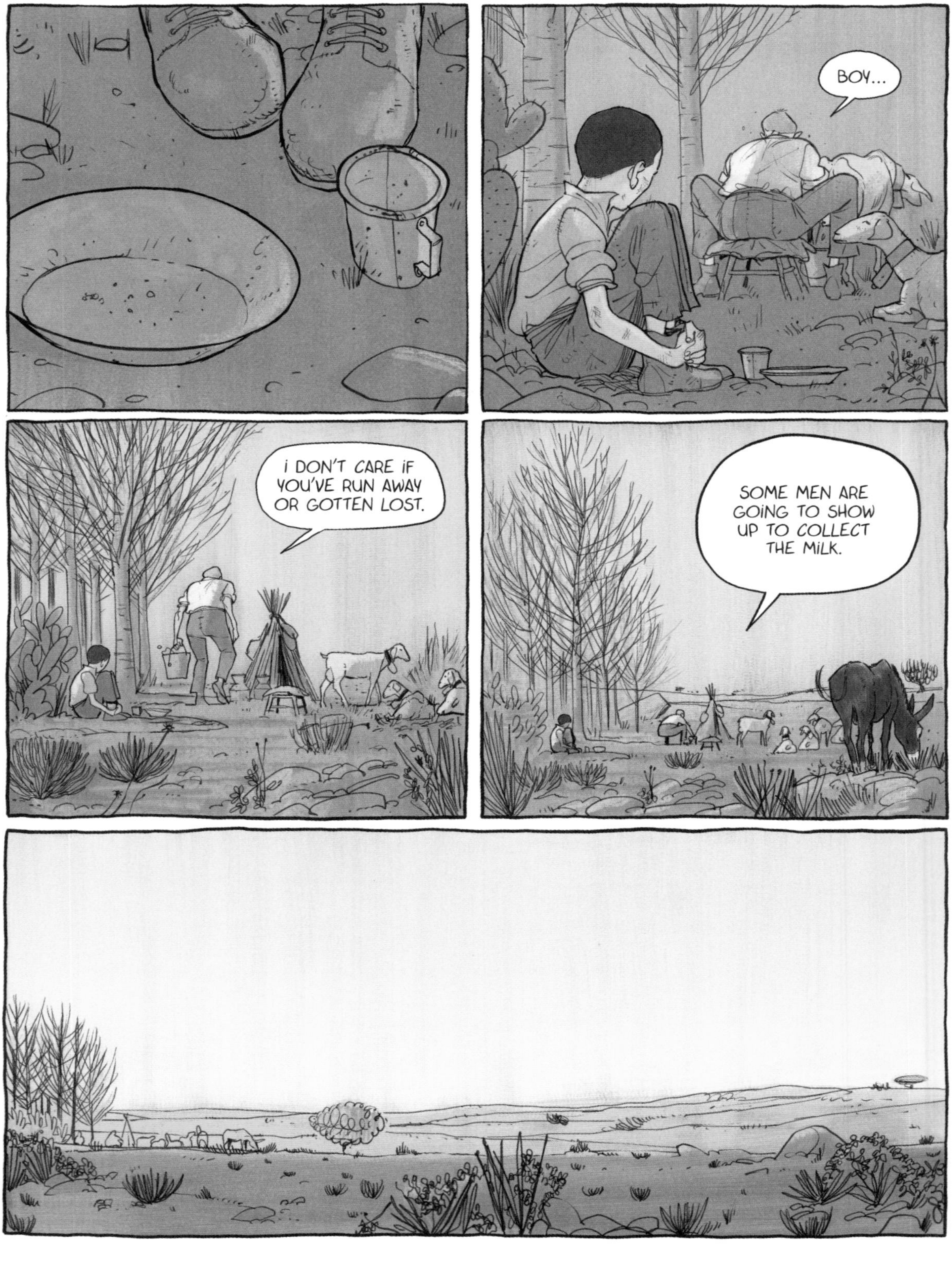
BOY...
I DON'T CARE IF YOU'VE RUN AWAY OR GOTTEN LOST.
SOME MEN ARE GOING TO SHOW UP TO COLLECT THE MILK.

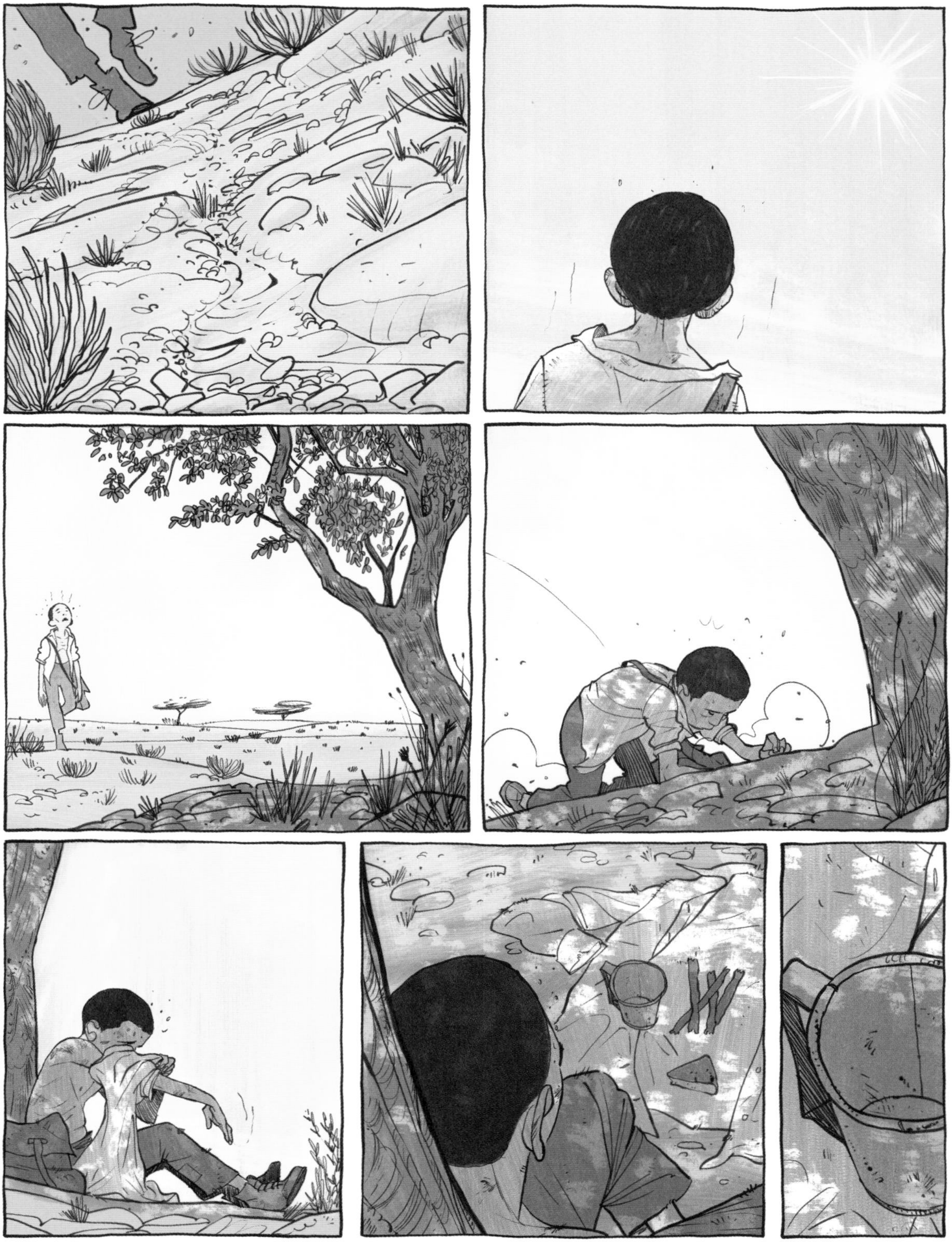

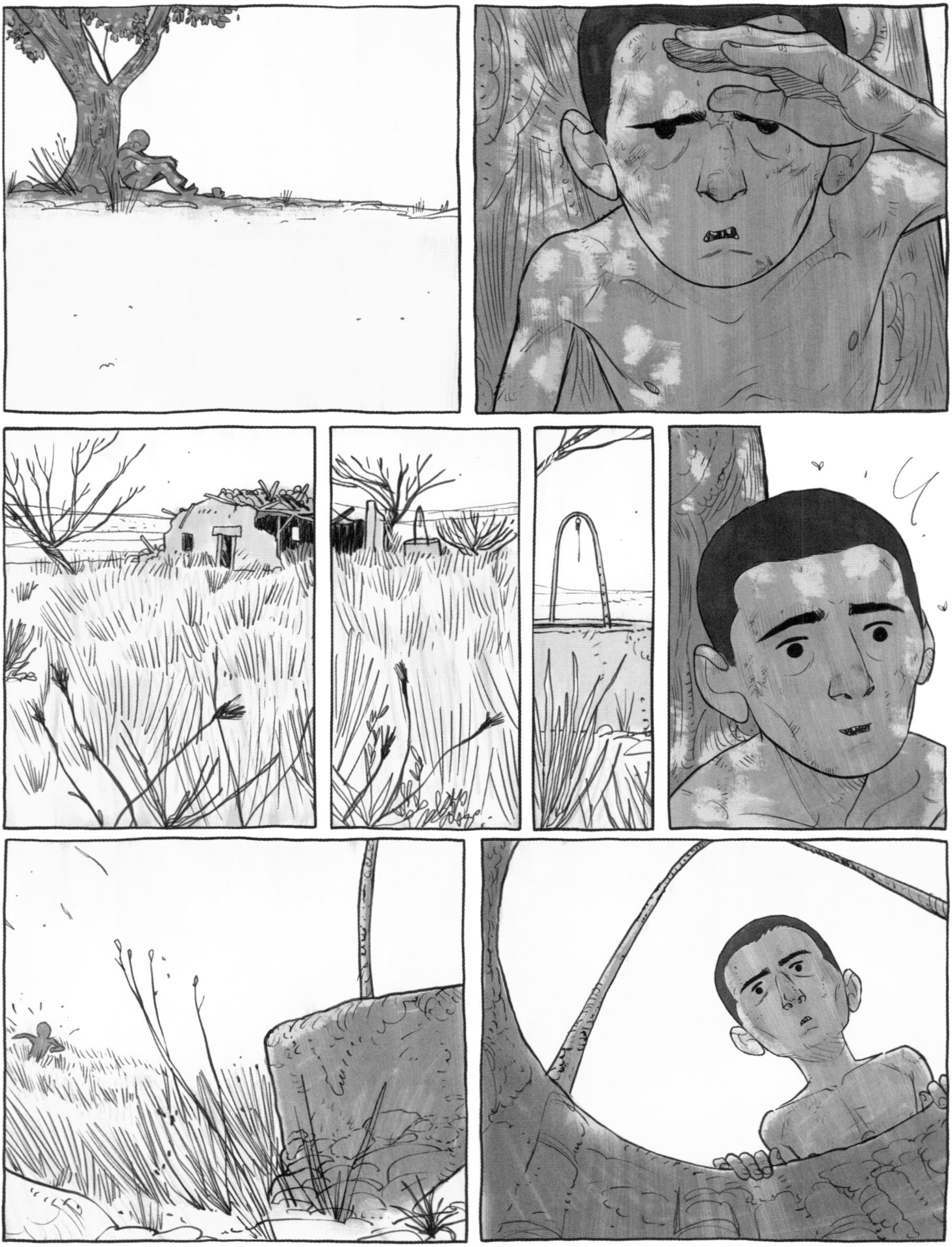

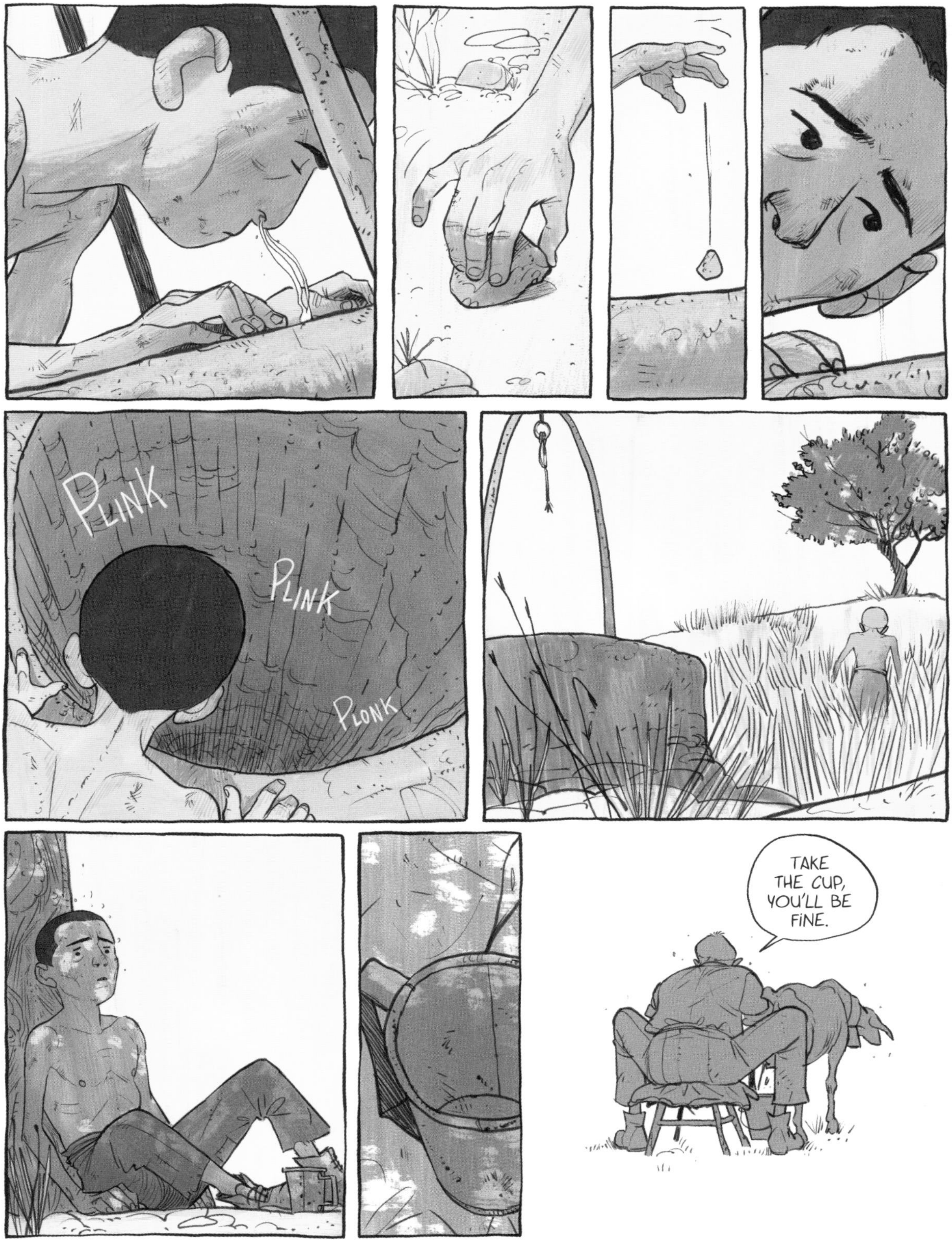
PLINK
PLINK
PLONK
TAKE THE CUP, YOU'LL BE FINE.

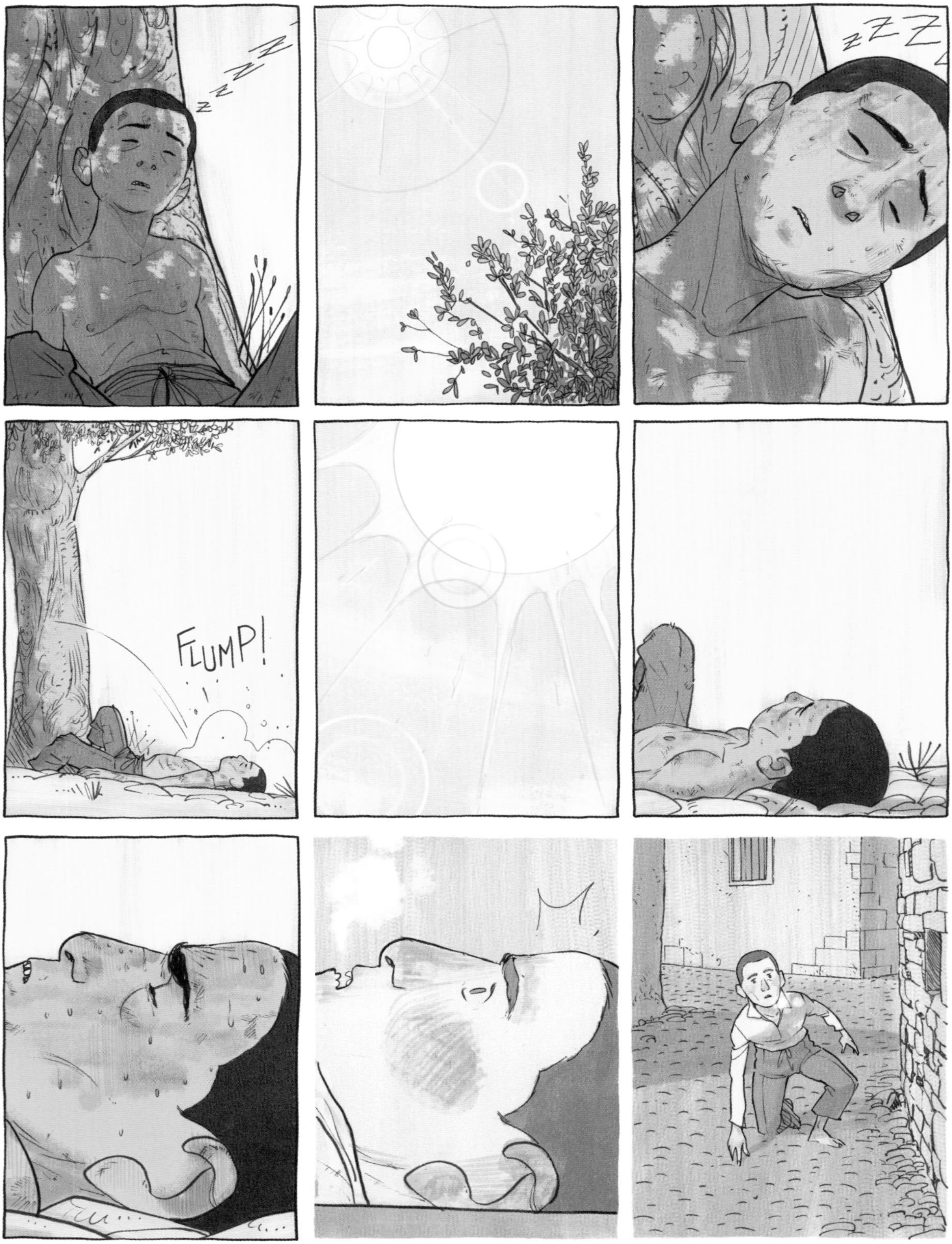

ZZZ
ZZZ
FLUMP!

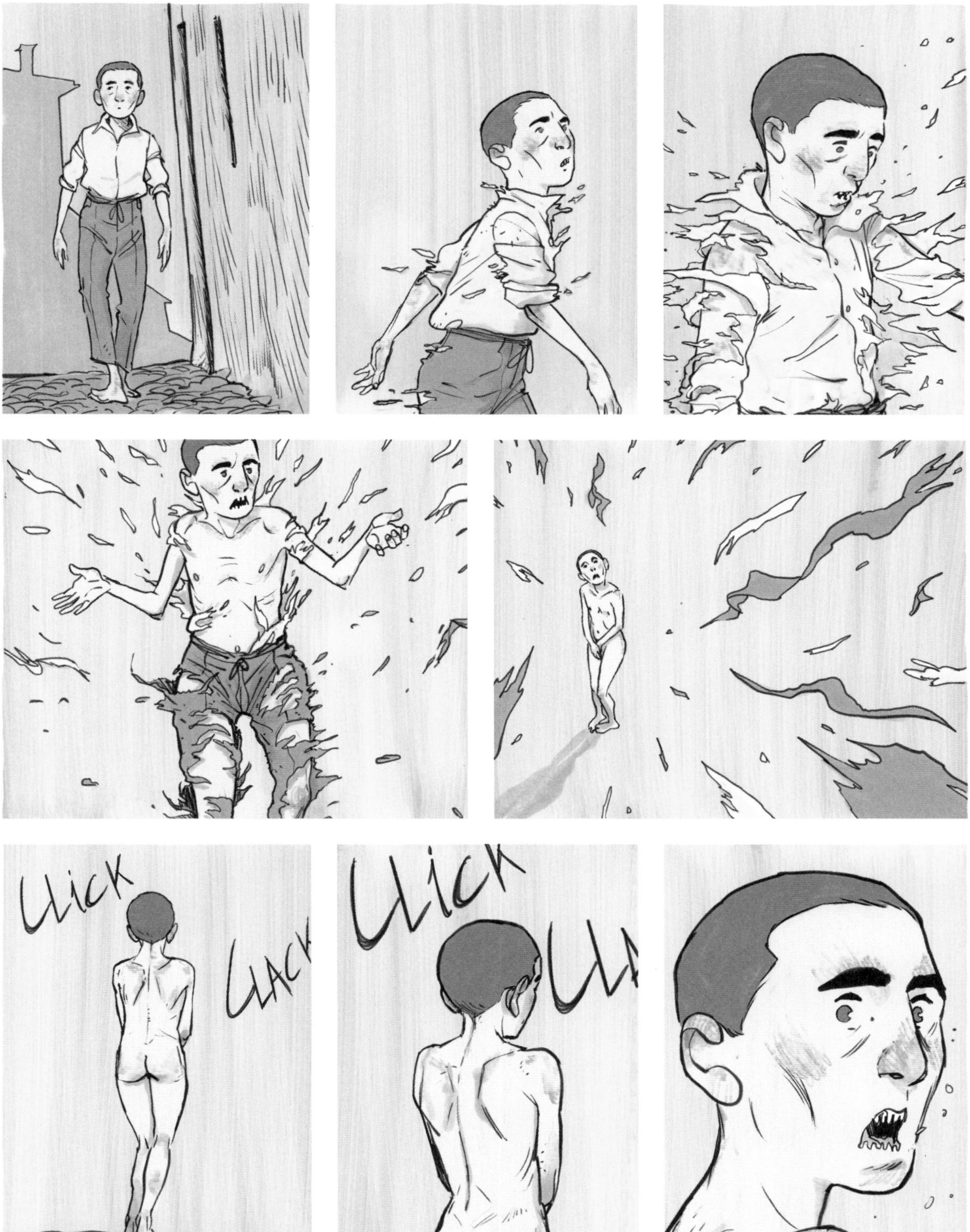
CLICK
CLACK
CLICK

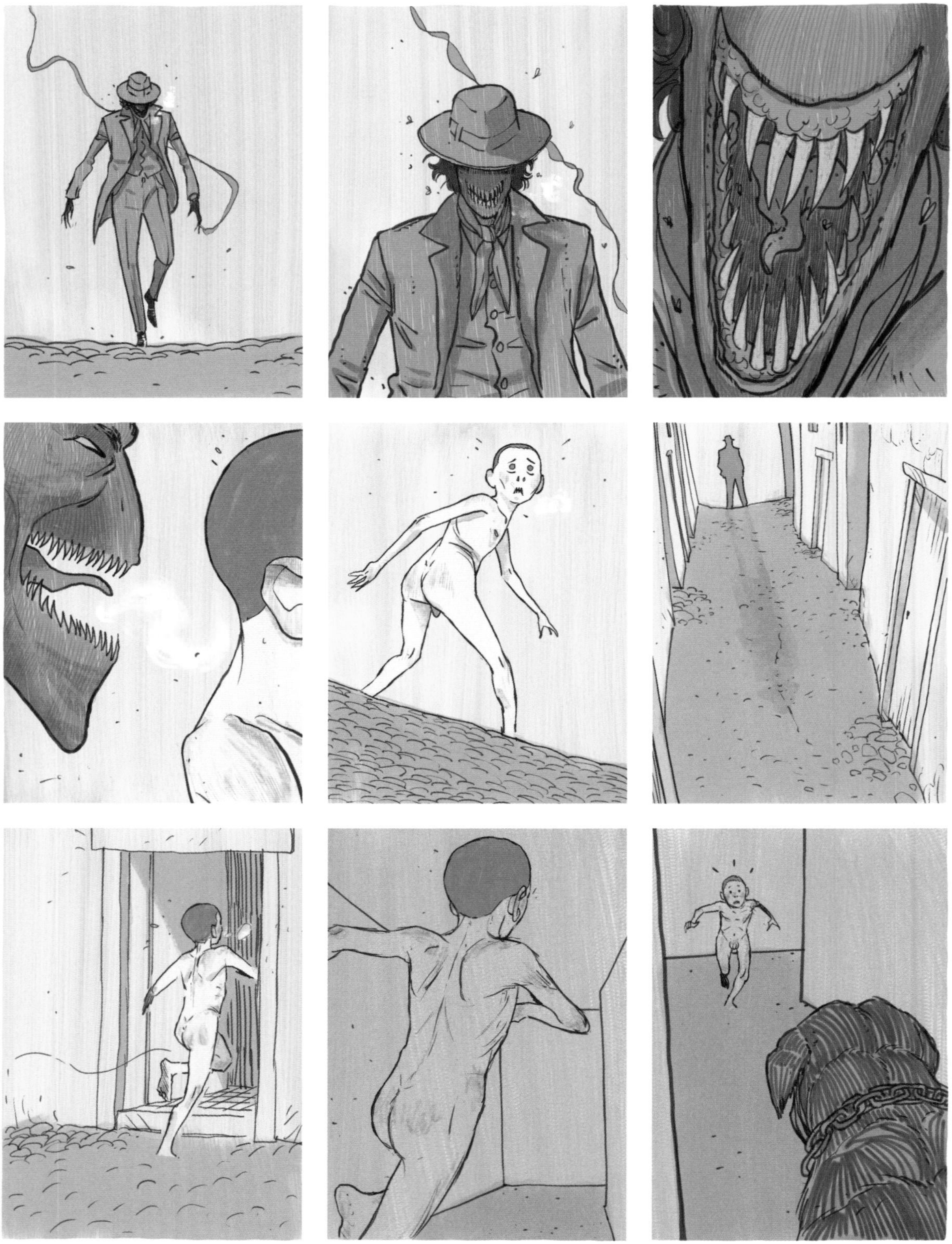

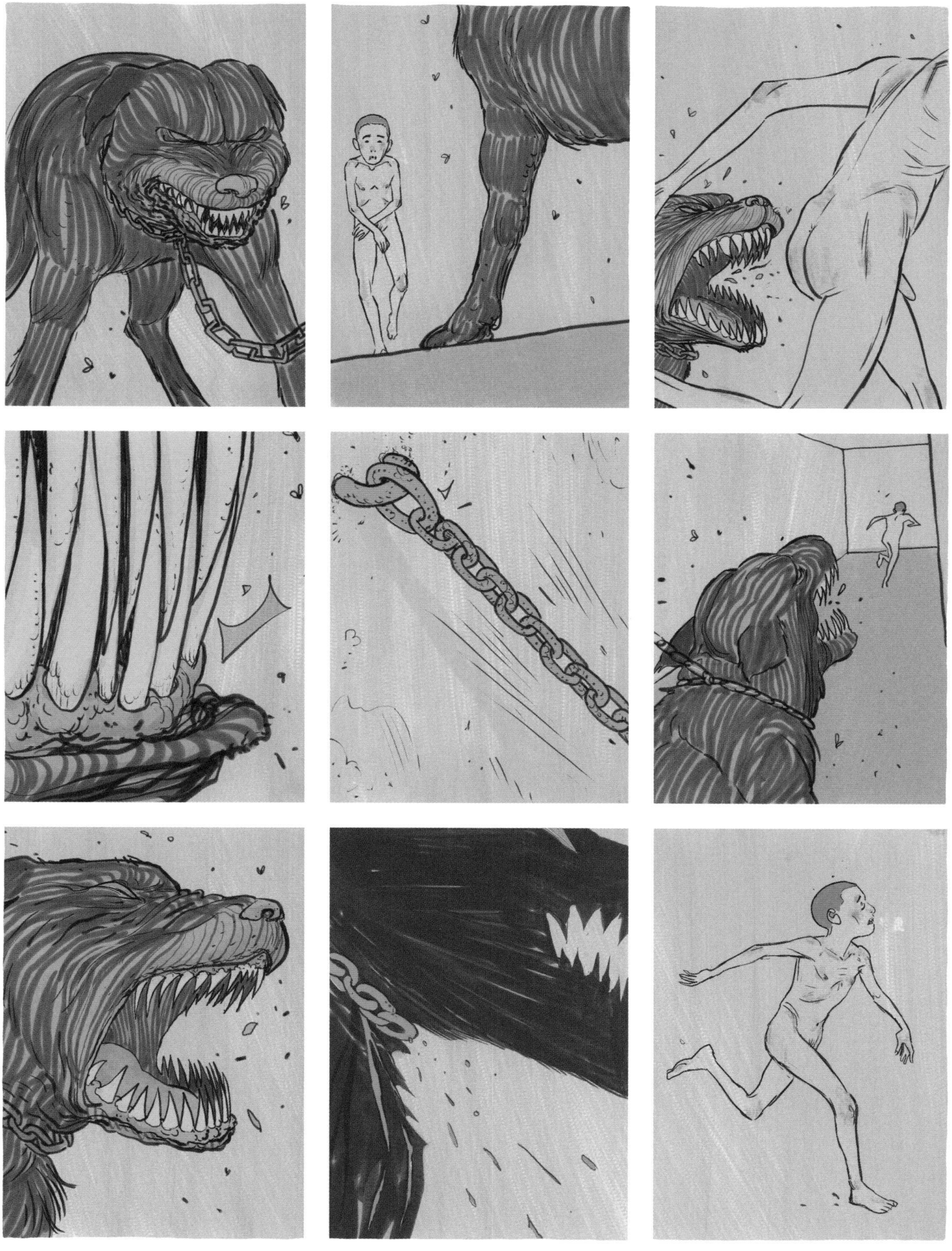

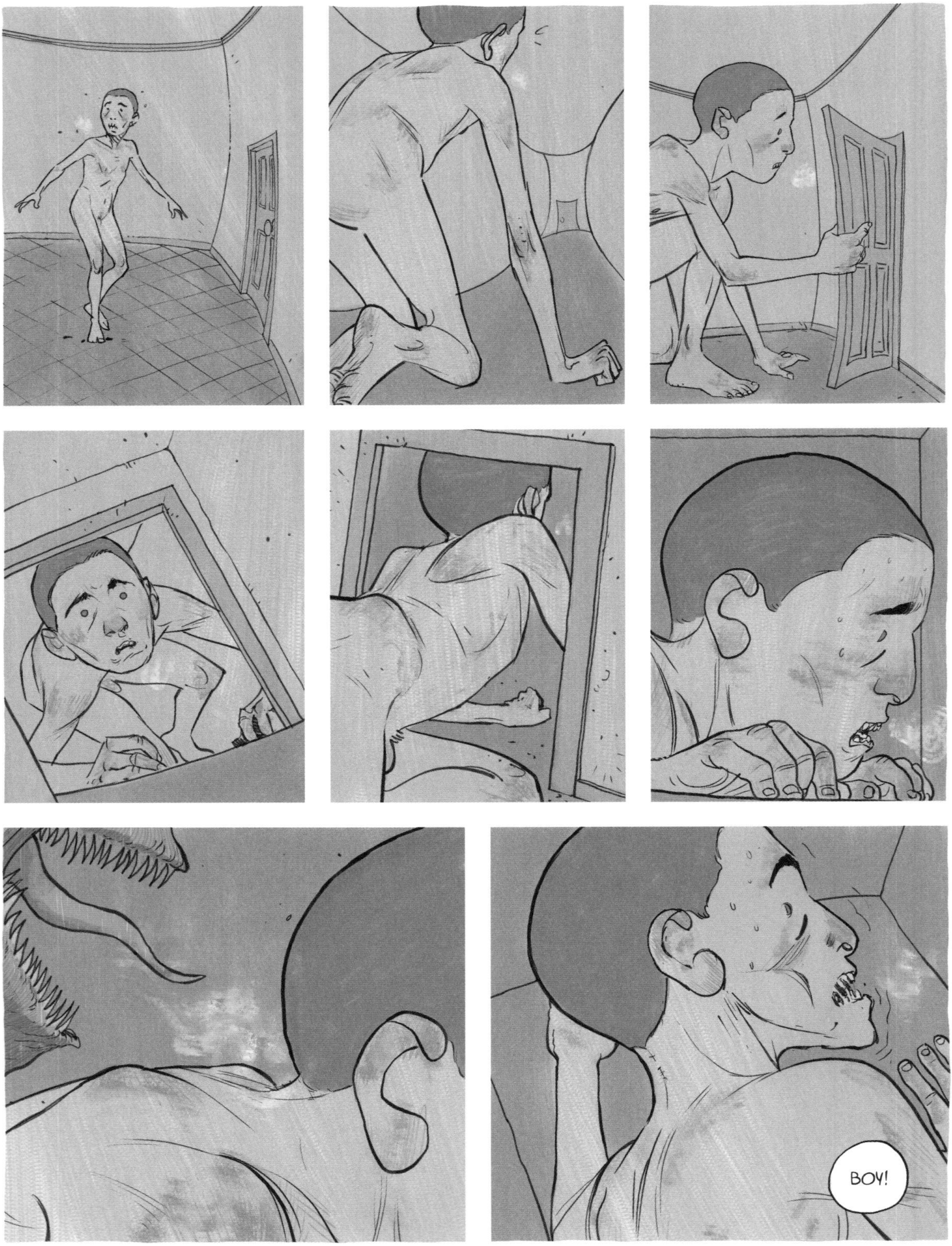
BOY!

CREeeeeeeeaK!

SIT UP, BOY!

PFFFFT!!

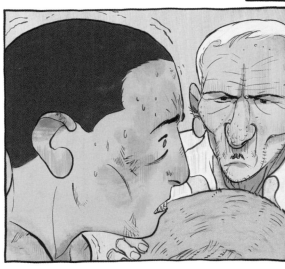

AAAAAAAA....

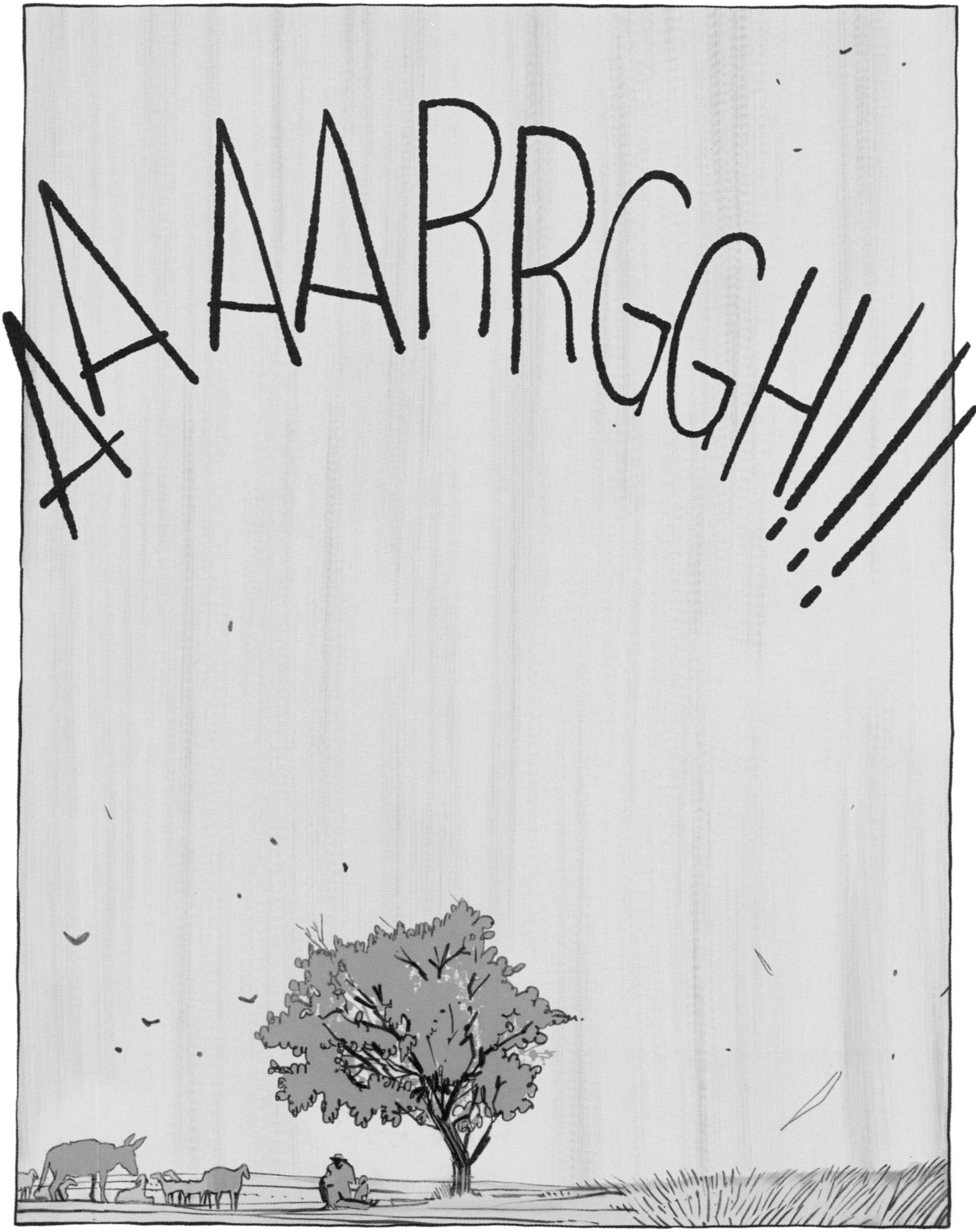
AAAARRGGH!!!

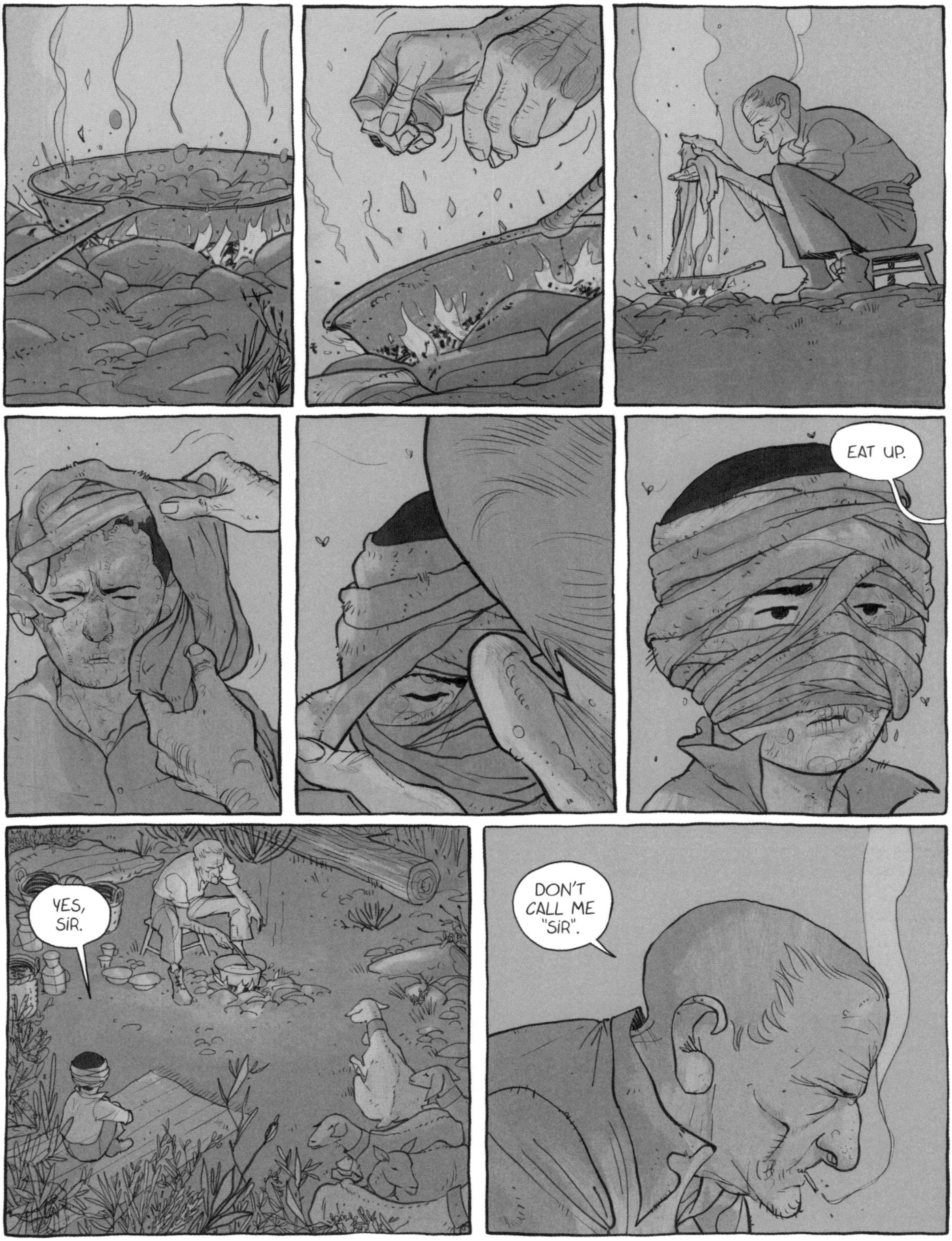
EAT UP.
YES, SIR.
DON'T CALL ME "SIR".

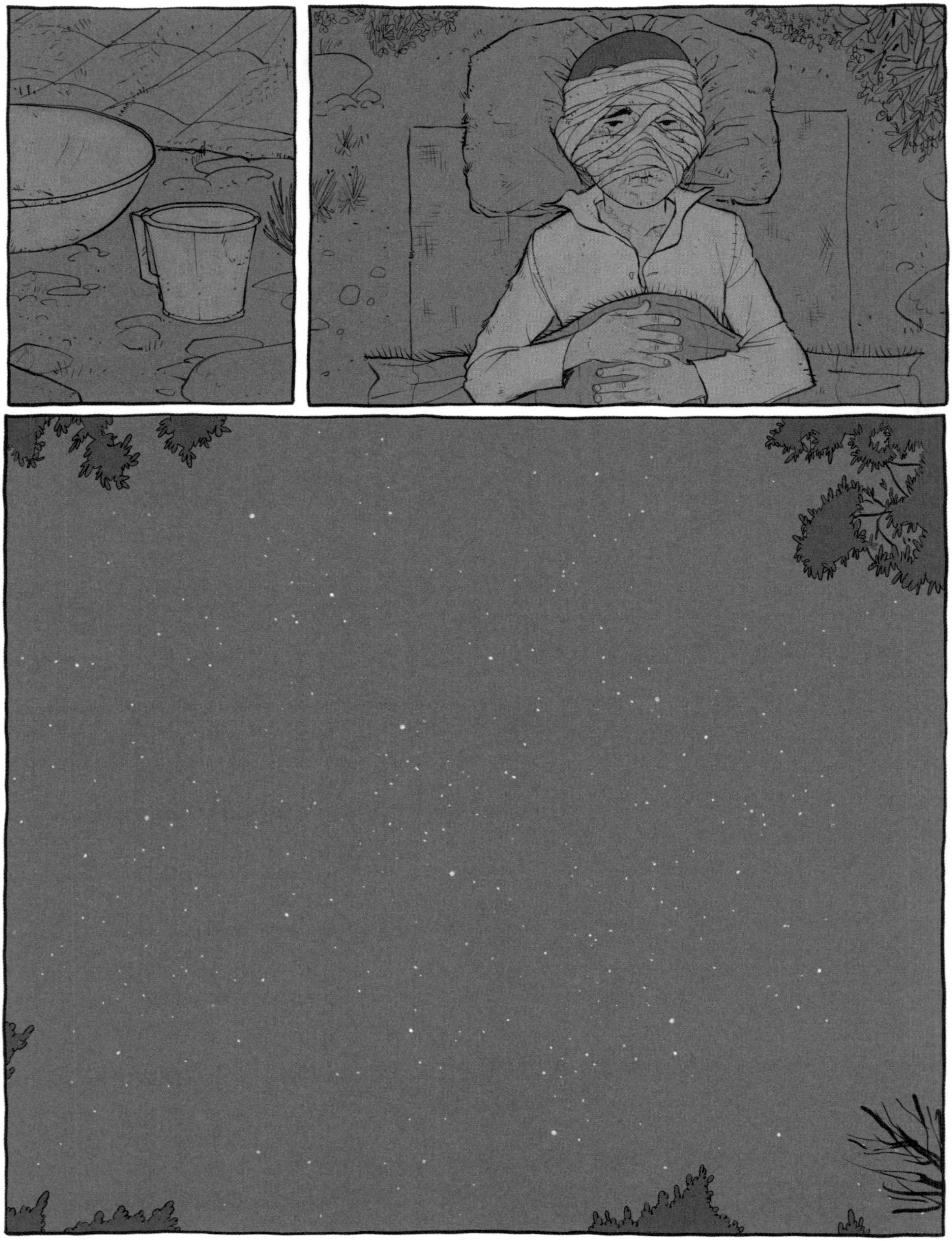

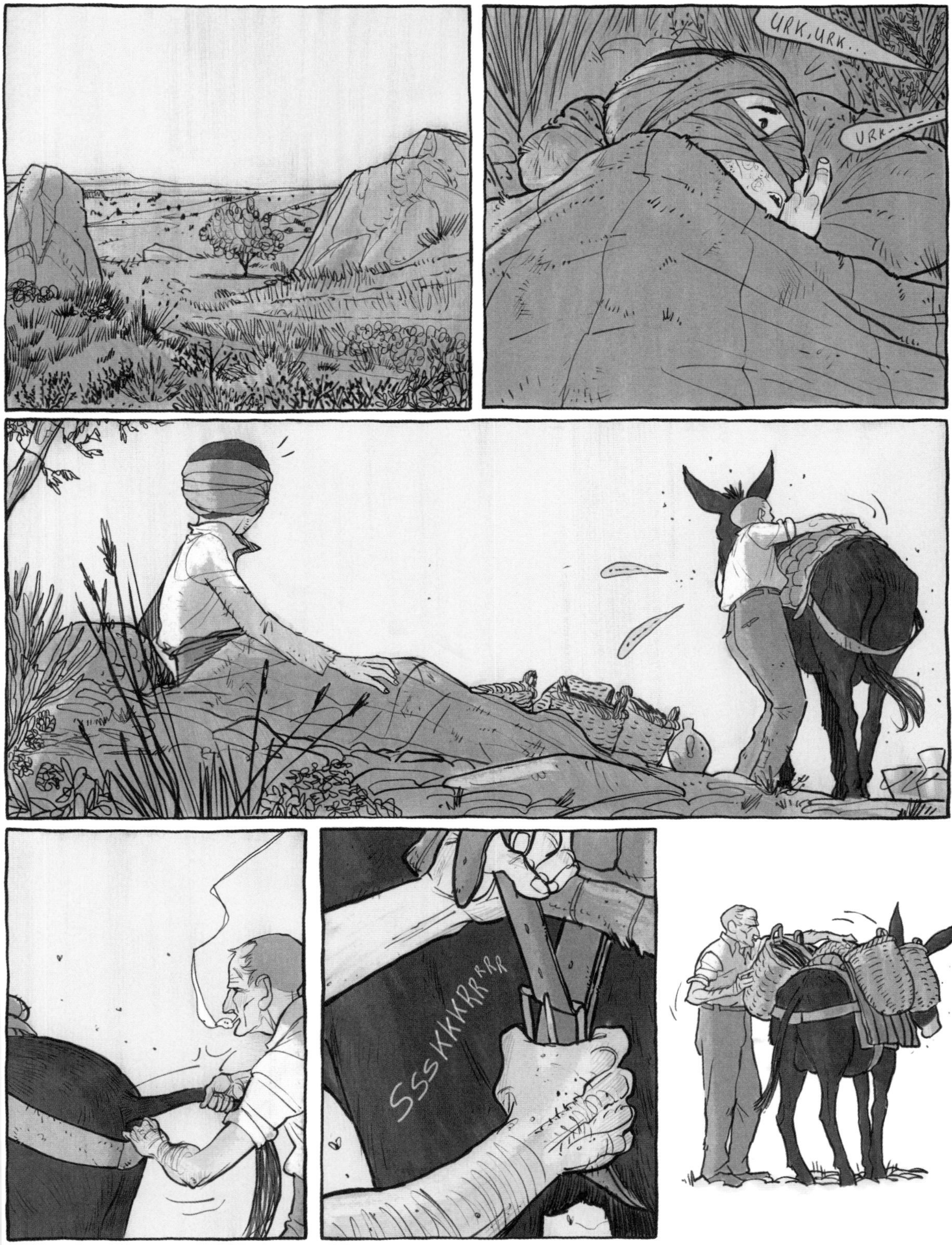
URK, URK...
URK-
SssKKKRRRRR

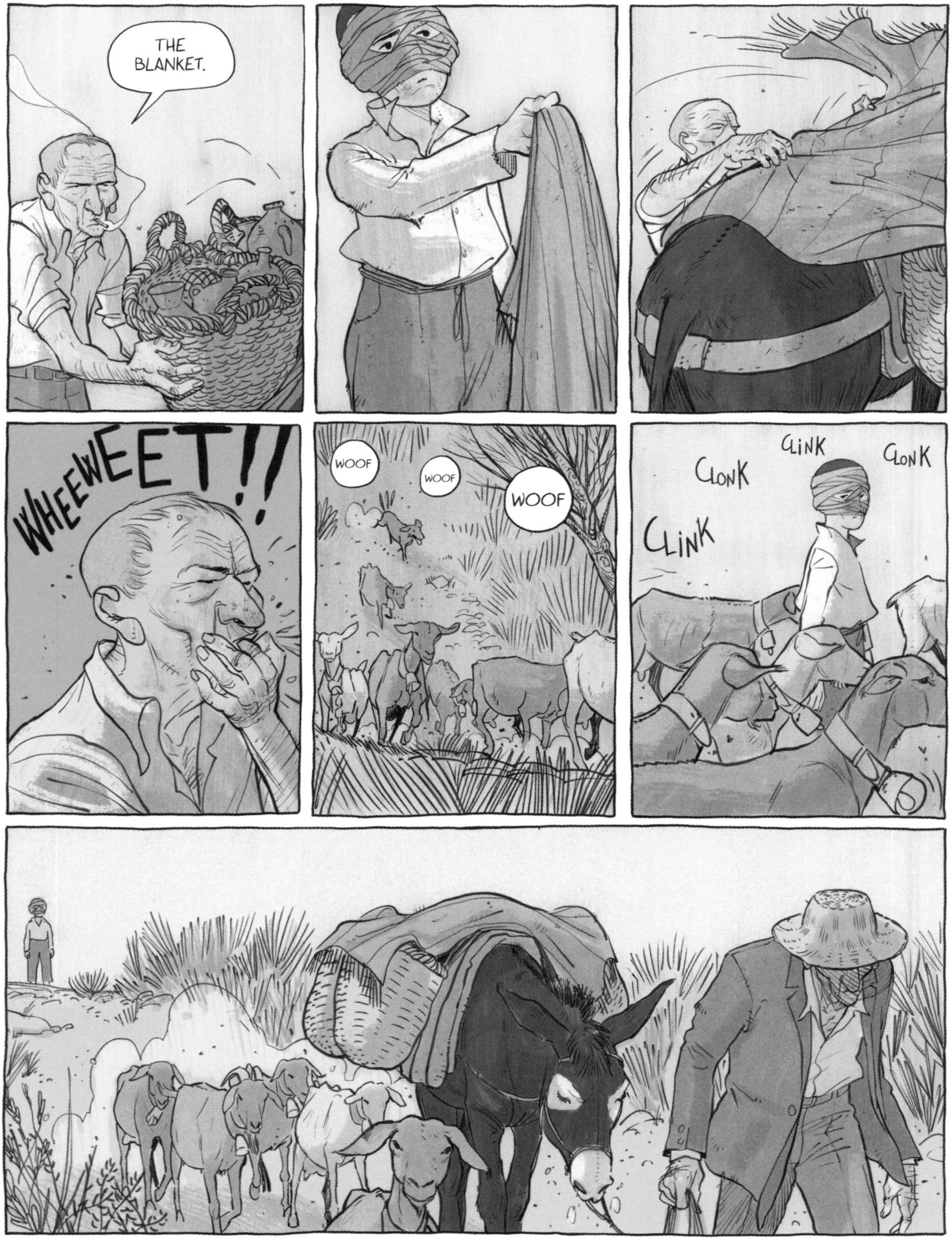
THE BLANKET.
WHEEWEET!!
WOOF
WOOF
WOOF
CLINK
CLONK
CLINK
CLONK

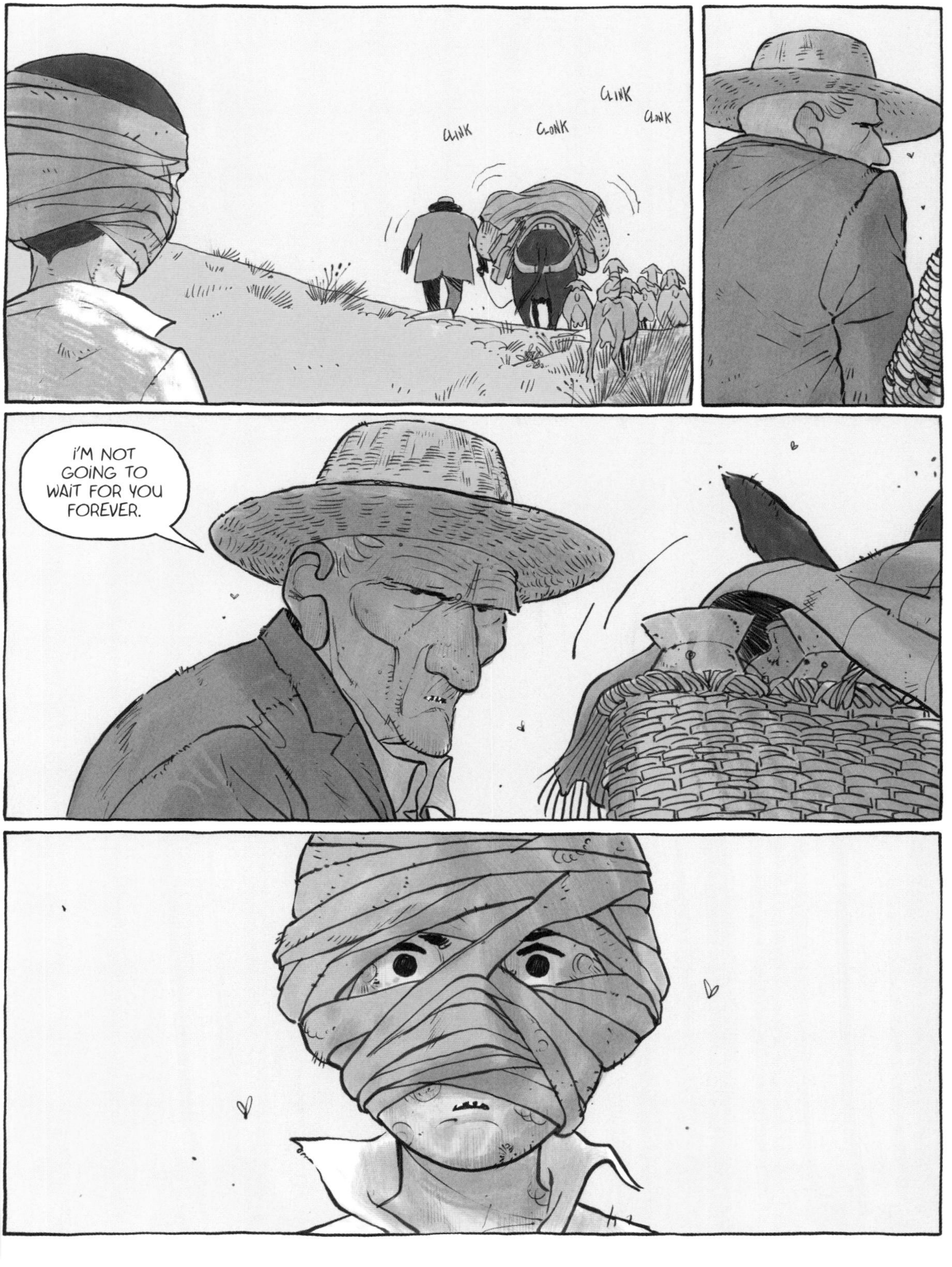
CLINK
CLONK
CLINK
CLONK
I'M NOT GOING TO WAIT FOR YOU FOREVER.

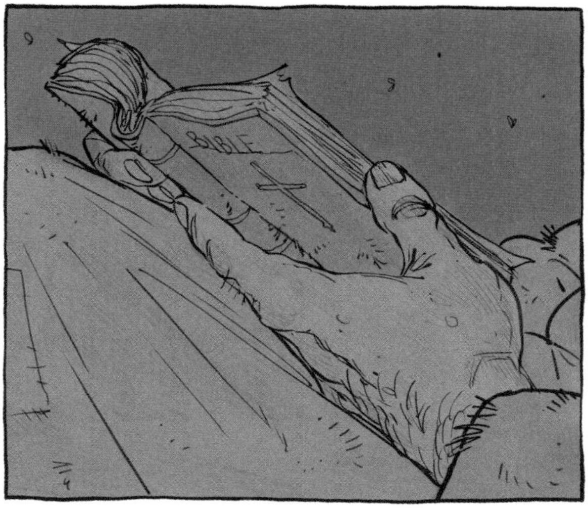
BIBLE

II

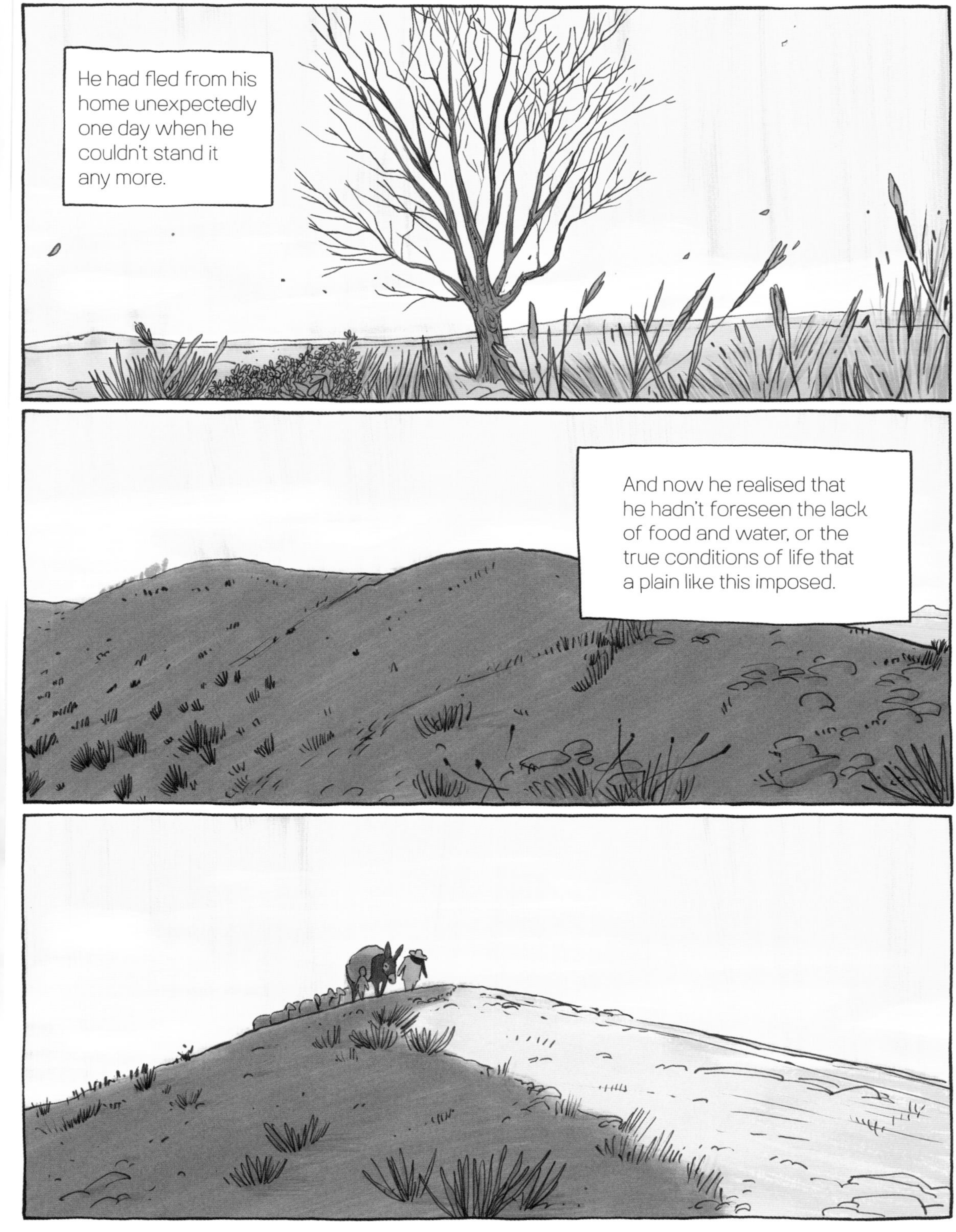
He had fled from his home unexpectedly one day when he couldn't stand it any more.
And now he realised that he hadn't foreseen the lack of food and water, or the true conditions of life that a plain like this imposed.

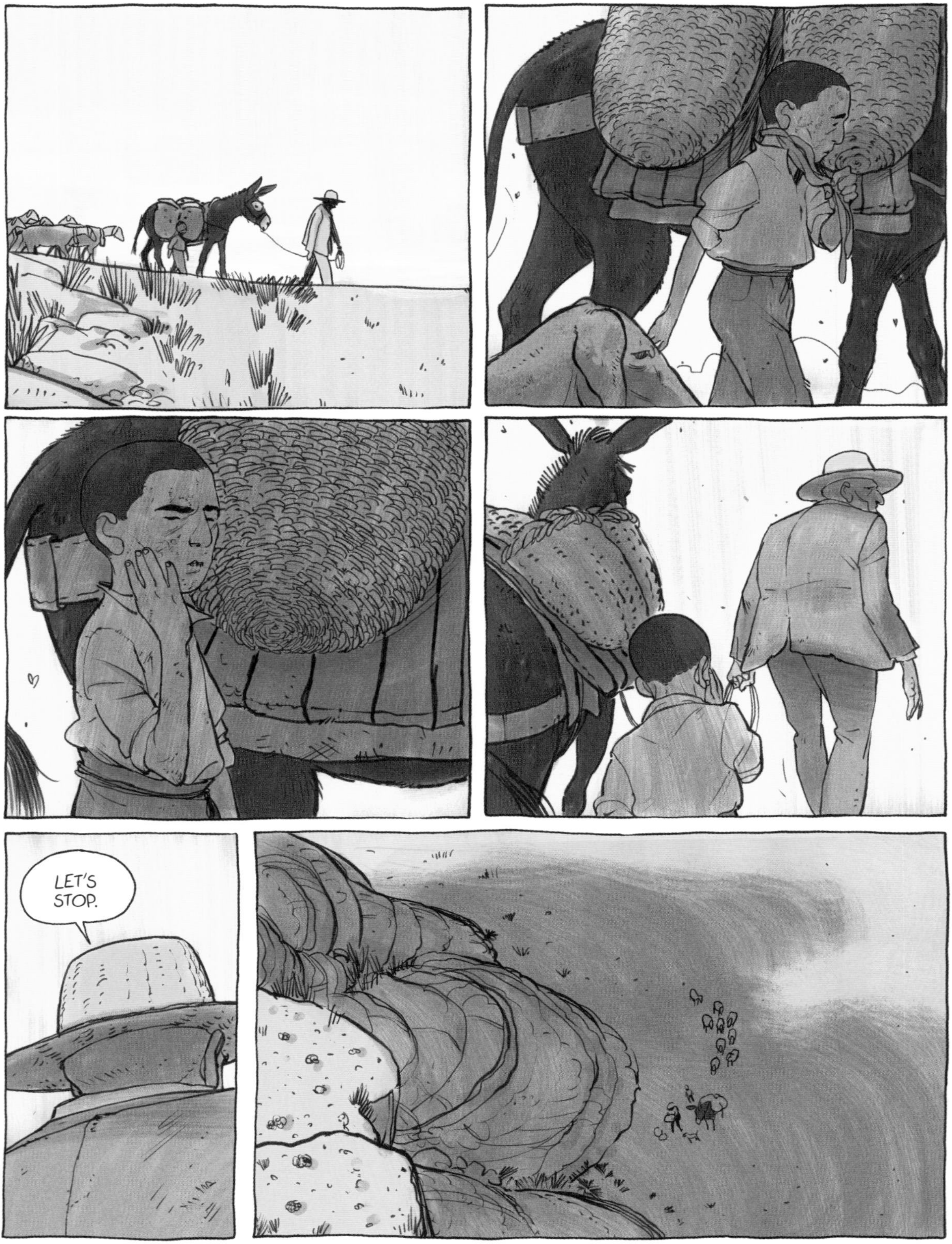
LET'S STOP.

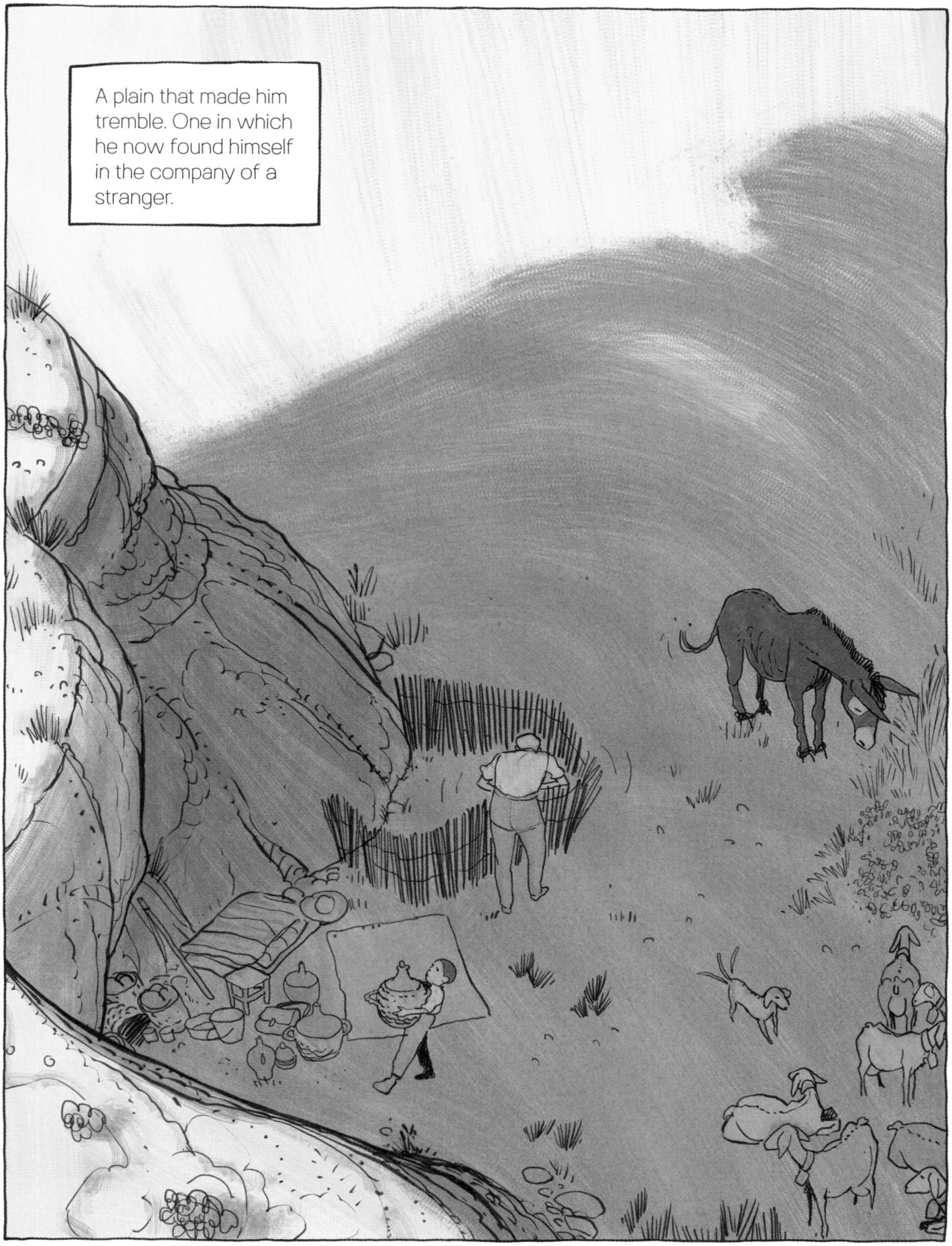
A plain that made him tremble. One in which he now found himself in the company of a stranger.

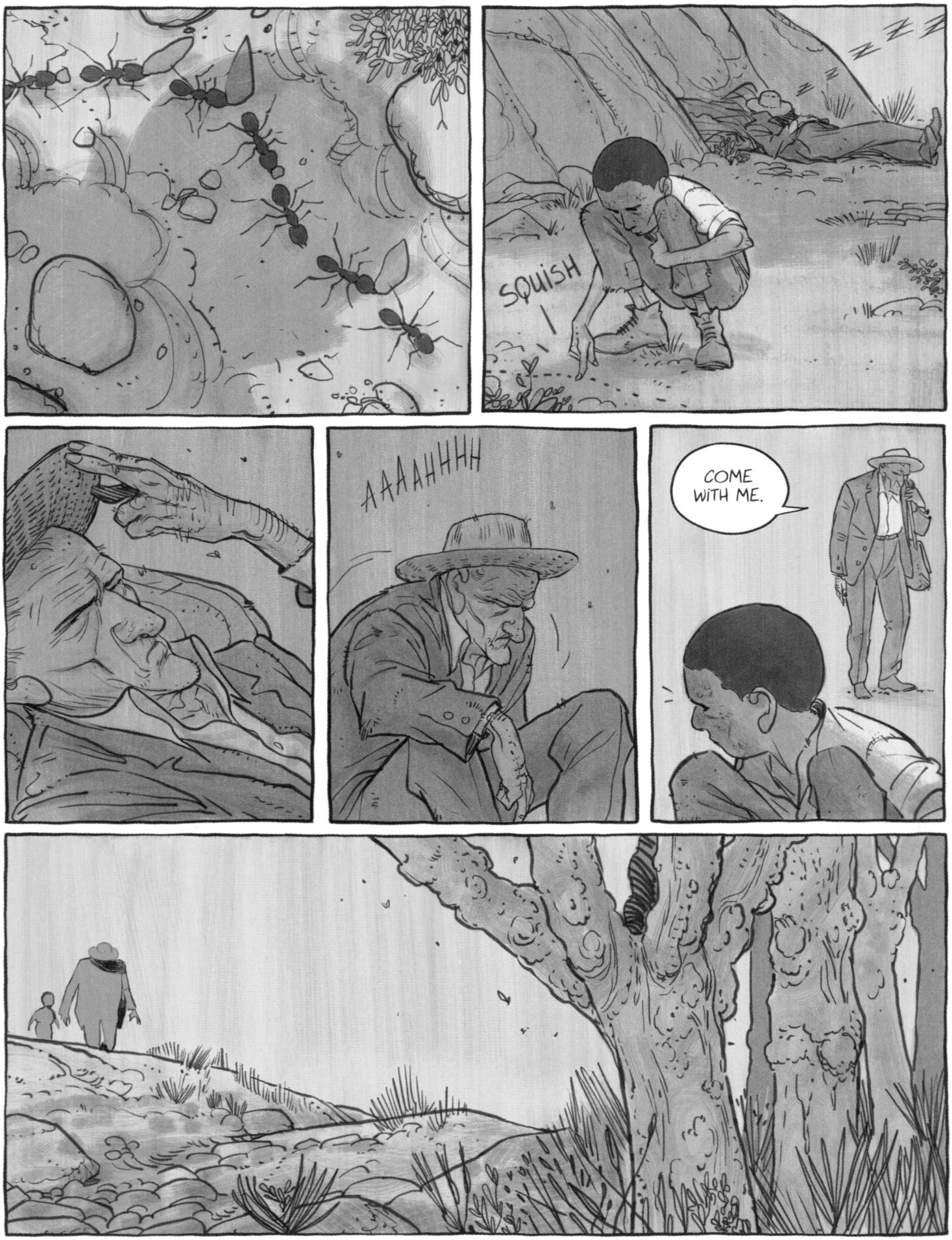
SQUISH
AAAAHHHH
COME WITH ME.

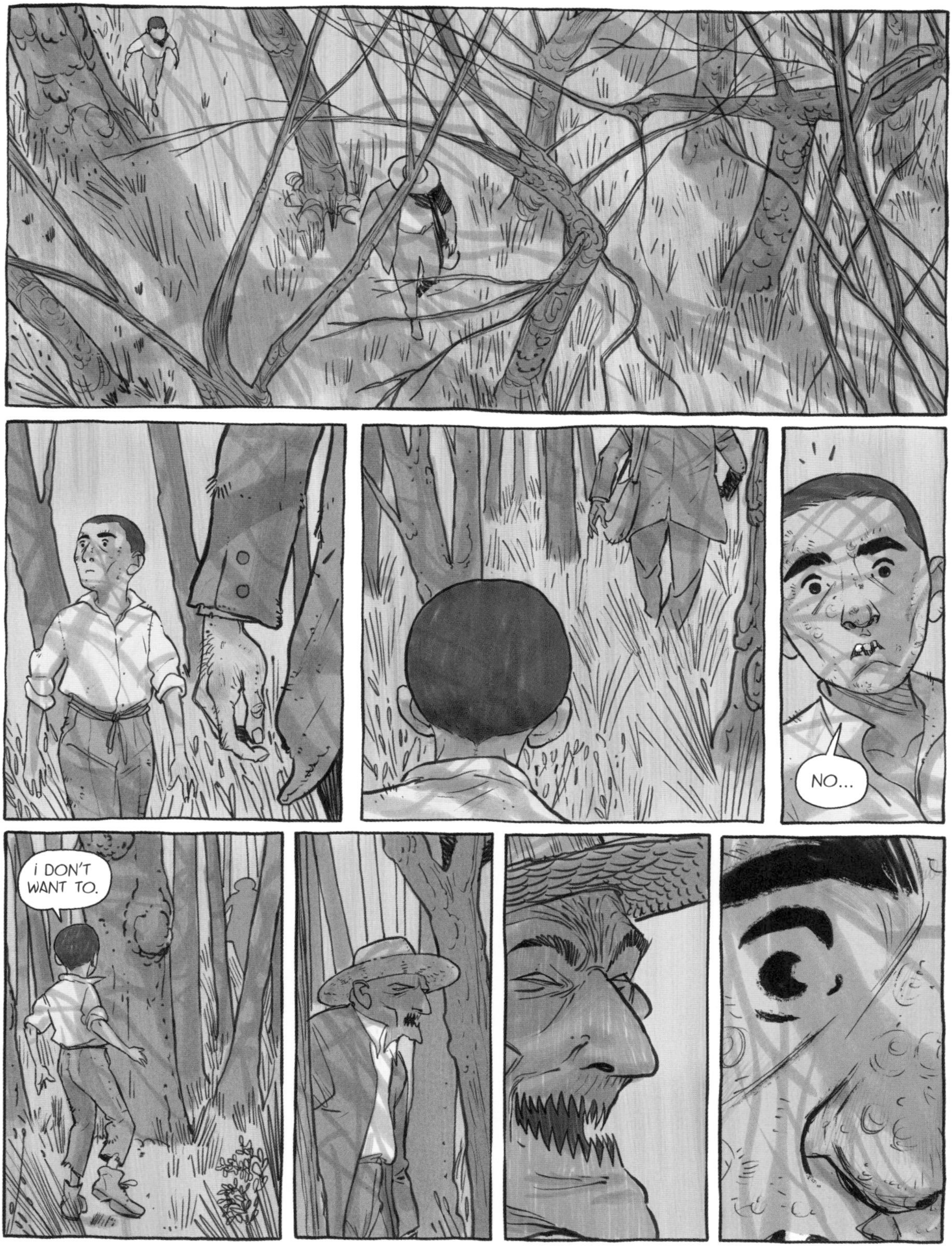
NO...
I DON'T WANT TO.

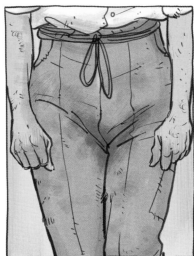

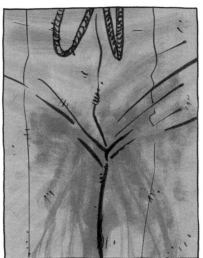

LISTEN.

IT HAS TO BE A CLEAN CUT.

SWISH

BRING ME A GOOD BUNDLE OF THESE.

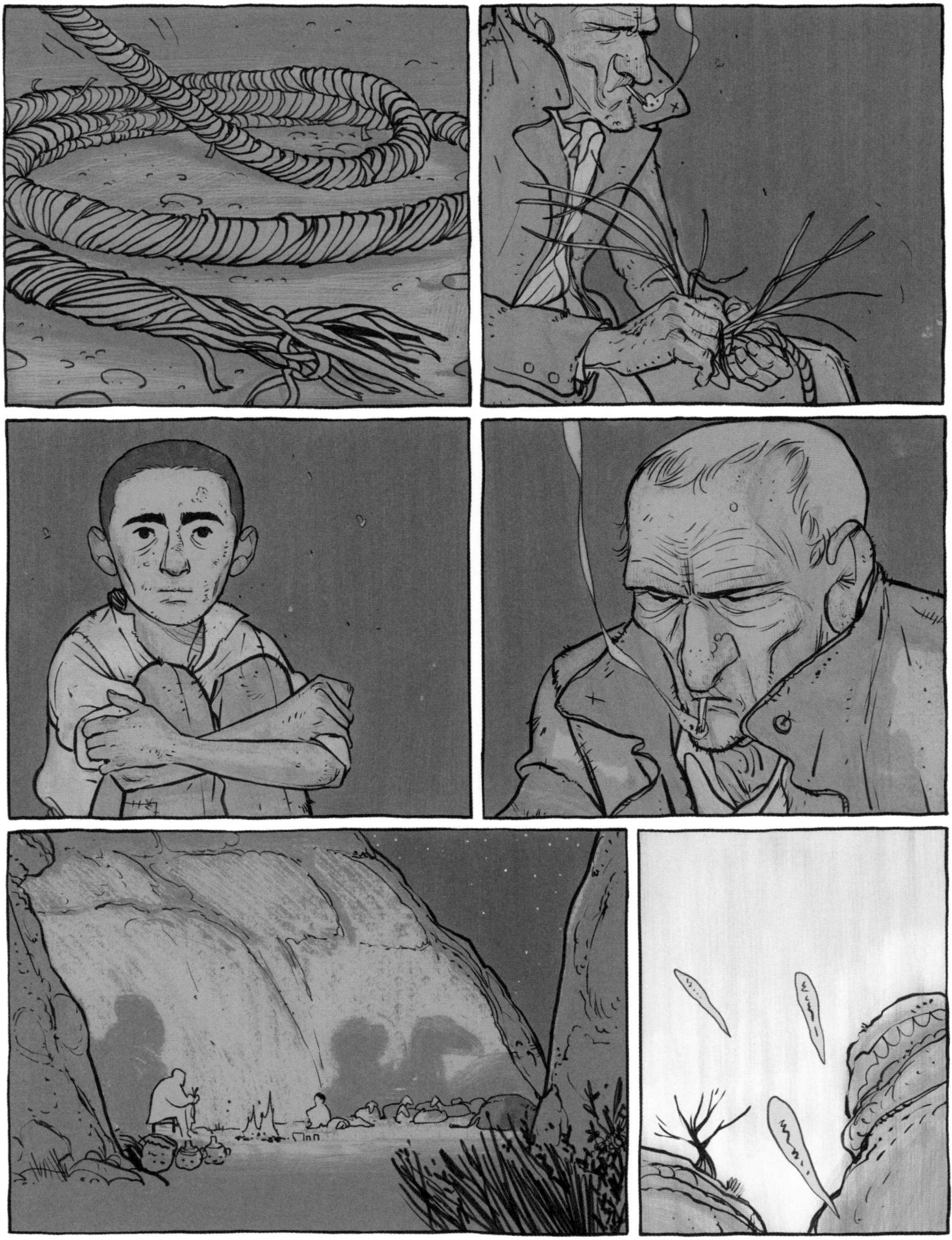

TAP!!

YOU'RE GOING TO HELP ME WITH THE MILKING.

I DON'T KNOW HOW.

JUST STAND AT THE ENTRANCE TO THE PEN AND PULL OUT THE GOATS.

ONE BY ONE, WHEN I TELL YOU TO.

SO LITTLE MILK...

IT'S NORMAL.

THIS TIME OF YEAR, BETWEEN THE HEAT AND THE LACK OF WATER, THE ANIMALS TURN MISERLY.

TSCHHH

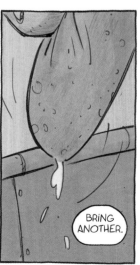

BRING ANOTHER.

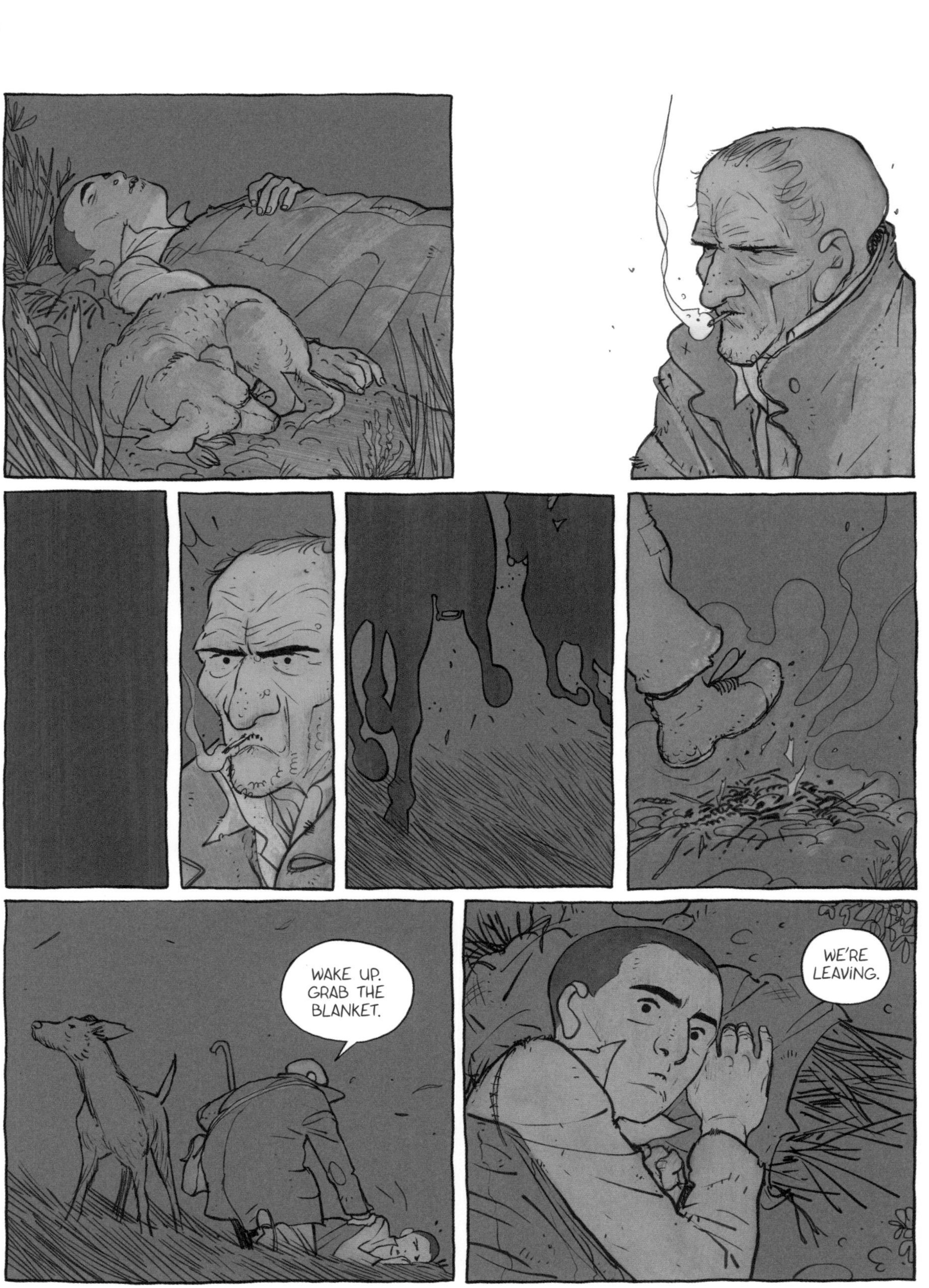
WAKE UP. GRAB THE BLANKET.
WE'RE LEAVING.

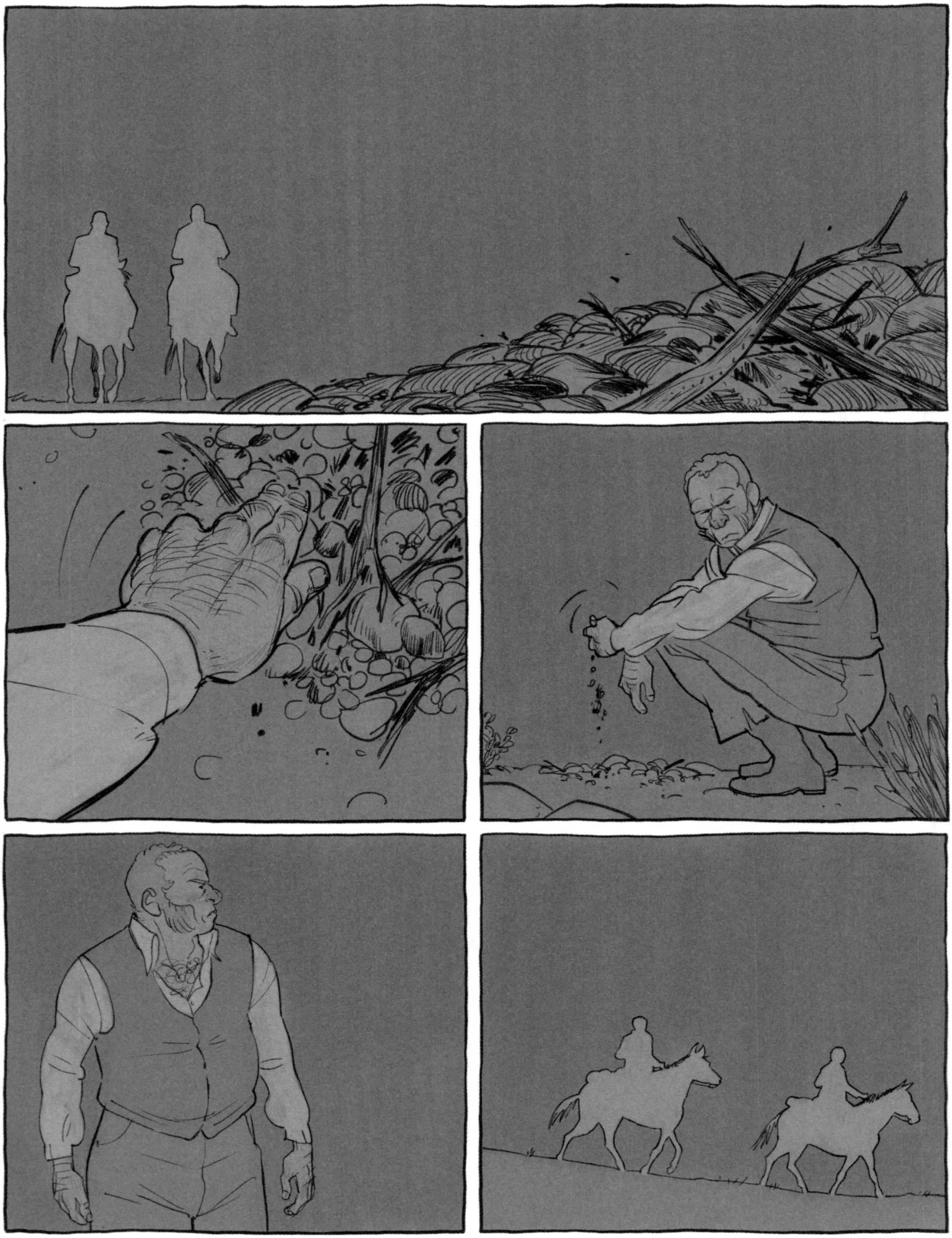

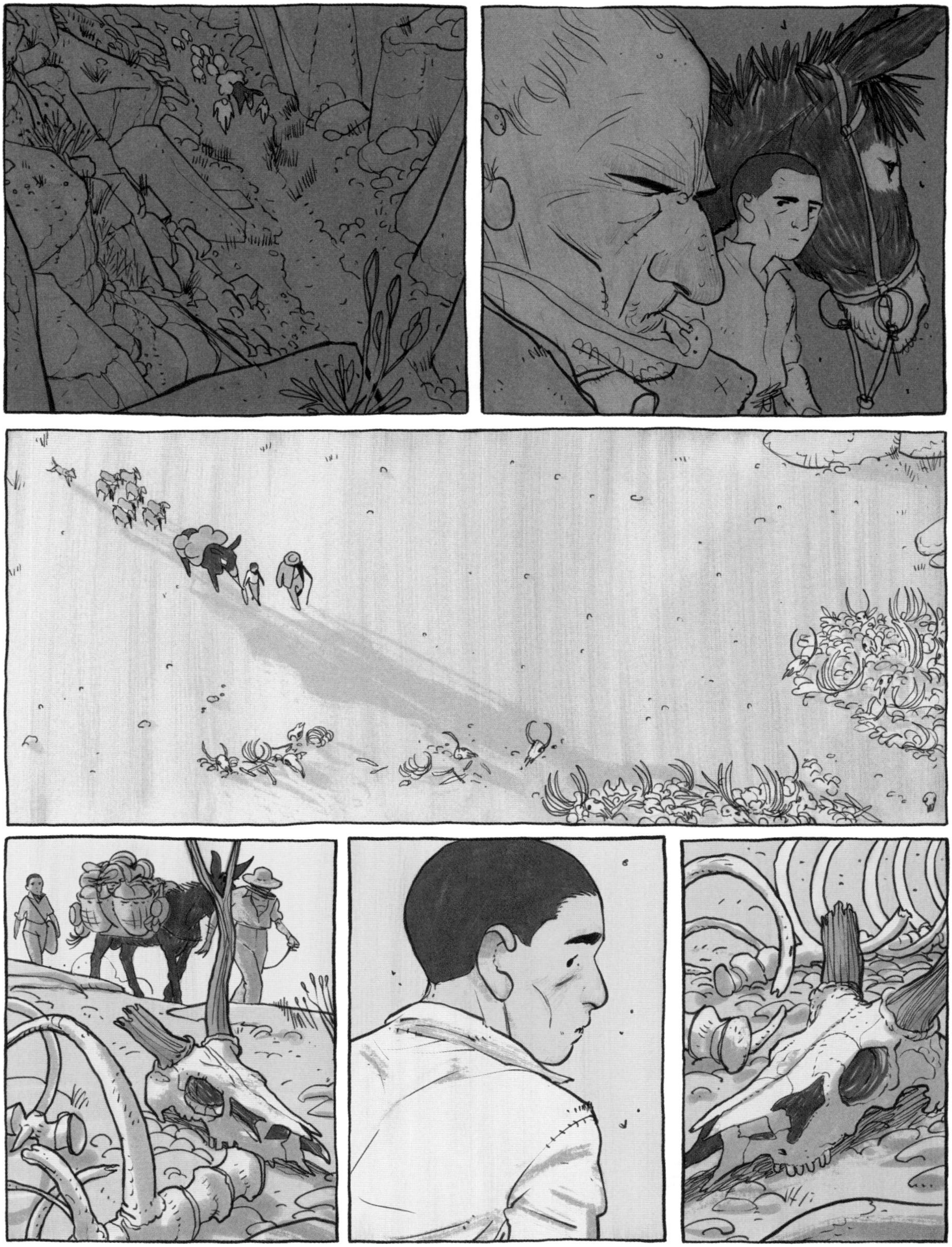

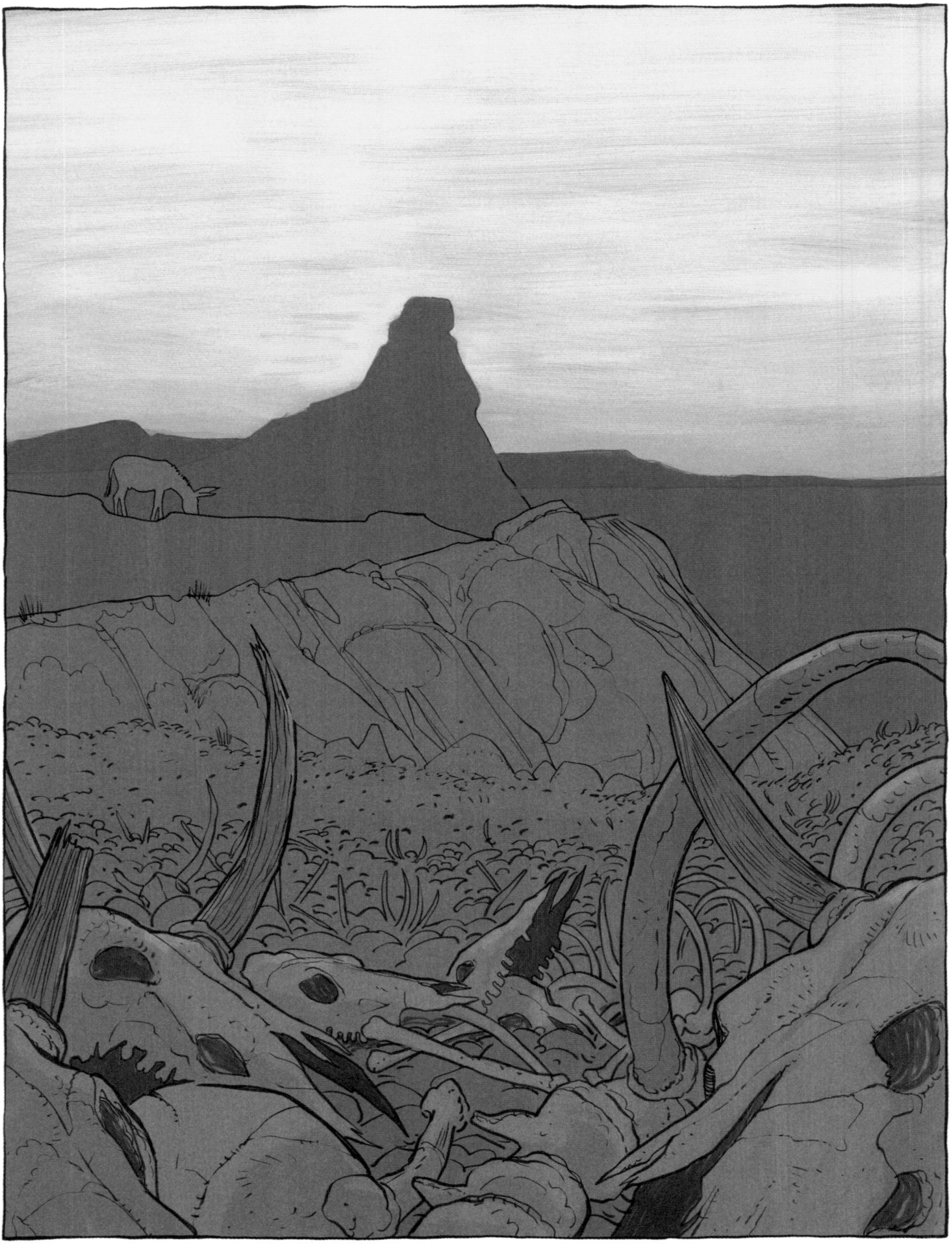

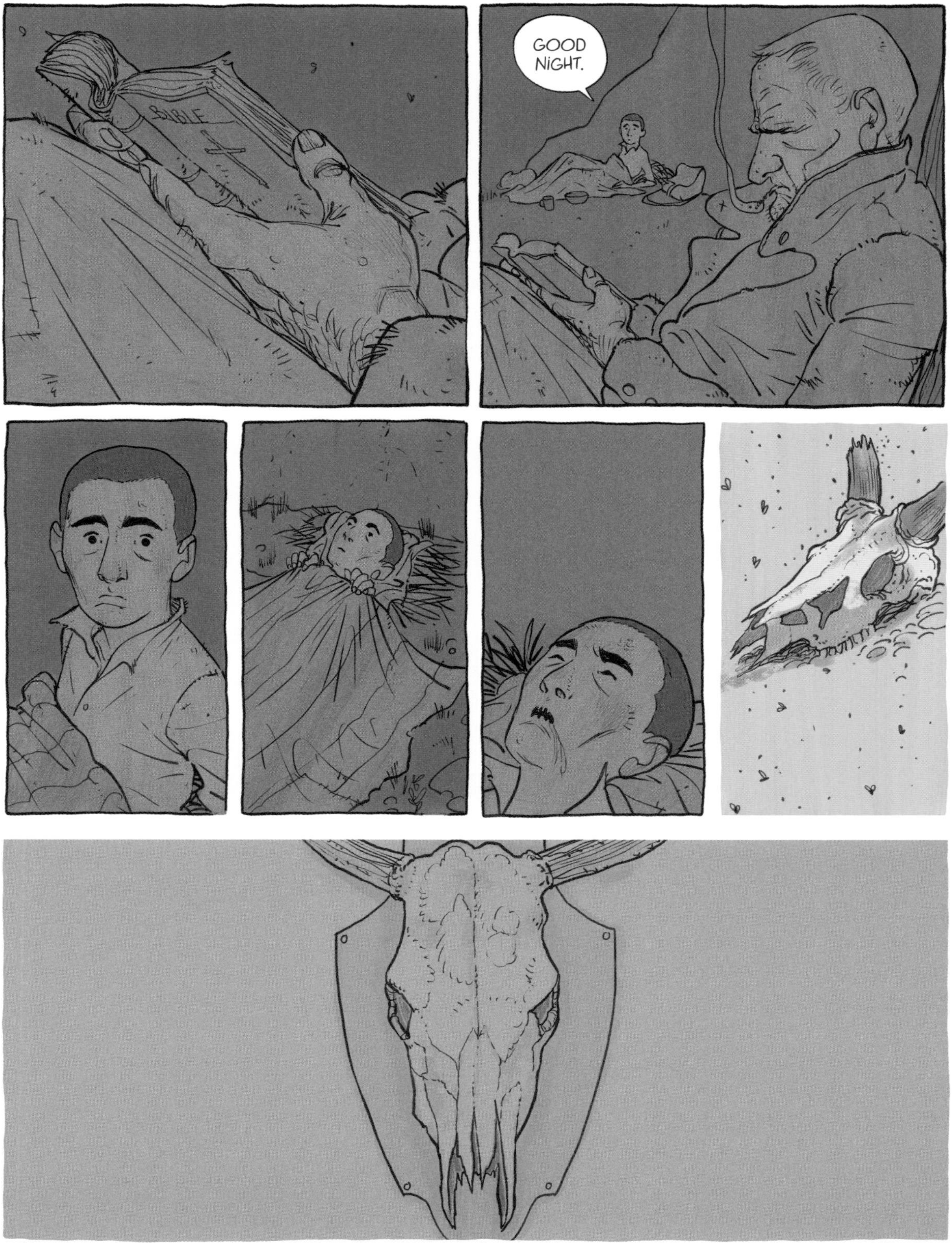
GOOD NIGHT.

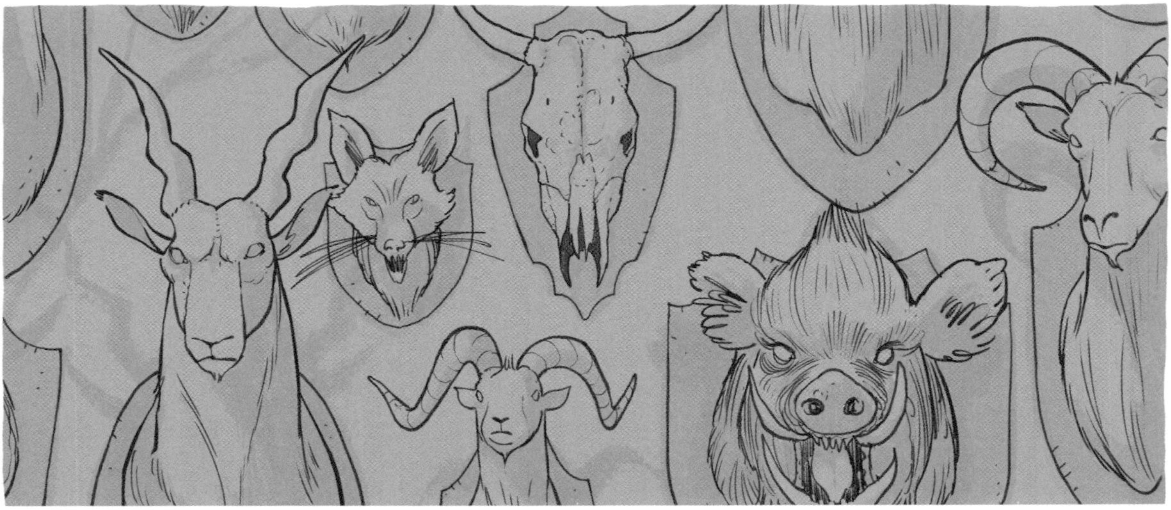
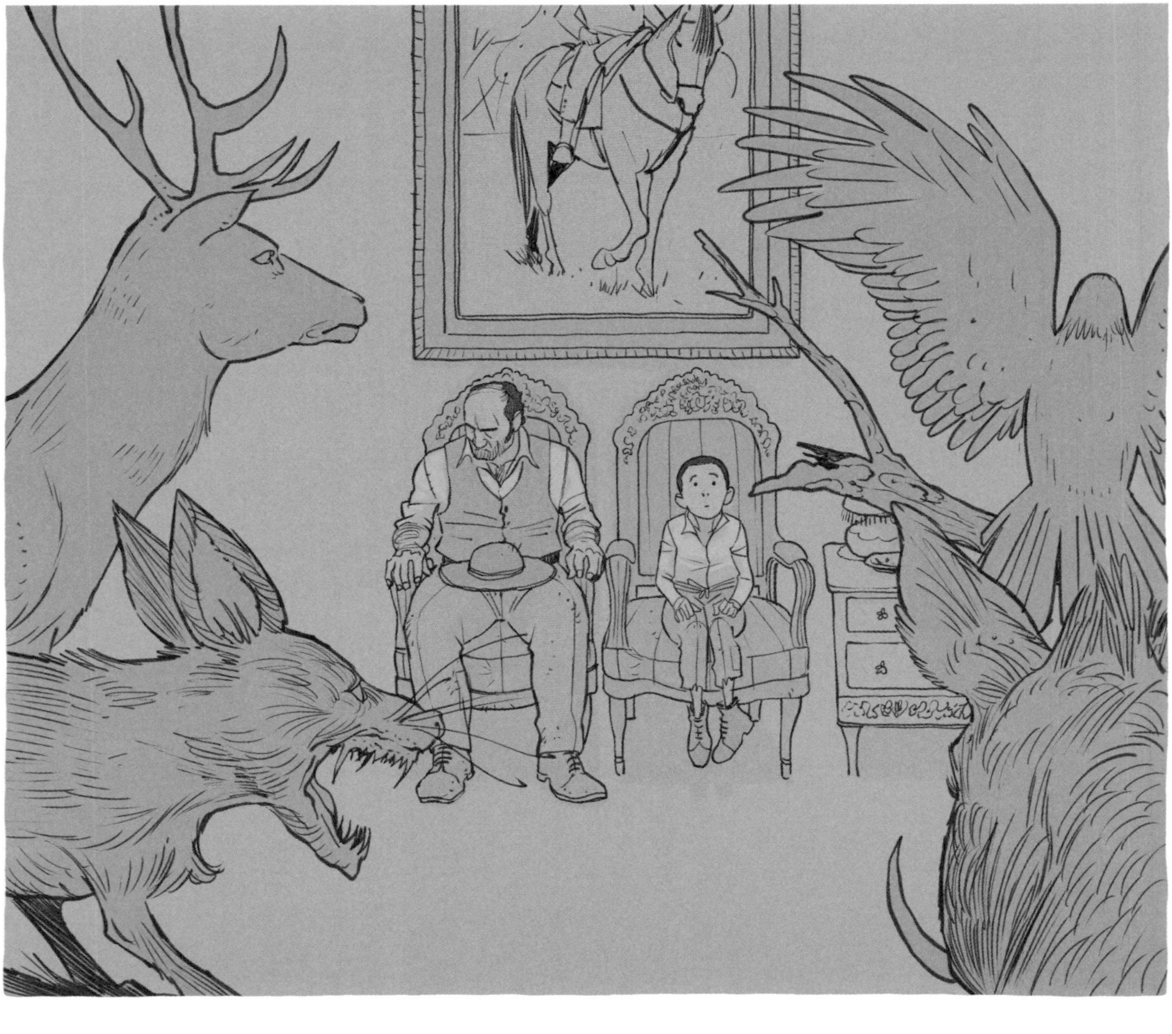

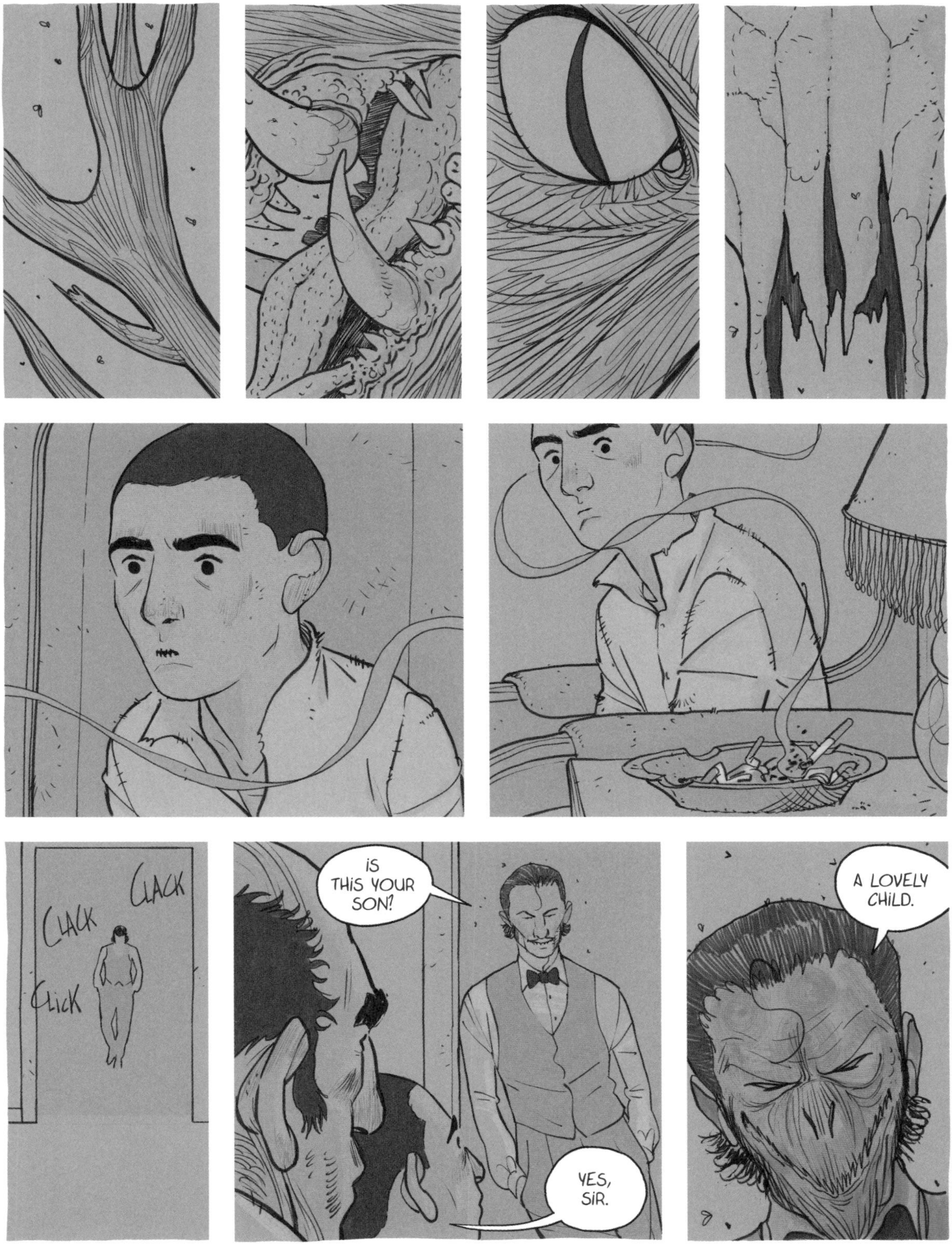
CLACK
CLACK
CLICK
IS THIS YOUR SON?
YES, SIR.
A LOVELY CHILD.

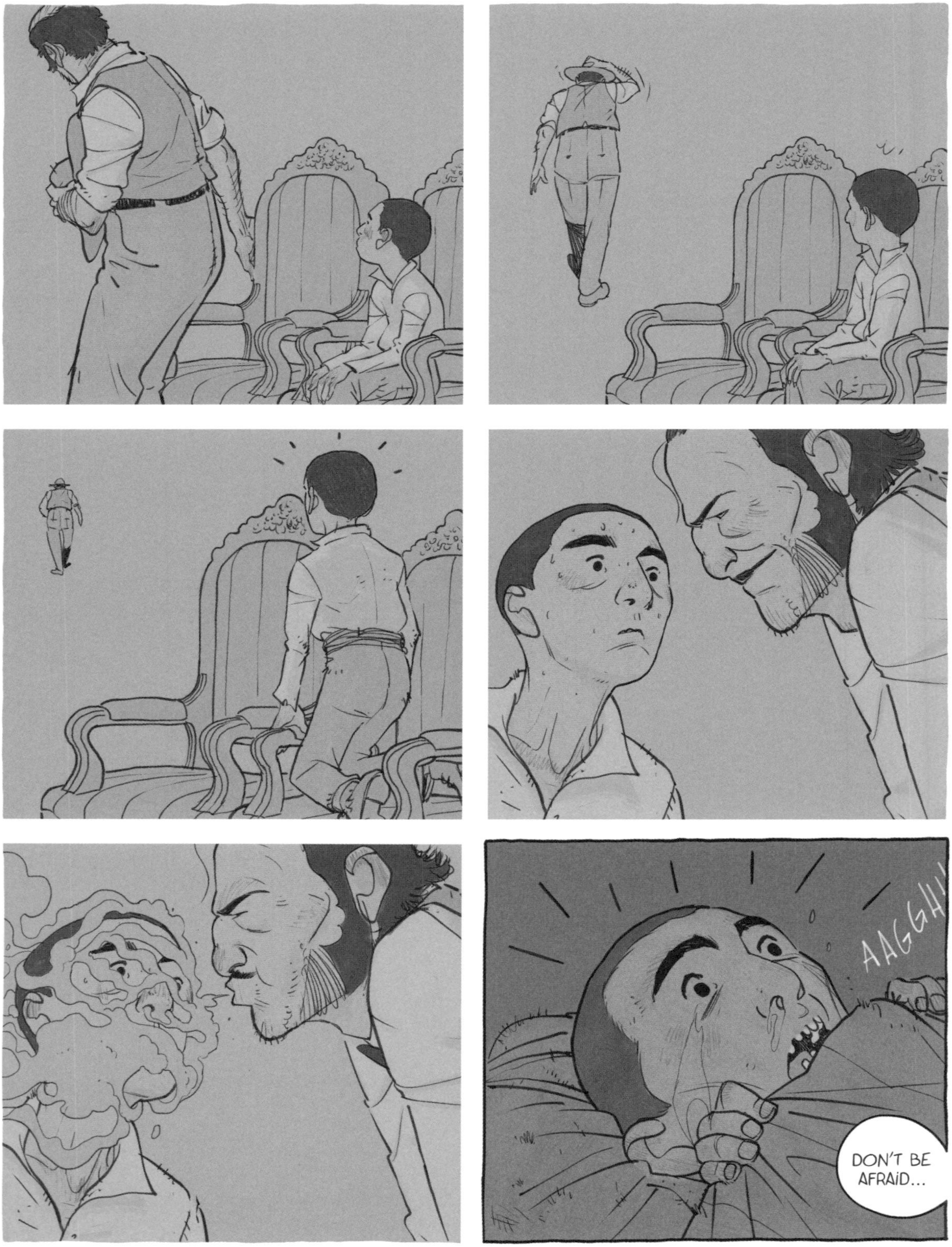
AAGHH
DON'T BE AFRAID...

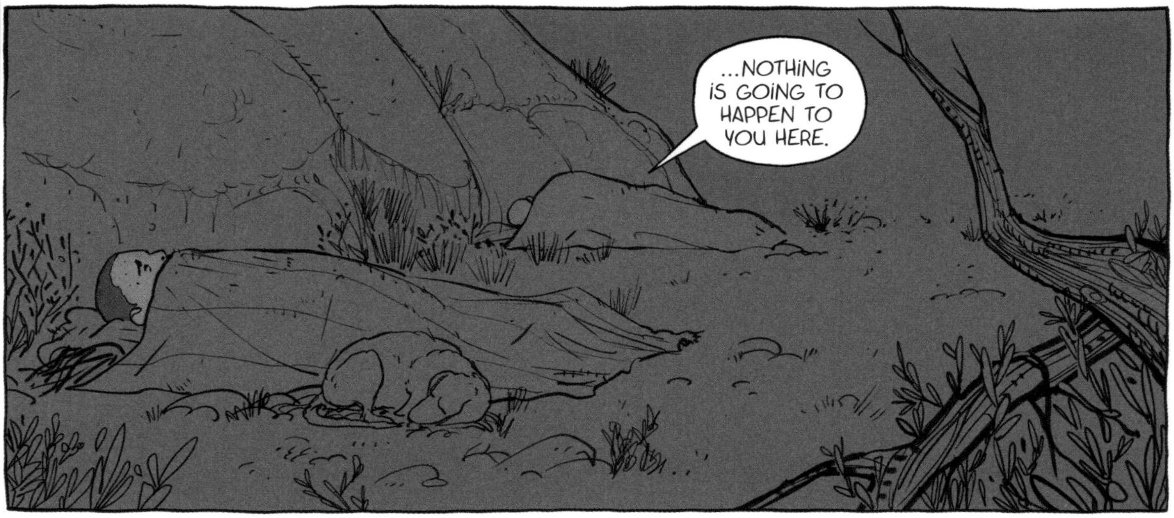
...NOTHING IS GOING TO HAPPEN TO YOU HERE.

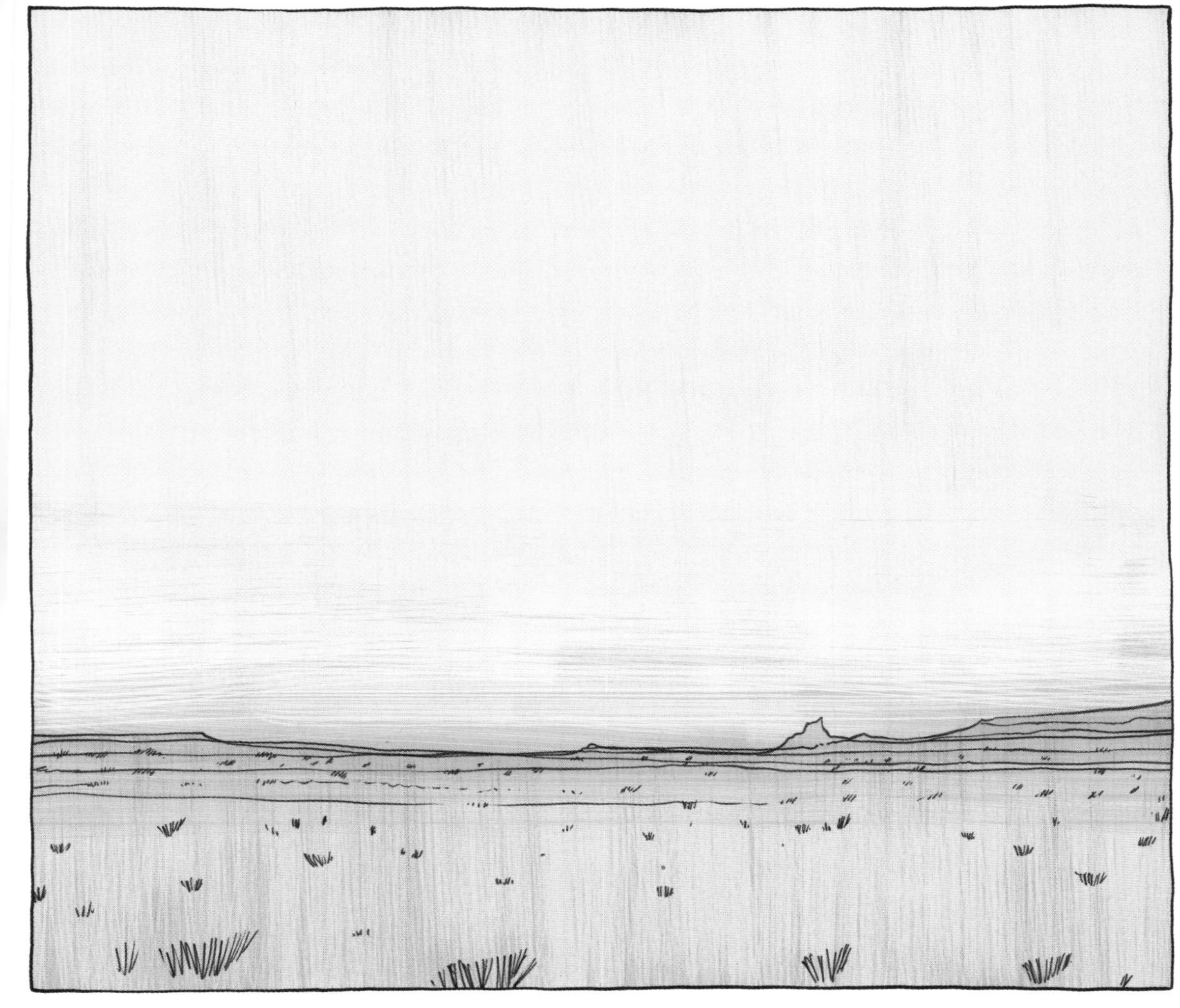

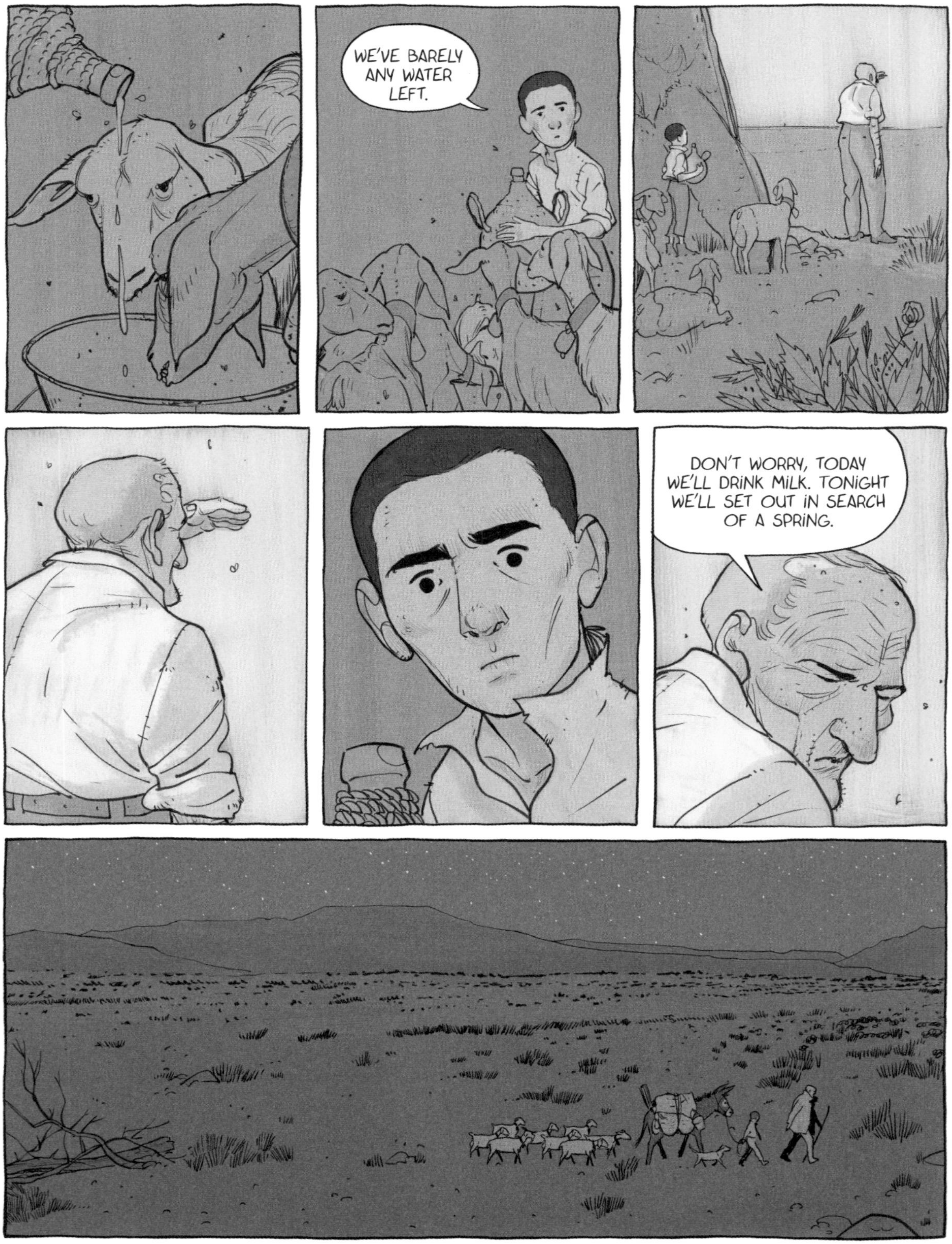
WE'VE BARELY ANY WATER LEFT.
DON'T WORRY, TODAY WE'LL DRINK MILK. TONIGHT WE'LL SET OUT IN SEARCH OF A SPRING.

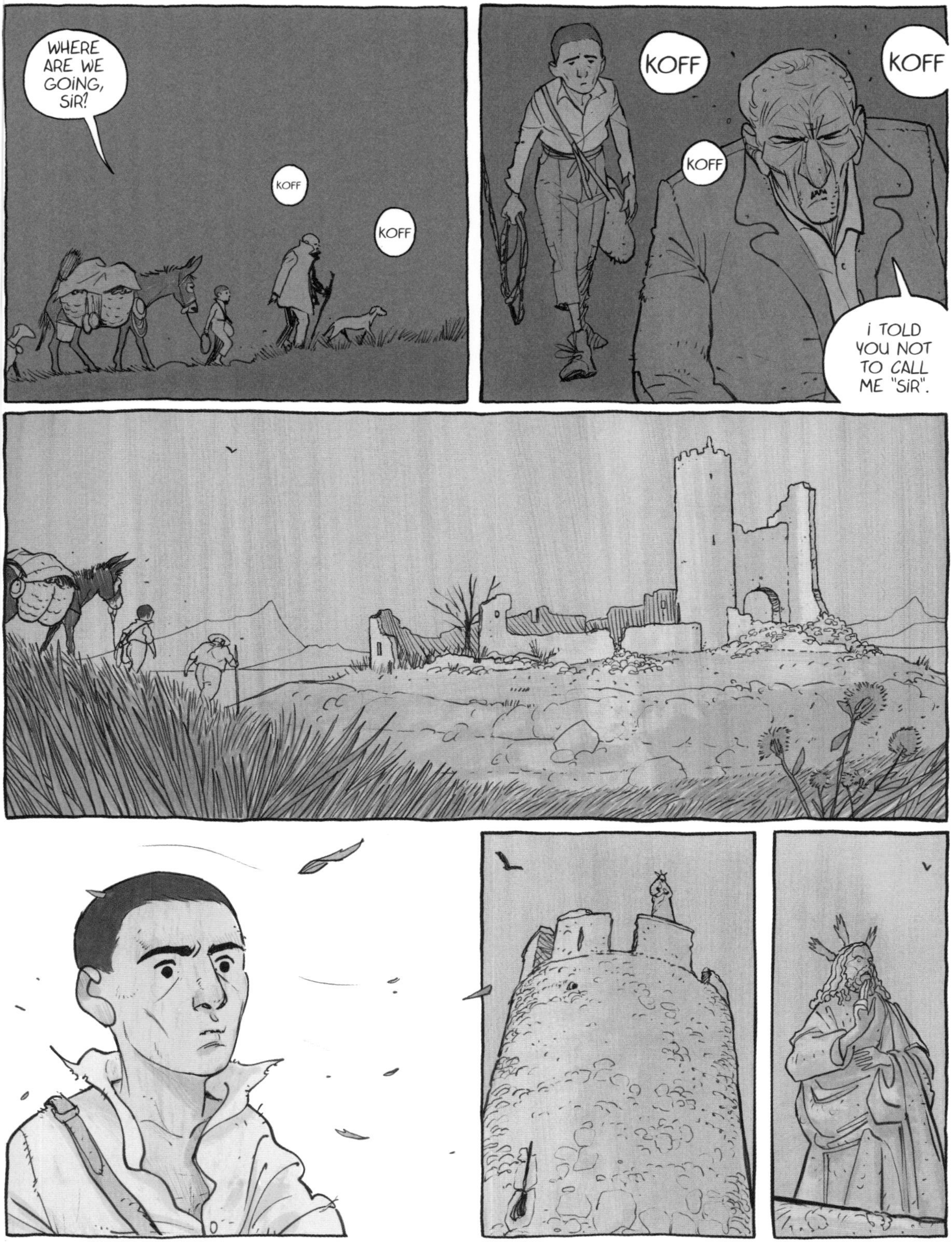
WHERE ARE WE GOING, SIR?
KOFF
KOFF
KOFF
KOFF
KOFF
I TOLD YOU NOT TO CALL ME "SIR".

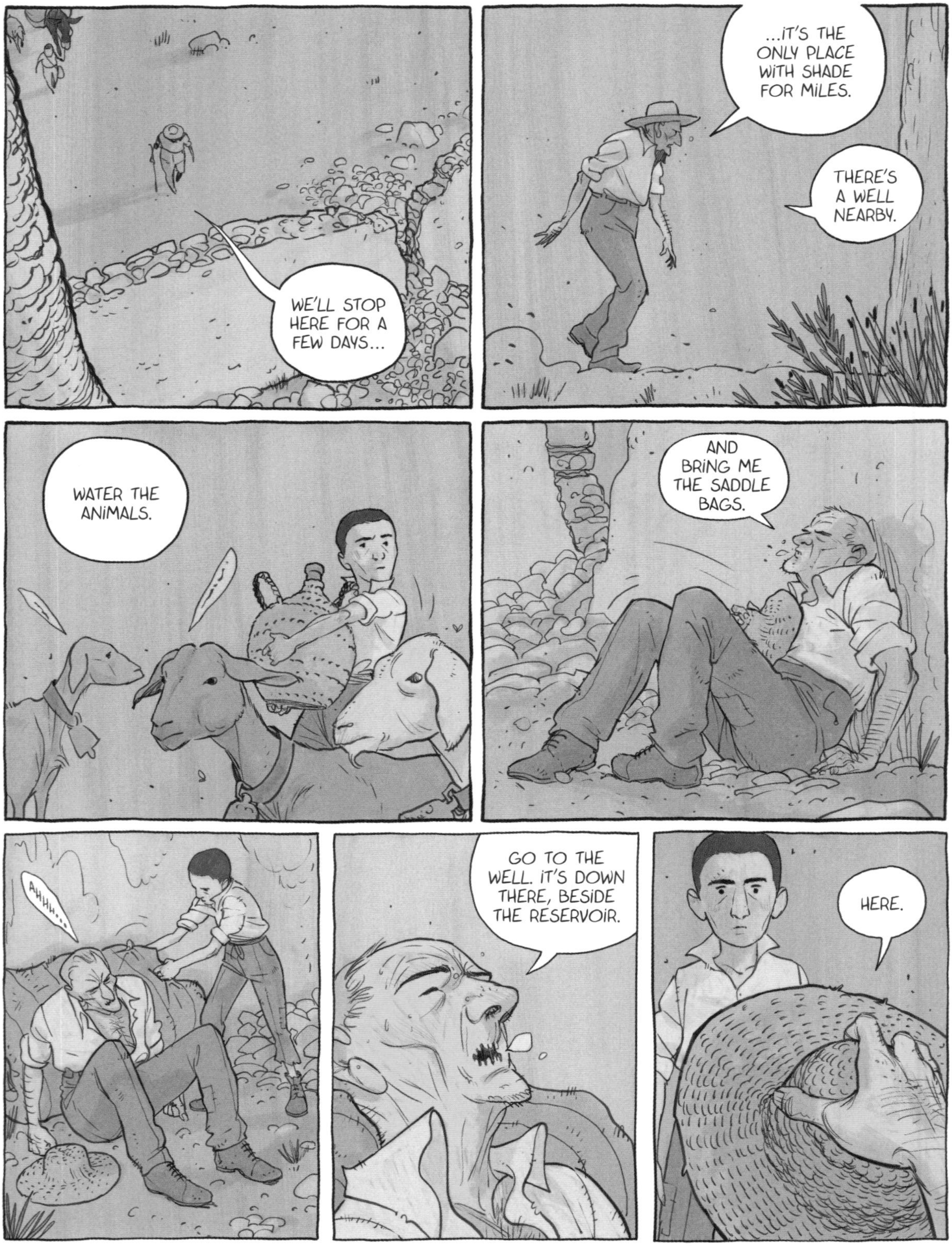
WE'LL STOP HERE FOR A FEW DAYS...
...IT'S THE ONLY PLACE WITH SHADE FOR MILES.
THERE'S A WELL NEARBY.
WATER THE ANIMALS.
AND BRING ME THE SADDLE BAGS.
AHHH...
GO TO THE WELL. IT'S DOWN THERE, BESIDE THE RESERVOIR.
HERE.

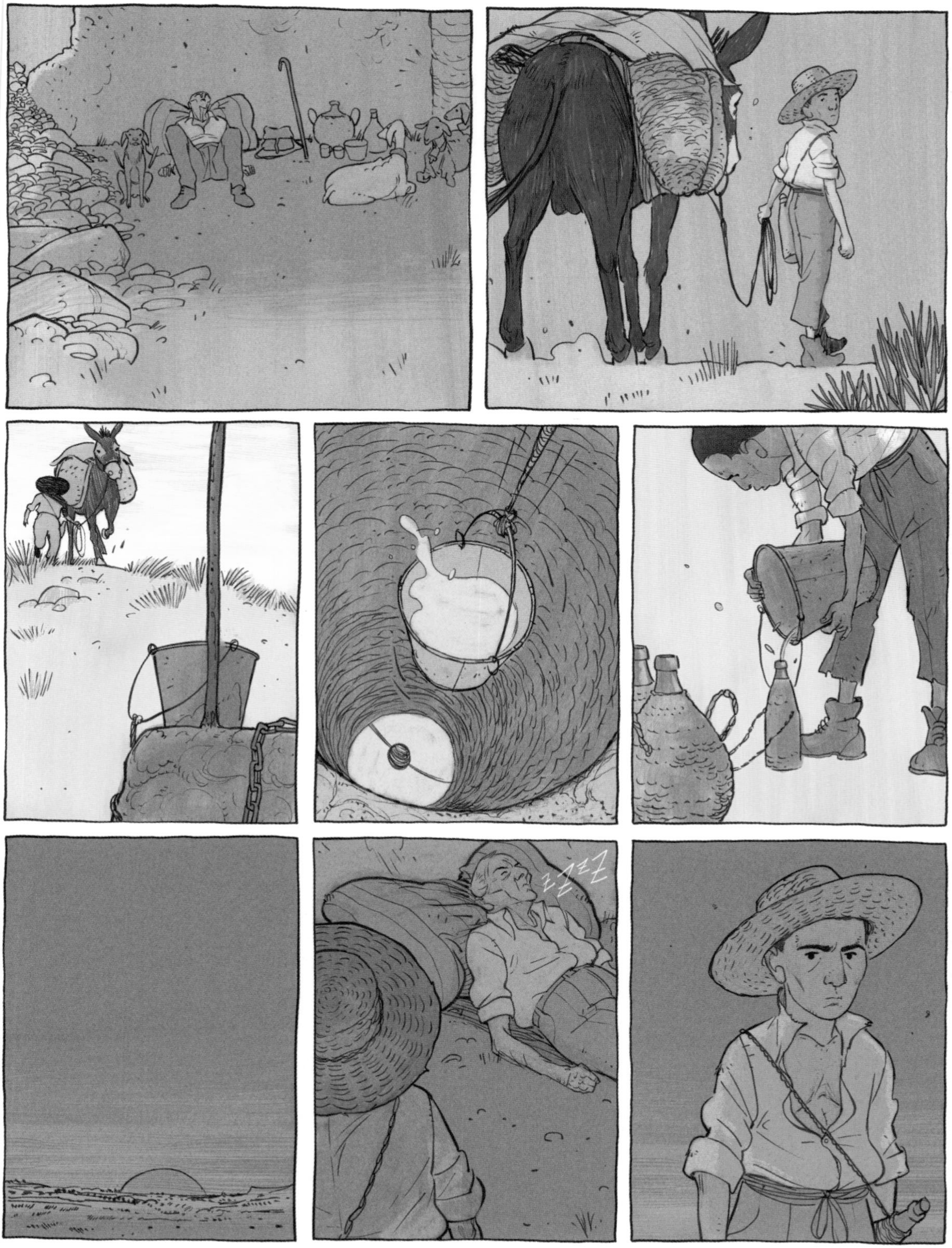
ZZZZ

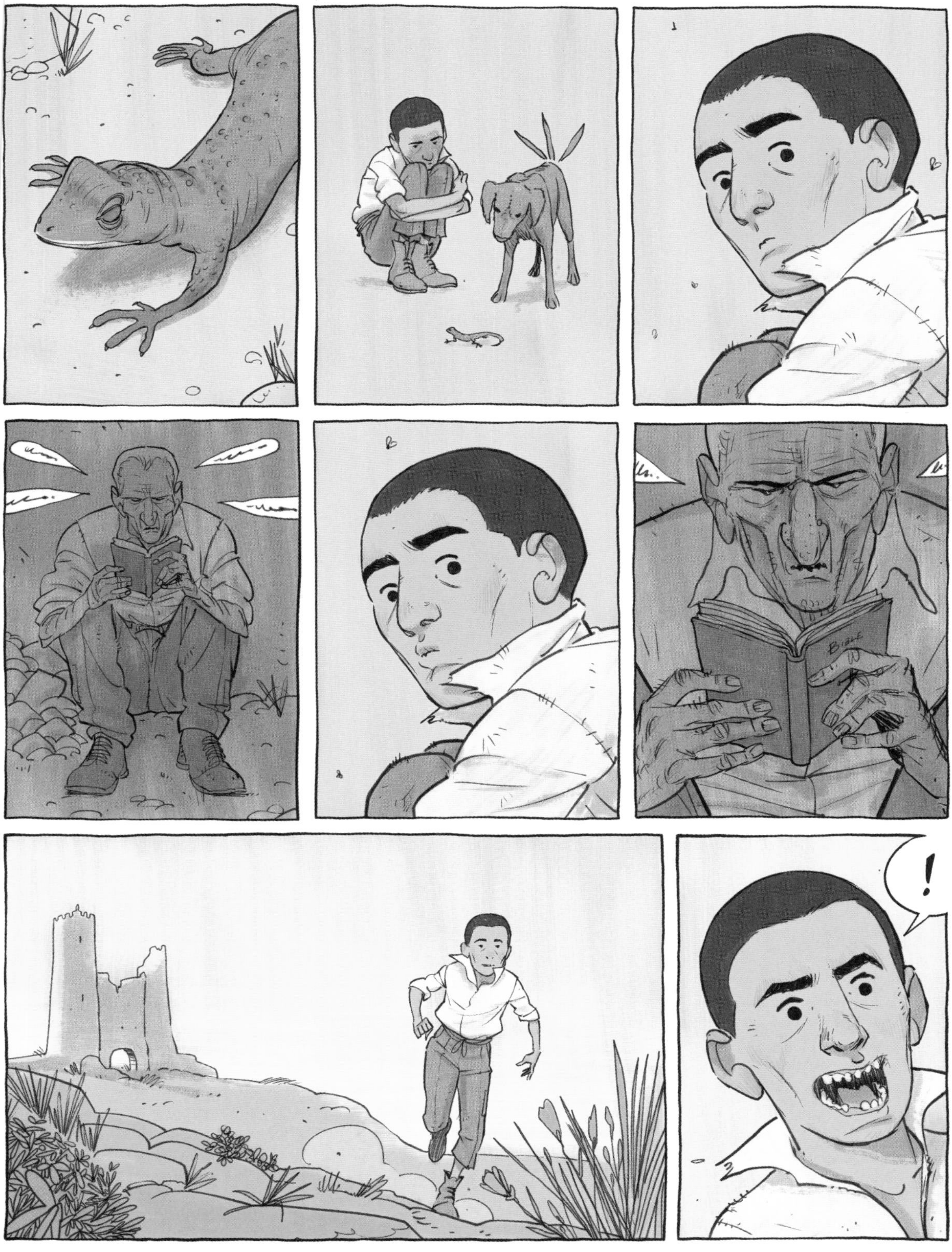
!

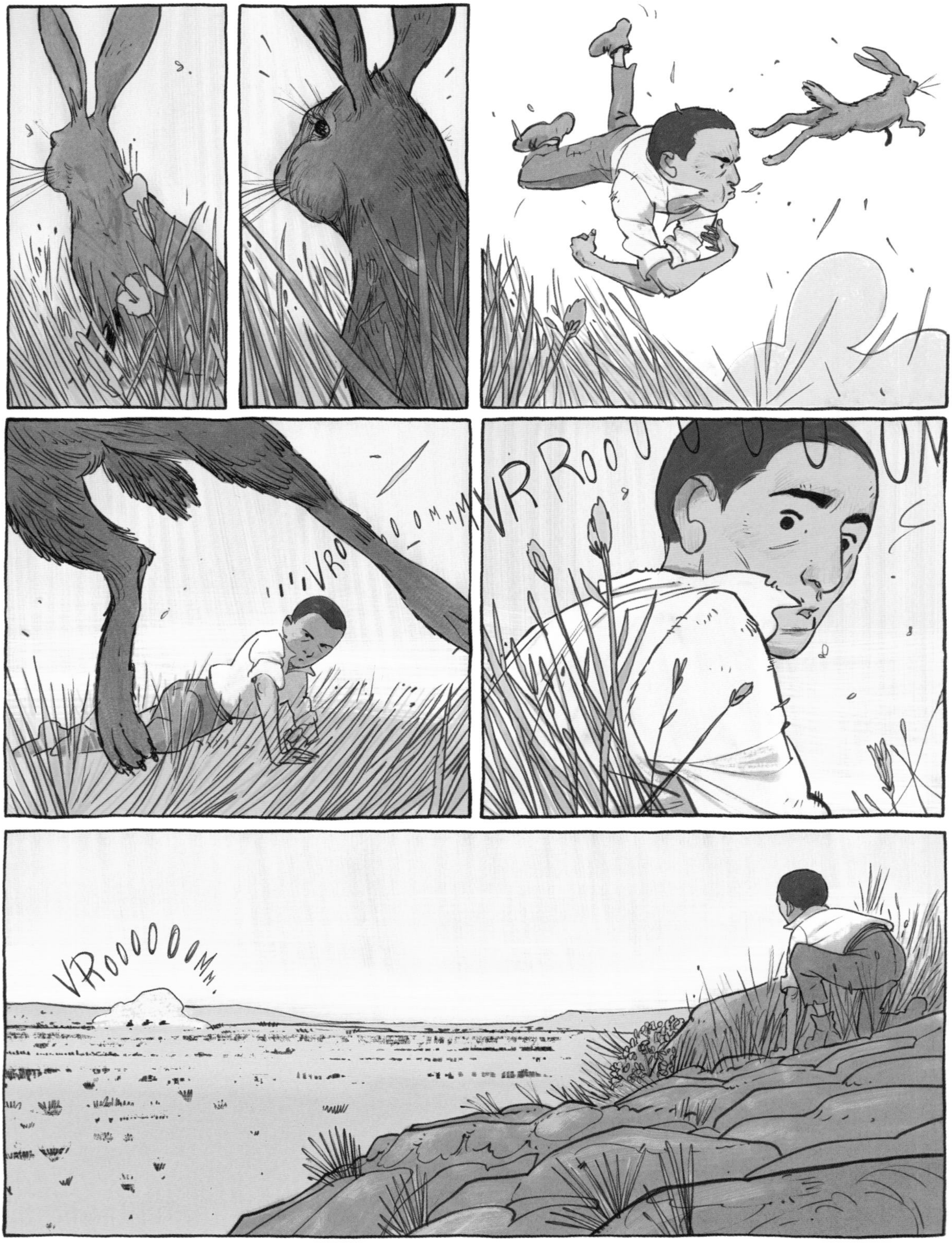
VROO_OMMM
VRROOOOOOM
VROOOOOMM

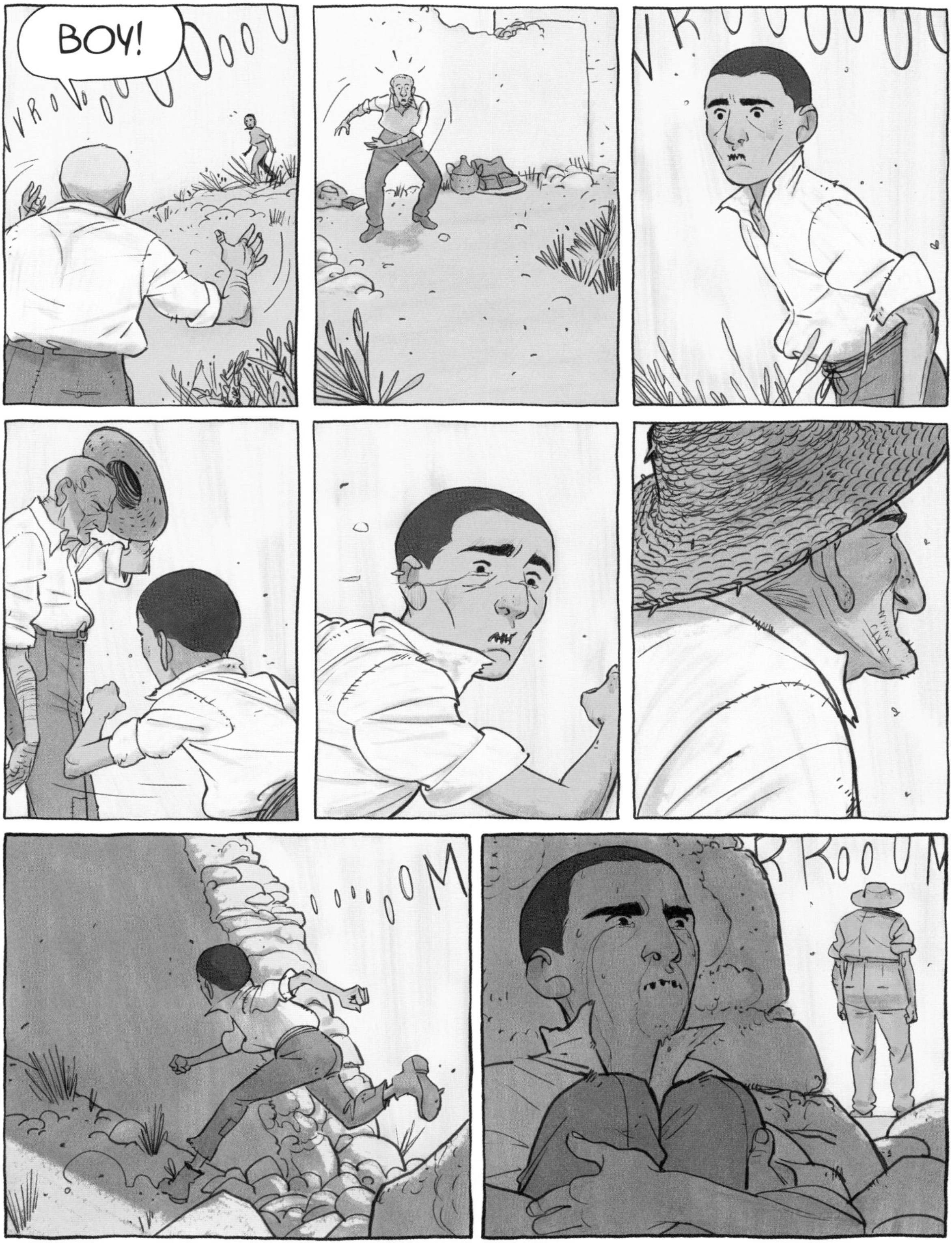
BOY!
VROOOOOOOO
VROOOOOOO
OOOOOOM
RROOOM

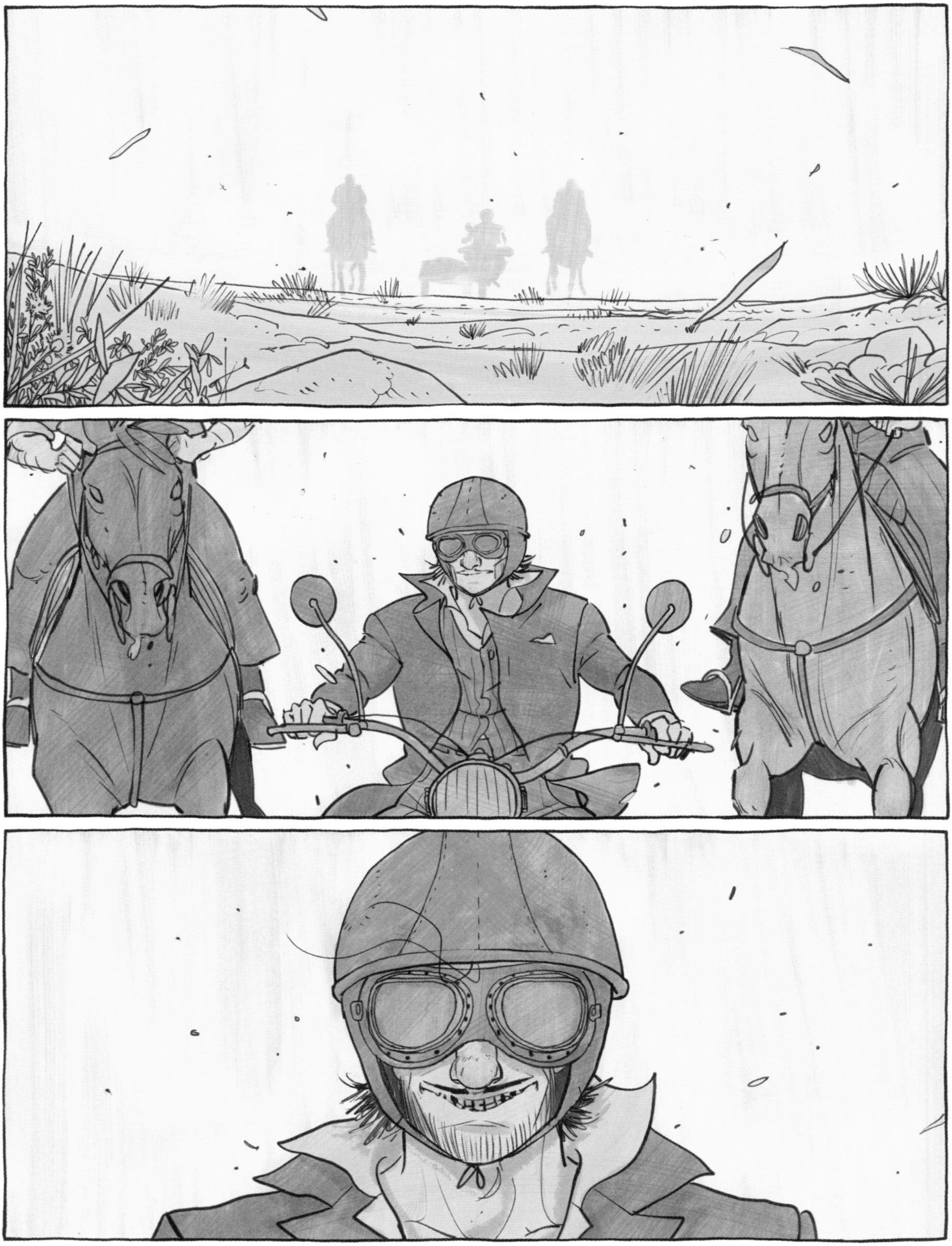

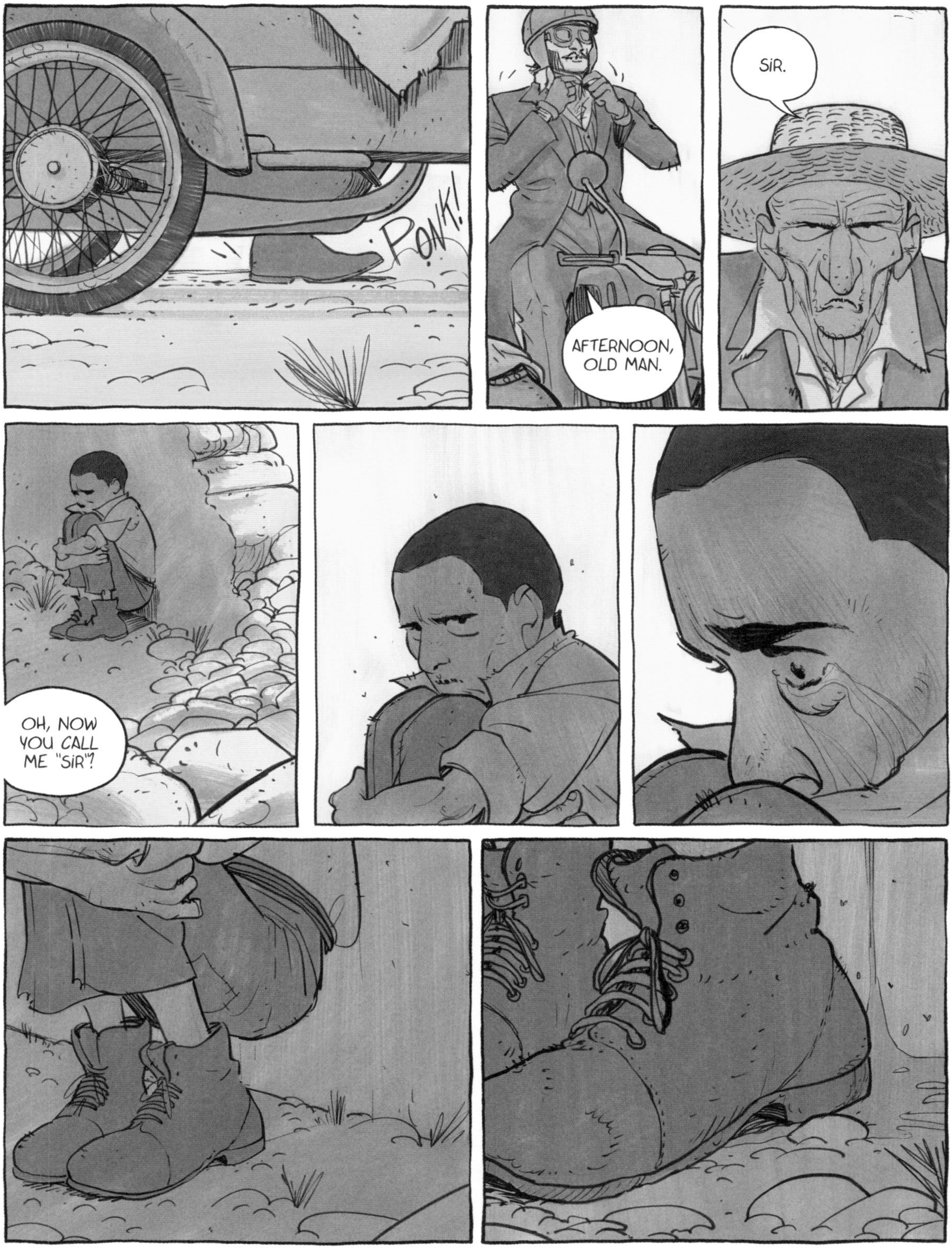
PONK!
AFTERNOON, OLD MAN.
SIR.
OH, NOW YOU CALL ME "SIR"?

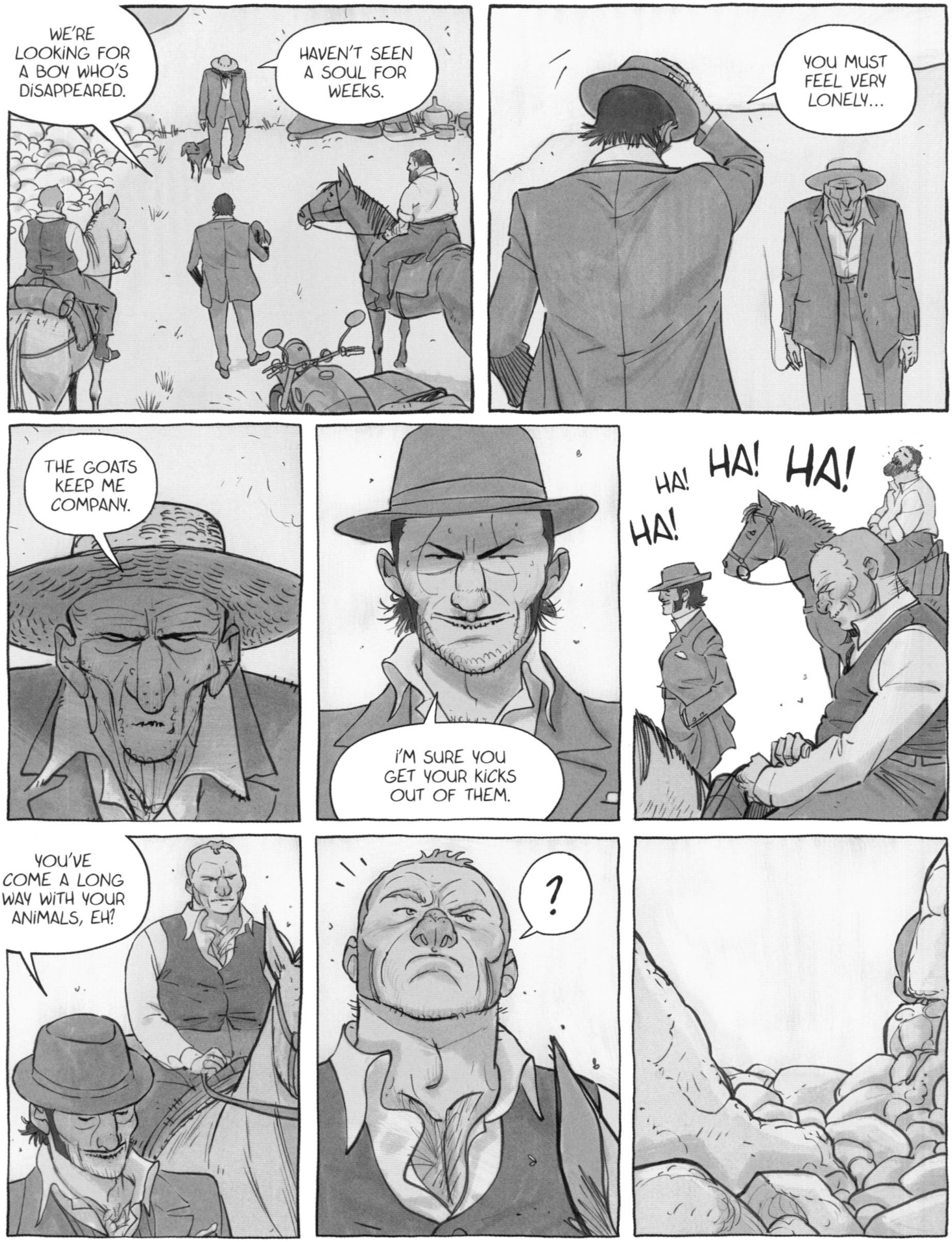
WE'RE LOOKING FOR A BOY WHO'S DISAPPEARED.
HAVEN'T SEEN A SOUL FOR WEEKS.
YOU MUST FEEL VERY LONELY...
THE GOATS KEEP ME COMPANY.
I'M SURE YOU GET YOUR KICKS OUT OF THEM.
HA! HA! HA! HA!
YOU'VE COME A LONG WAY WITH YOUR ANIMALS, EH?
?

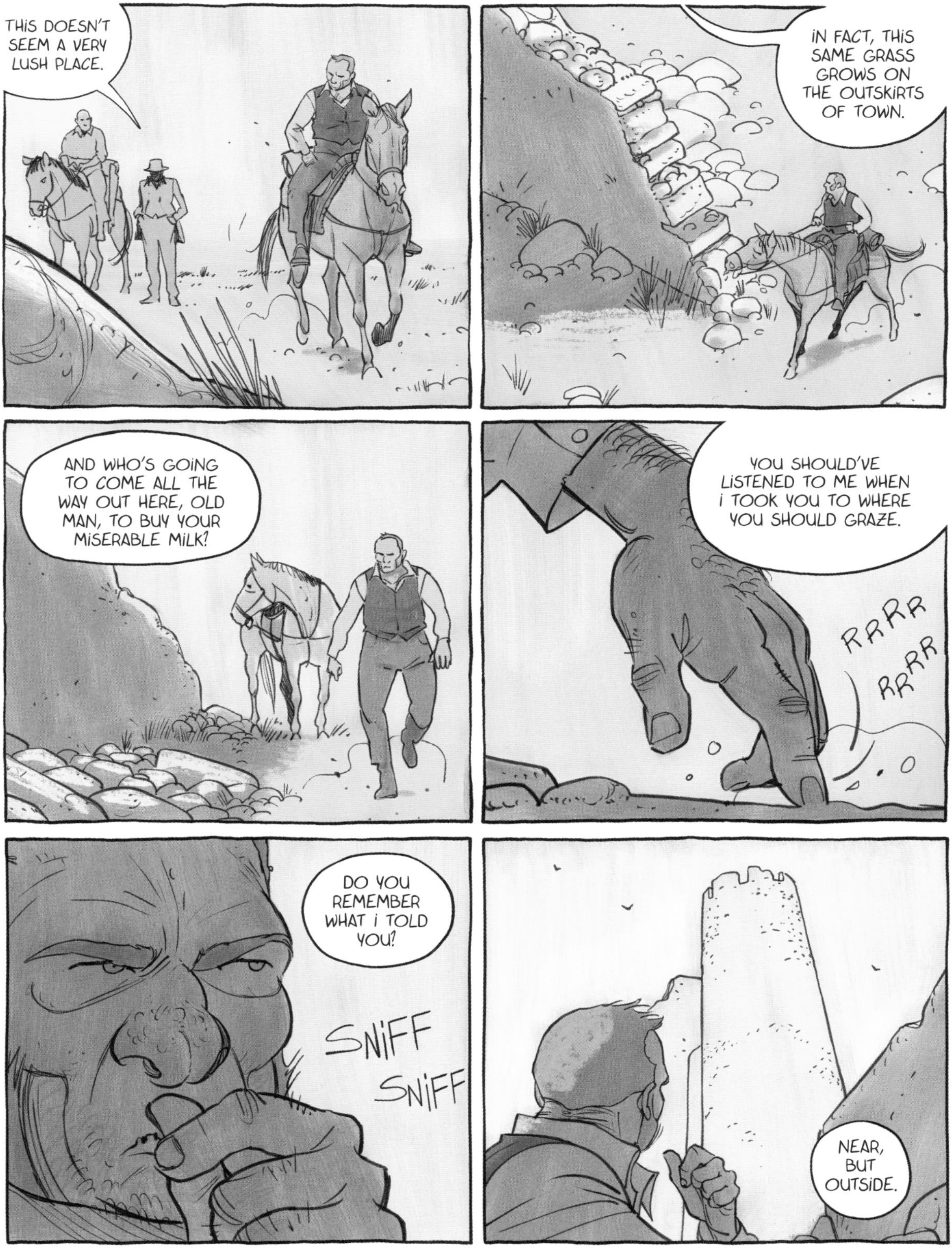
THIS DOESN'T SEEM A VERY LUSH PLACE.
IN FACT, THIS SAME GRASS GROWS ON THE OUTSKIRTS OF TOWN.
AND WHO'S GOING TO COME ALL THE WAY OUT HERE, OLD MAN, TO BUY YOUR MISERABLE MILK?
YOU SHOULD'VE LISTENED TO ME WHEN I TOOK YOU TO WHERE YOU SHOULD GRAZE.
RRRR
RRRR
DO YOU REMEMBER WHAT I TOLD YOU?
SNIFF
SNIFF
NEAR, BUT OUTSIDE.

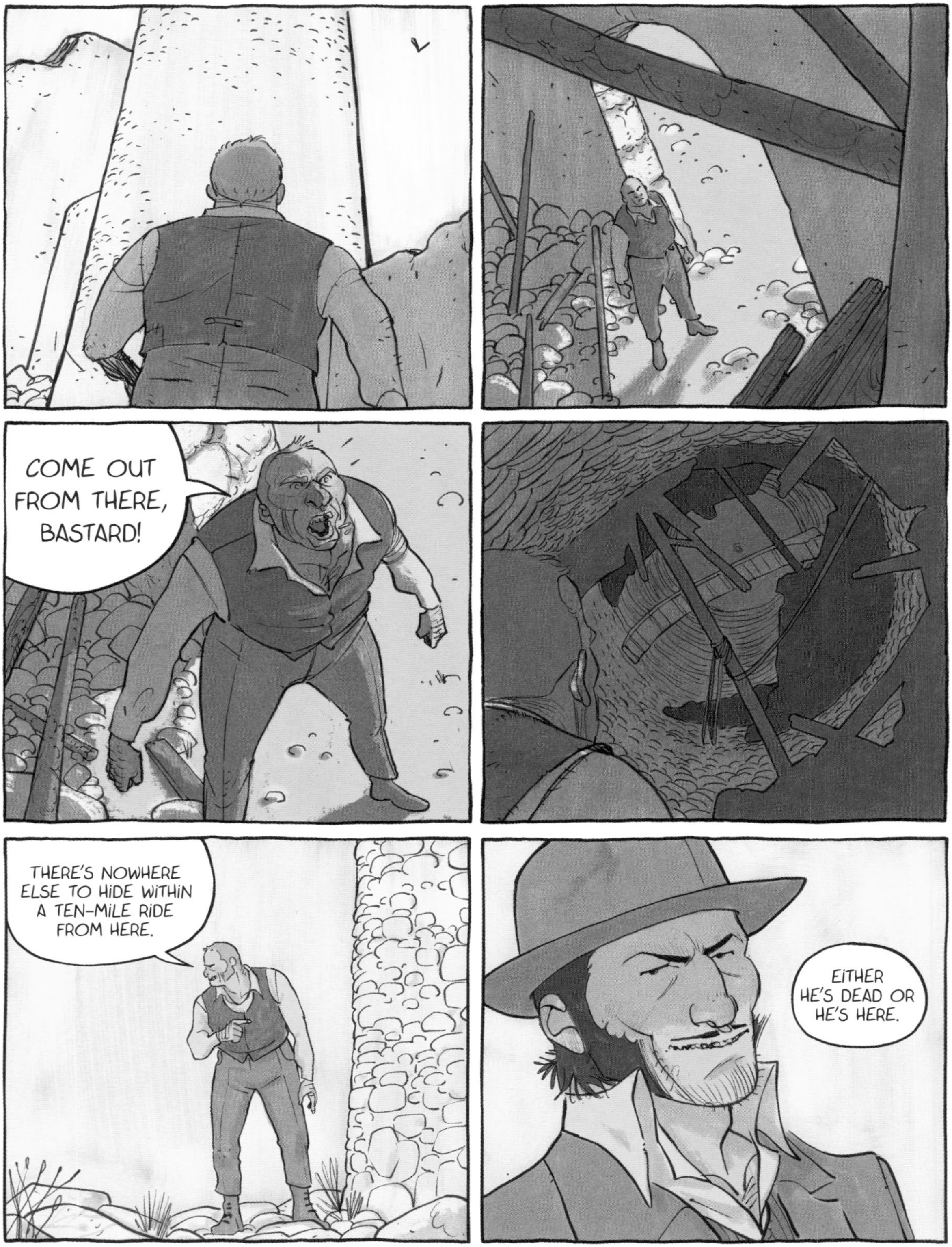
COME OUT FROM THERE, BASTARD!
THERE'S NOWHERE ELSE TO HIDE WITHIN A TEN-MILE RIDE FROM HERE.
EITHER HE'S DEAD OR HE'S HERE.

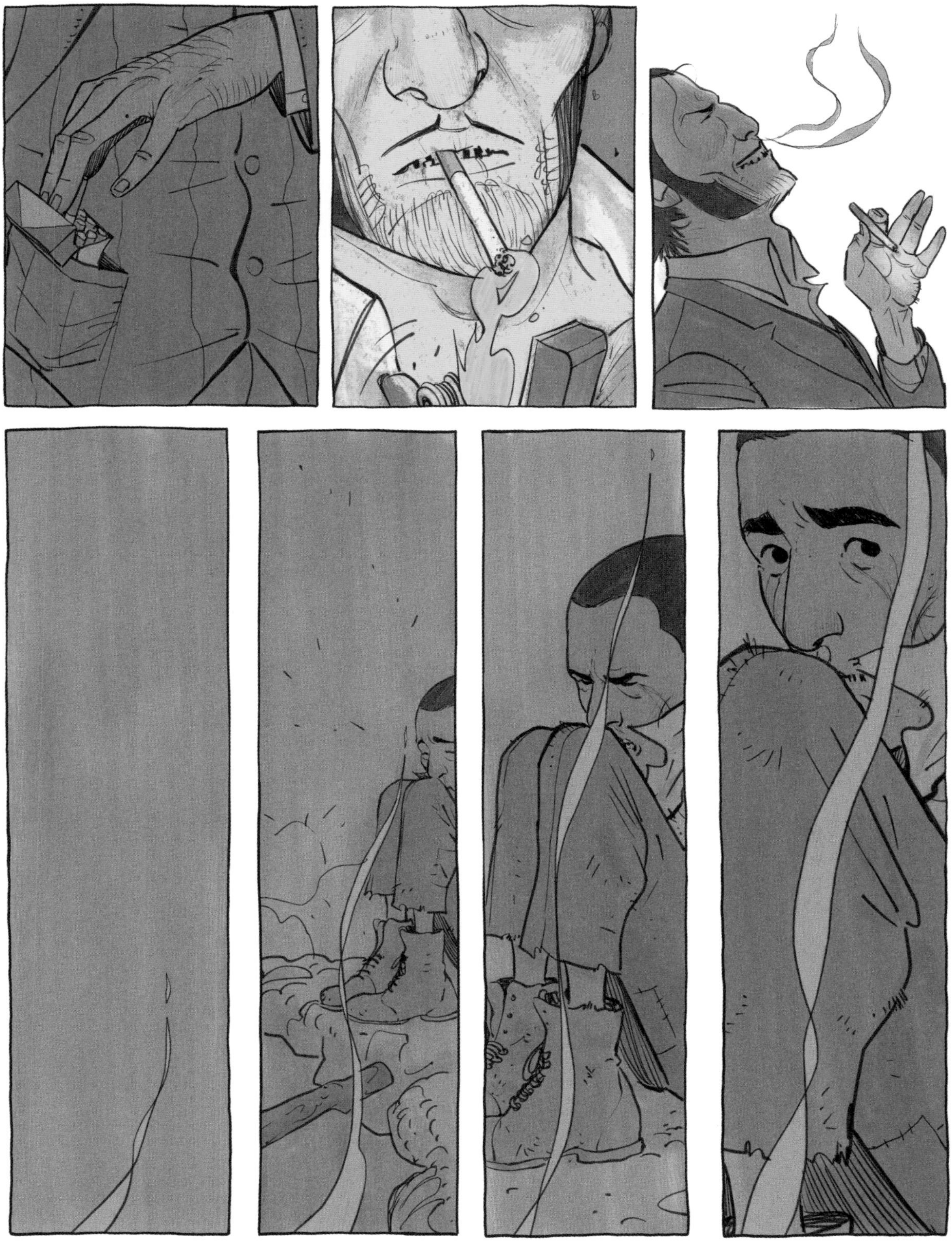

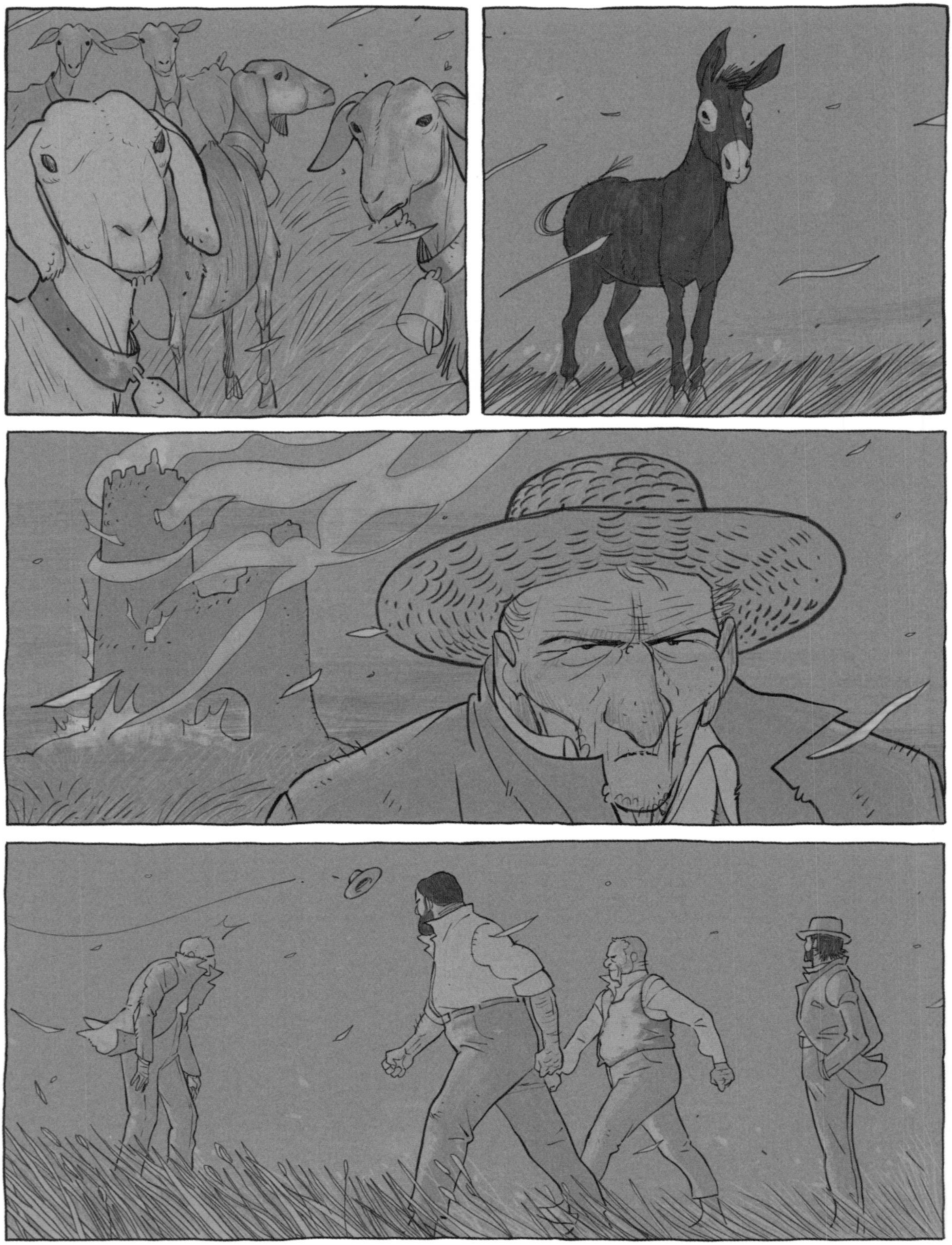

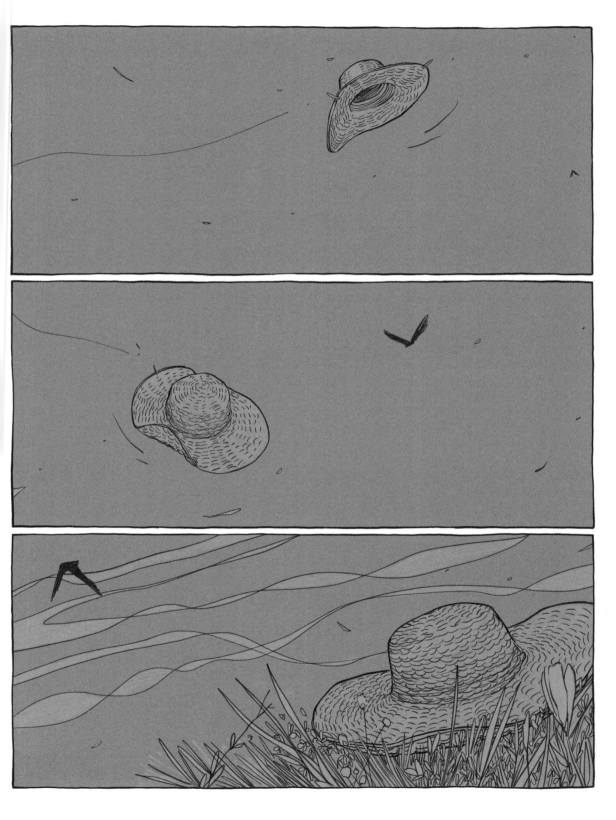

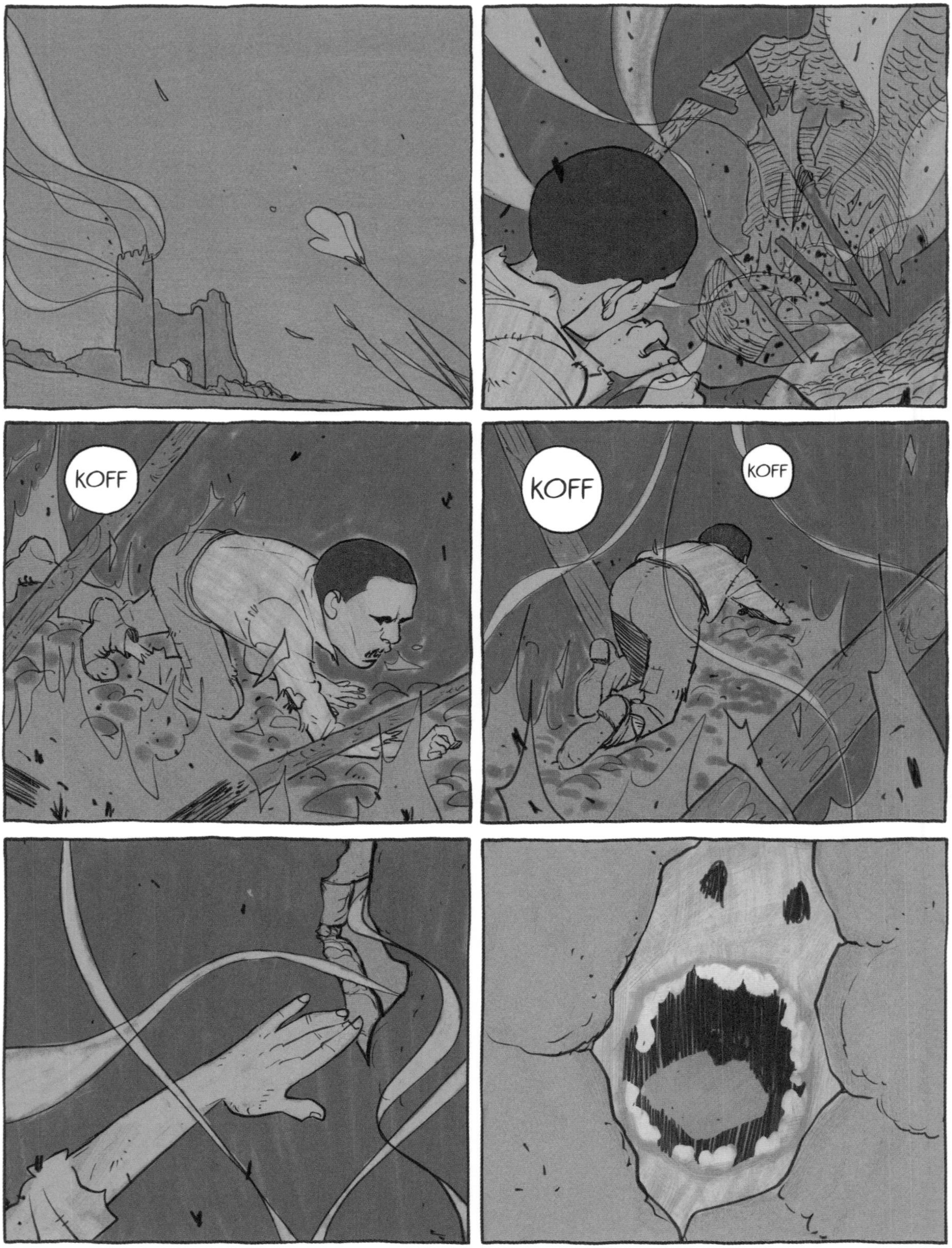
KOFF
KOFF
KOFF

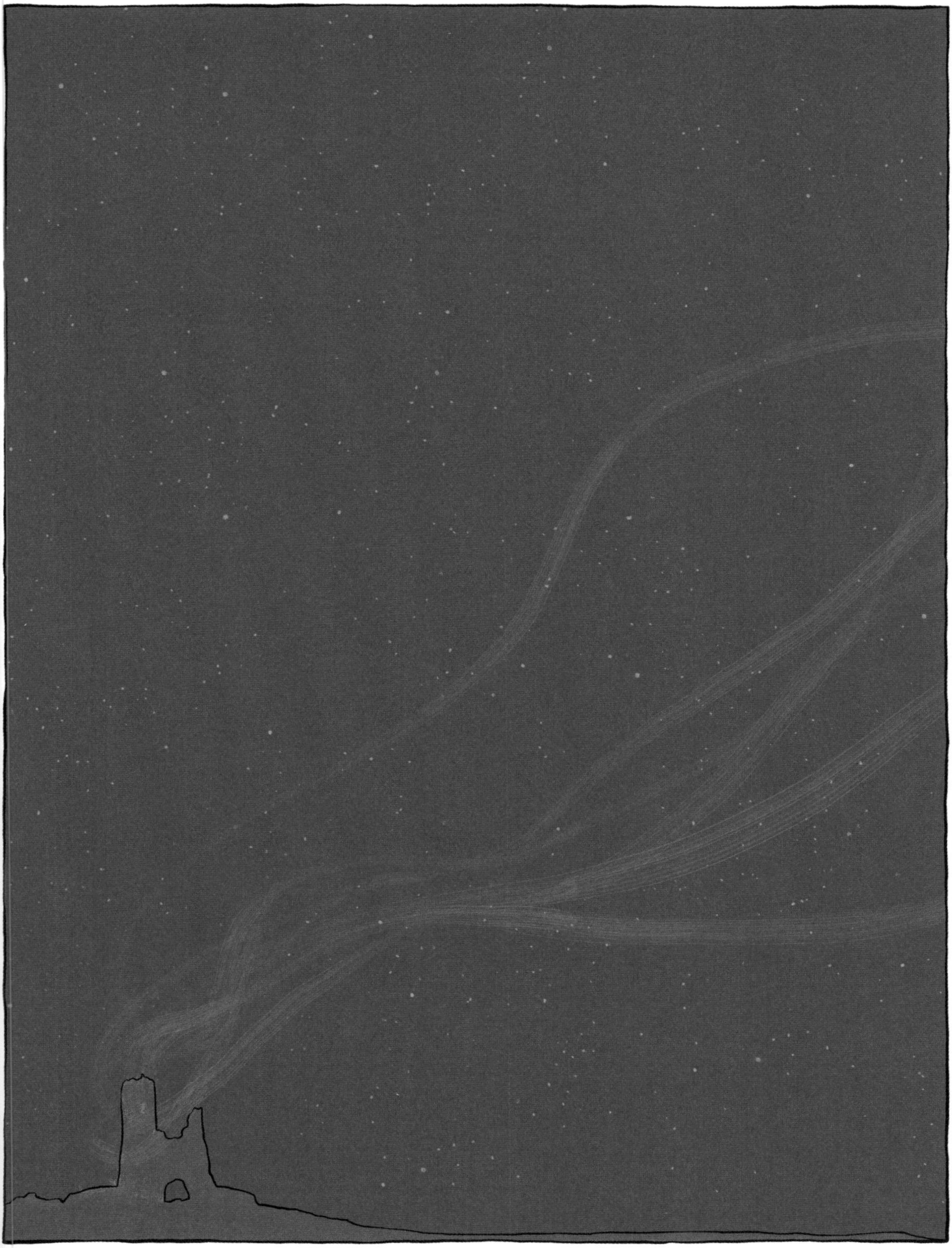

    As the sun rose, the mountains in the distance began to become visible. The plain was like a sea that stopped at those foothills to the north. Right then, they were just a landmark, a reminder that a place existed where one could breathe better.

He imagined himself at the base of those first foothills. Accompanied by the goatherd and his animals. They moved forward, climbed up to a high plateau, advancing along a path that wound between trees he didn't recognise. Wooded slopes, shadowy gullies. They rested, and he amused himself by making little boats from the fallen bark of enormous pines.

In his daydream, the herd had grown and now spread all across the green and fragrant plateau. To the north, the mountains still raised themselves like nipples of washed stone above the treeline and the bushes. Then the peaks, white.

In the afternoons, after finishing his chores with the goats, he sat on the edge of a balcony and watched the plain. He summoned angels and archangels to bring rain to his town, restoring to the wheat fields their lost fertility. All would swim in those riches, the Sheriff would get his tributes and nobody would ever remember the boy who disappeared.

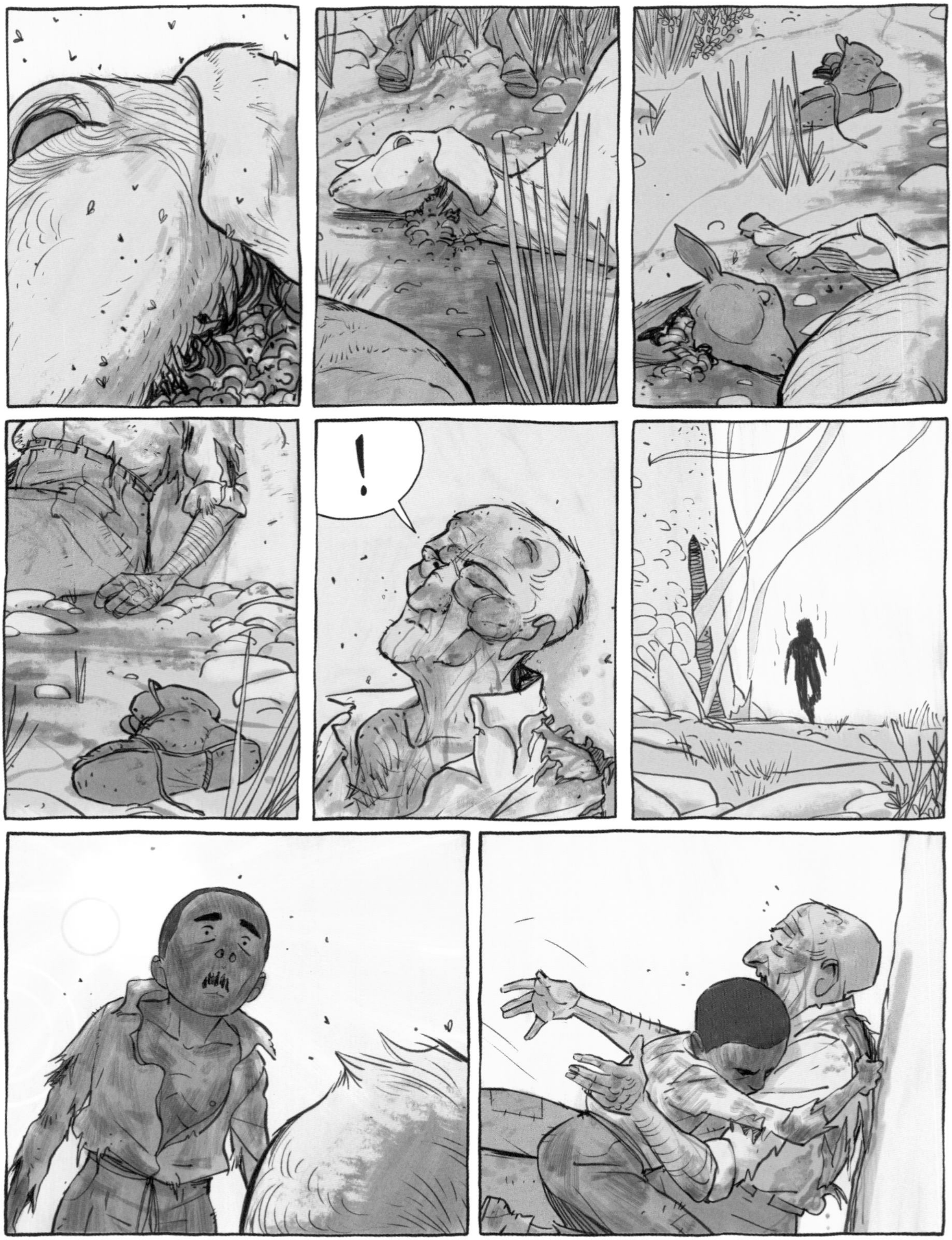
!

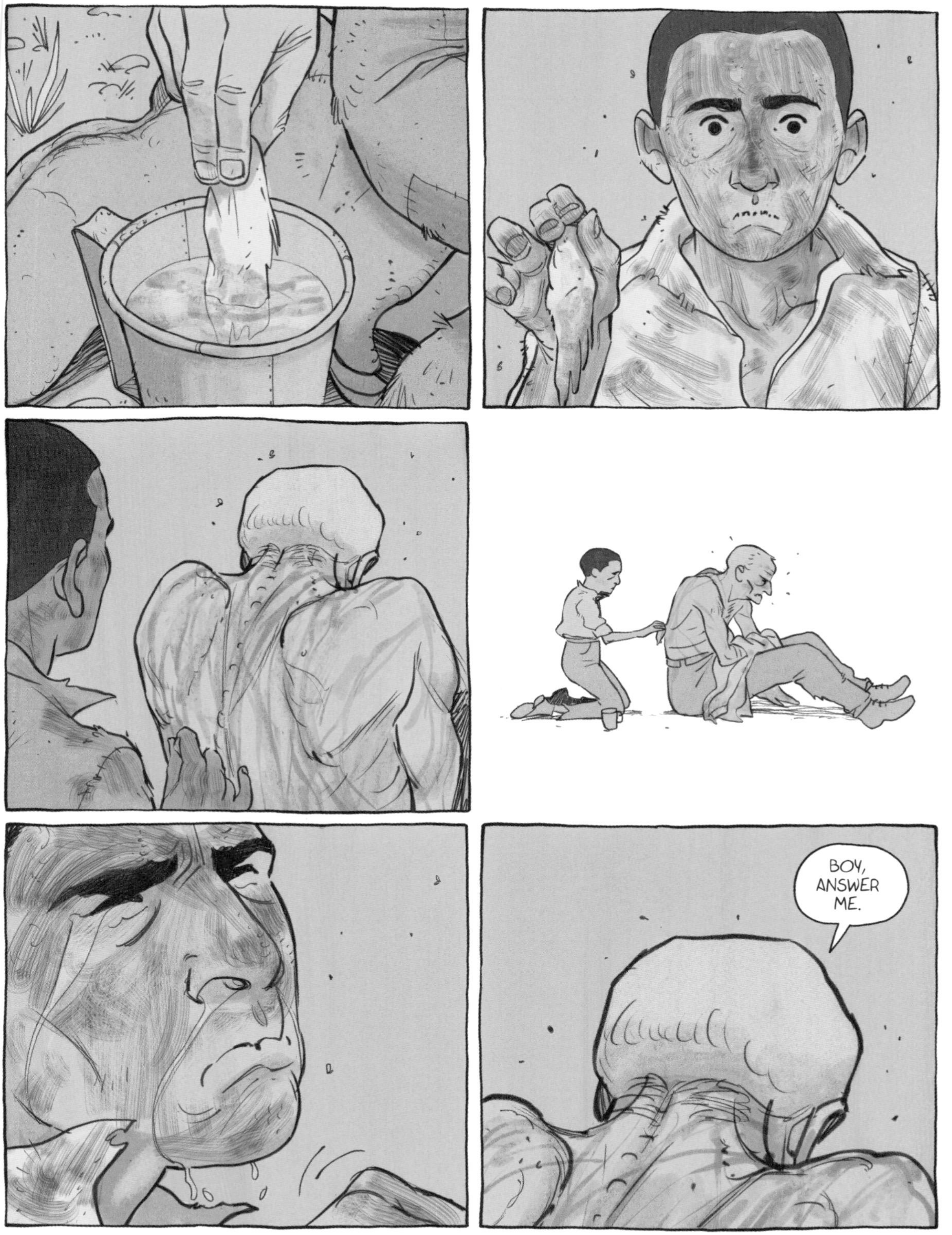
BOY, ANSWER ME.

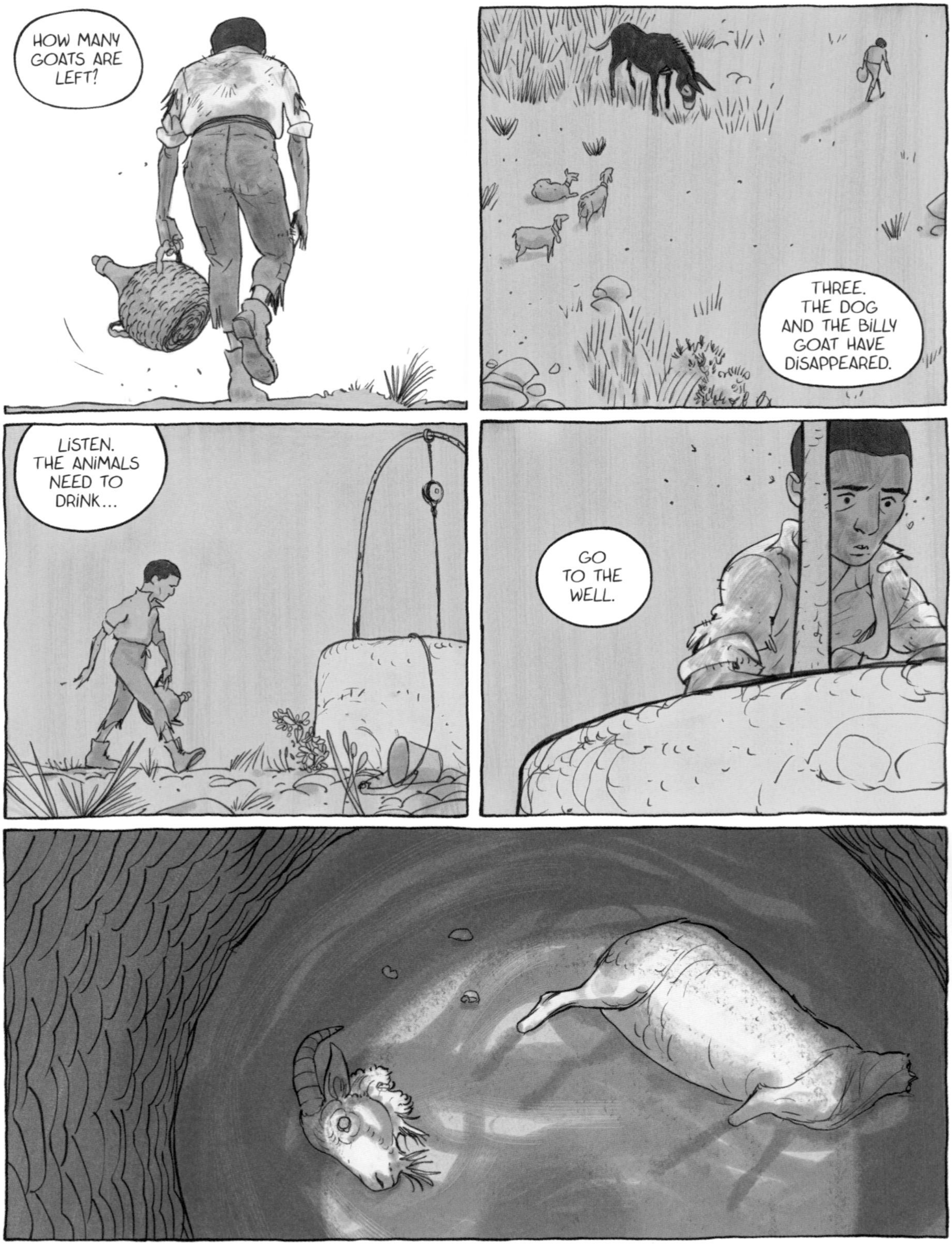
HOW MANY GOATS ARE LEFT?
THREE. THE DOG AND THE BILLY GOAT HAVE DISAPPEARED.
LISTEN. THE ANIMALS NEED TO DRINK...
GO TO THE WELL.

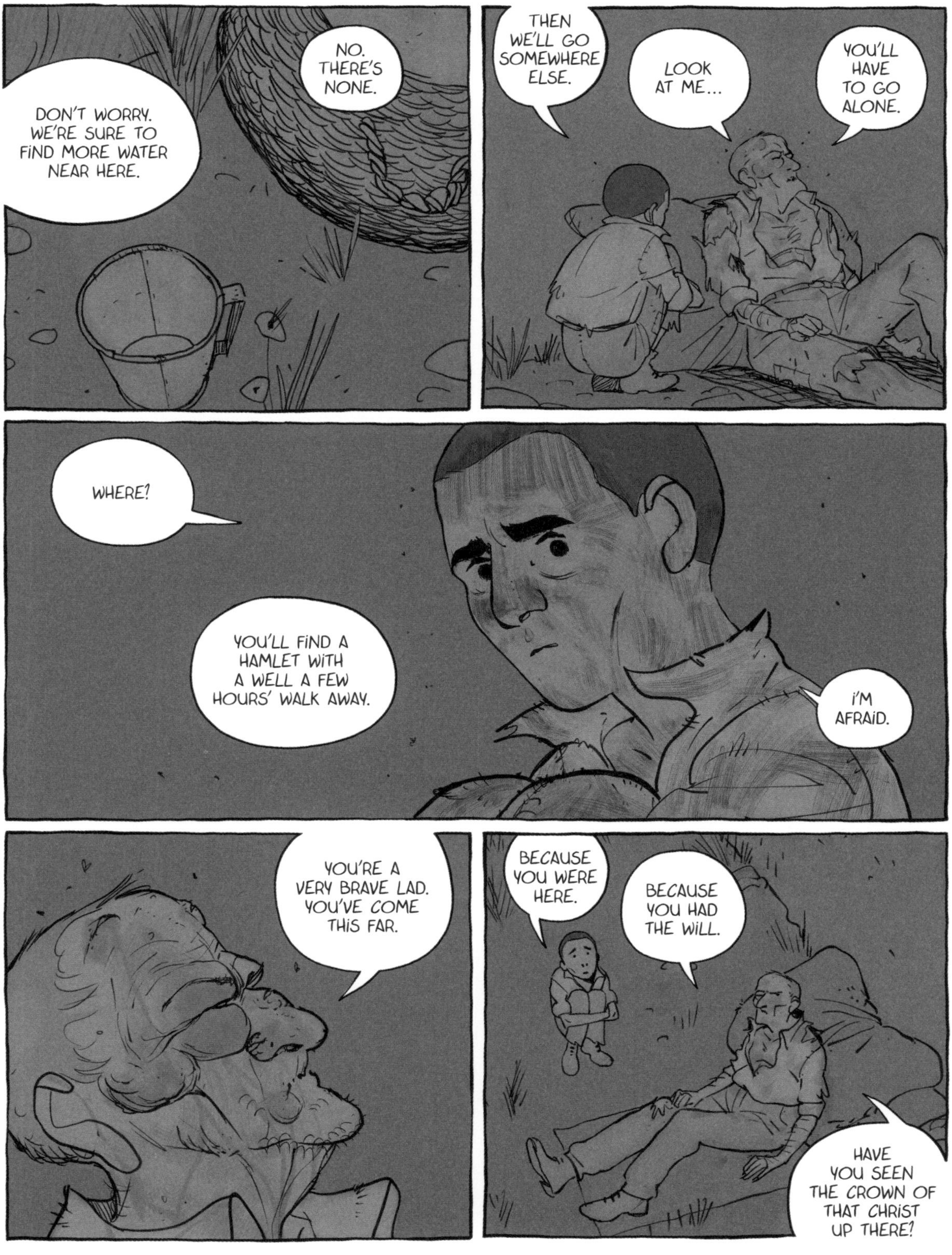
DON'T WORRY. WE'RE SURE TO FIND MORE WATER NEAR HERE.
NO. THERE'S NONE.
THEN WE'LL GO SOMEWHERE ELSE.
LOOK AT ME...
YOU'LL HAVE TO GO ALONE.
WHERE?
YOU'LL FIND A HAMLET WITH A WELL A FEW HOURS' WALK AWAY.
I'M AFRAID.
YOU'RE A VERY BRAVE LAD. YOU'VE COME THIS FAR.
BECAUSE YOU WERE HERE.
BECAUSE YOU HAD THE WILL.
HAVE YOU SEEN THE CROWN OF THAT CHRIST UP THERE?

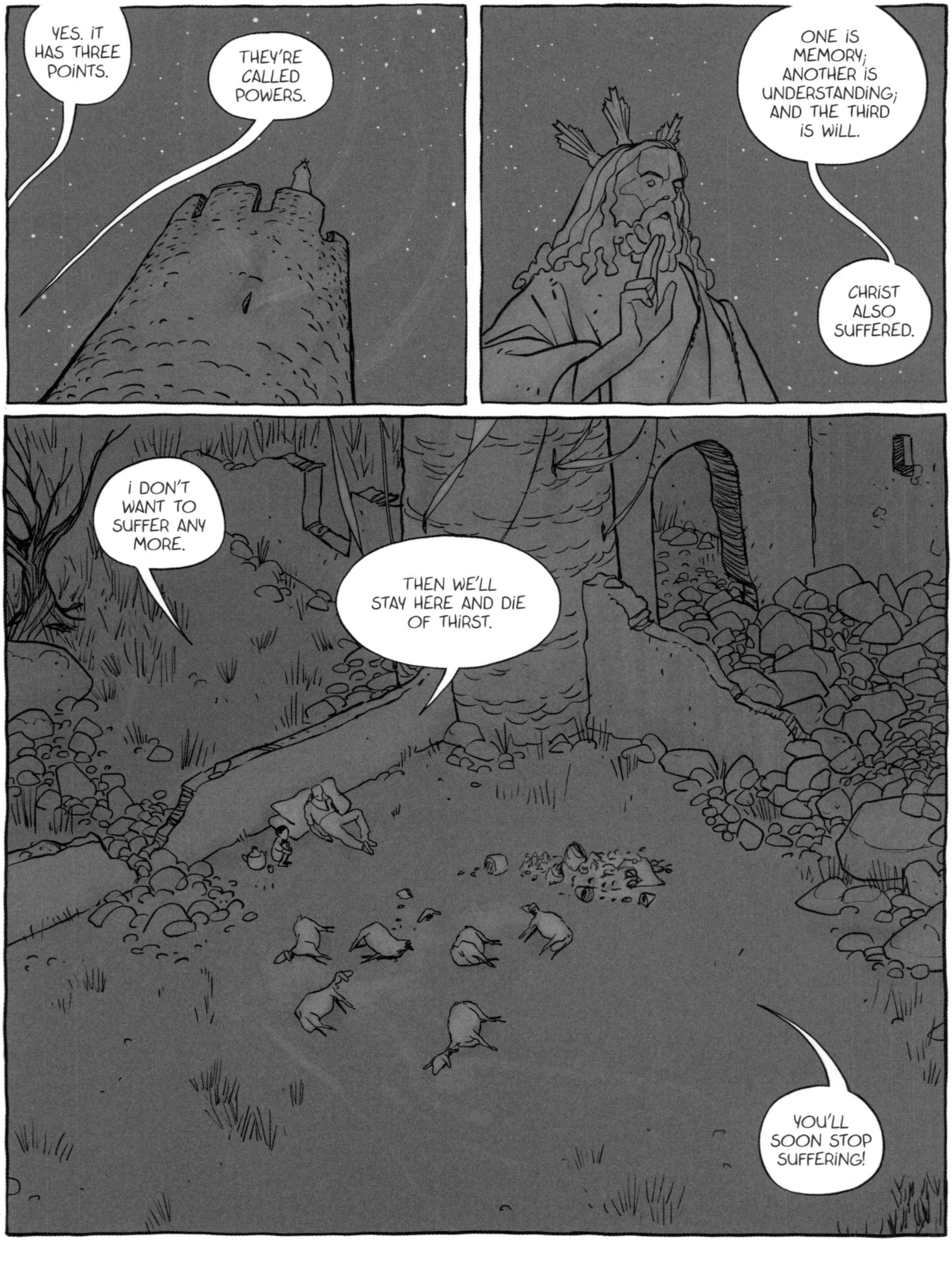
YES. IT HAS THREE POINTS.
THEY'RE CALLED POWERS.
ONE IS MEMORY; ANOTHER IS UNDERSTANDING; AND THE THIRD IS WILL.
CHRIST ALSO SUFFERED.
I DON'T WANT TO SUFFER ANY MORE.
THEN WE'LL STAY HERE AND DIE OF THIRST.
YOU'LL SOON STOP SUFFERING!

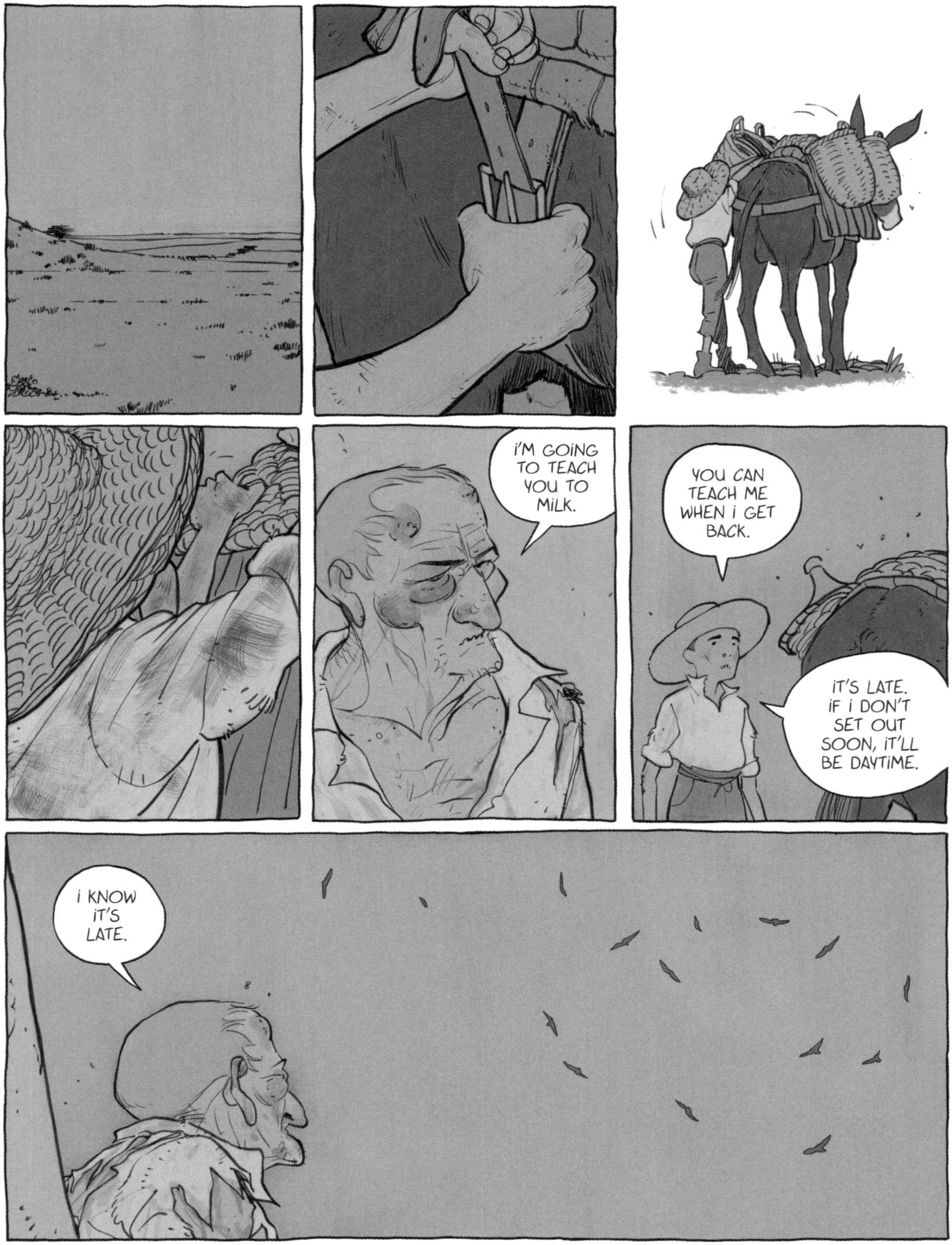
I'M GOING TO TEACH YOU TO MILK.
YOU CAN TEACH ME WHEN I GET BACK.
IT'S LATE. IF I DON'T SET OUT SOON, IT'LL BE DAYTIME.
I KNOW IT'S LATE.

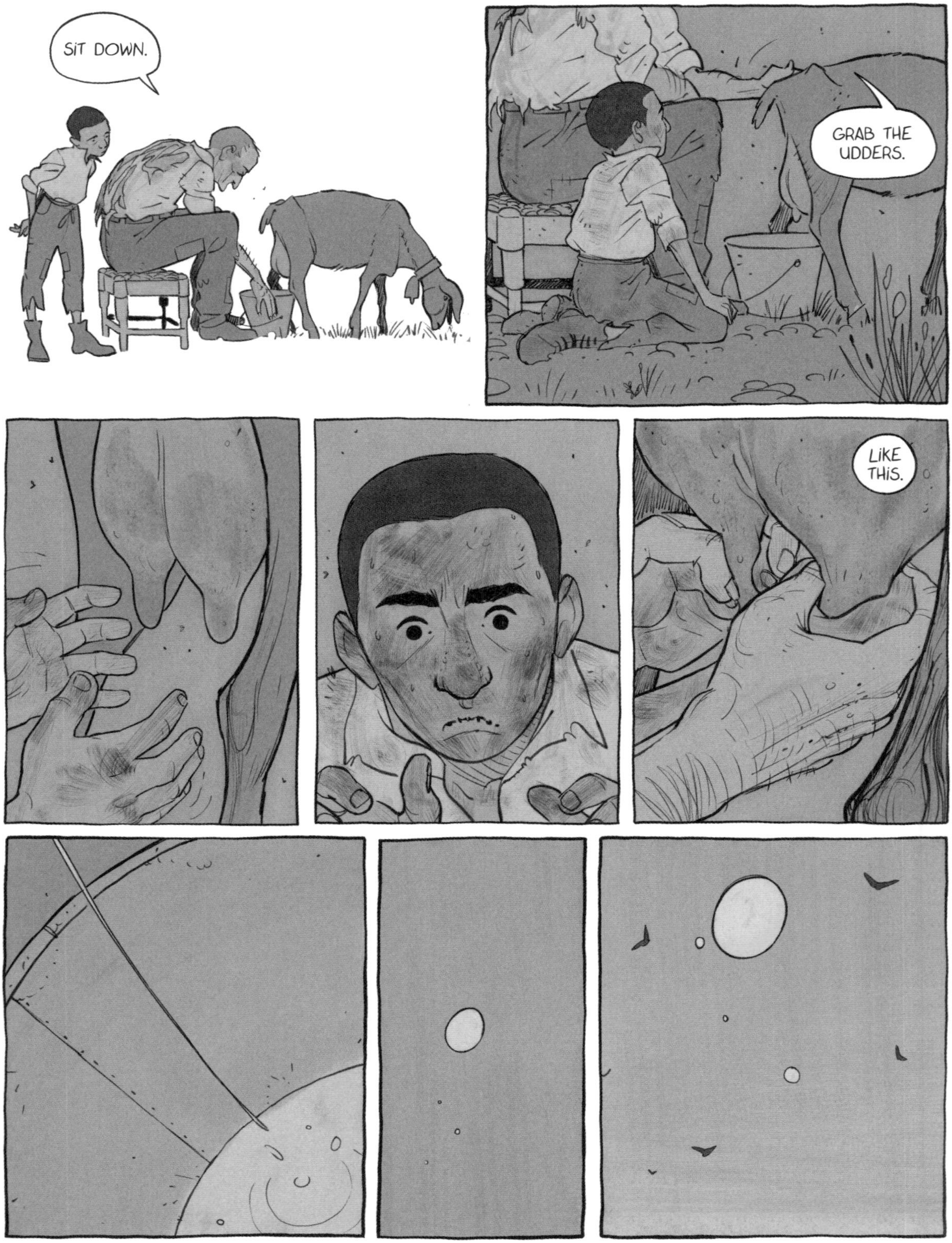
SIT DOWN.
GRAB THE UDDERS.
LIKE THIS.

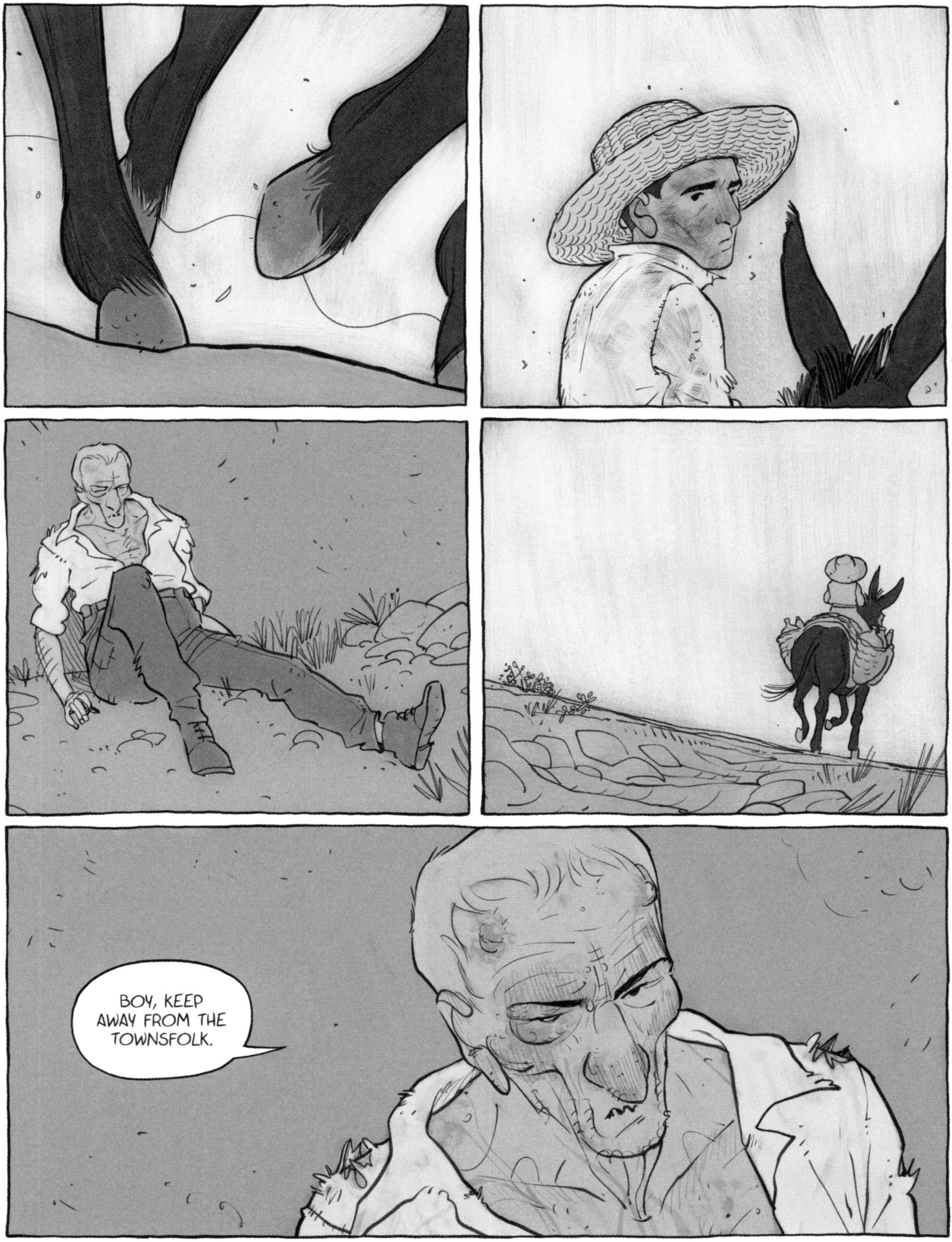
BOY, KEEP AWAY FROM THE TOWNSFOLK.

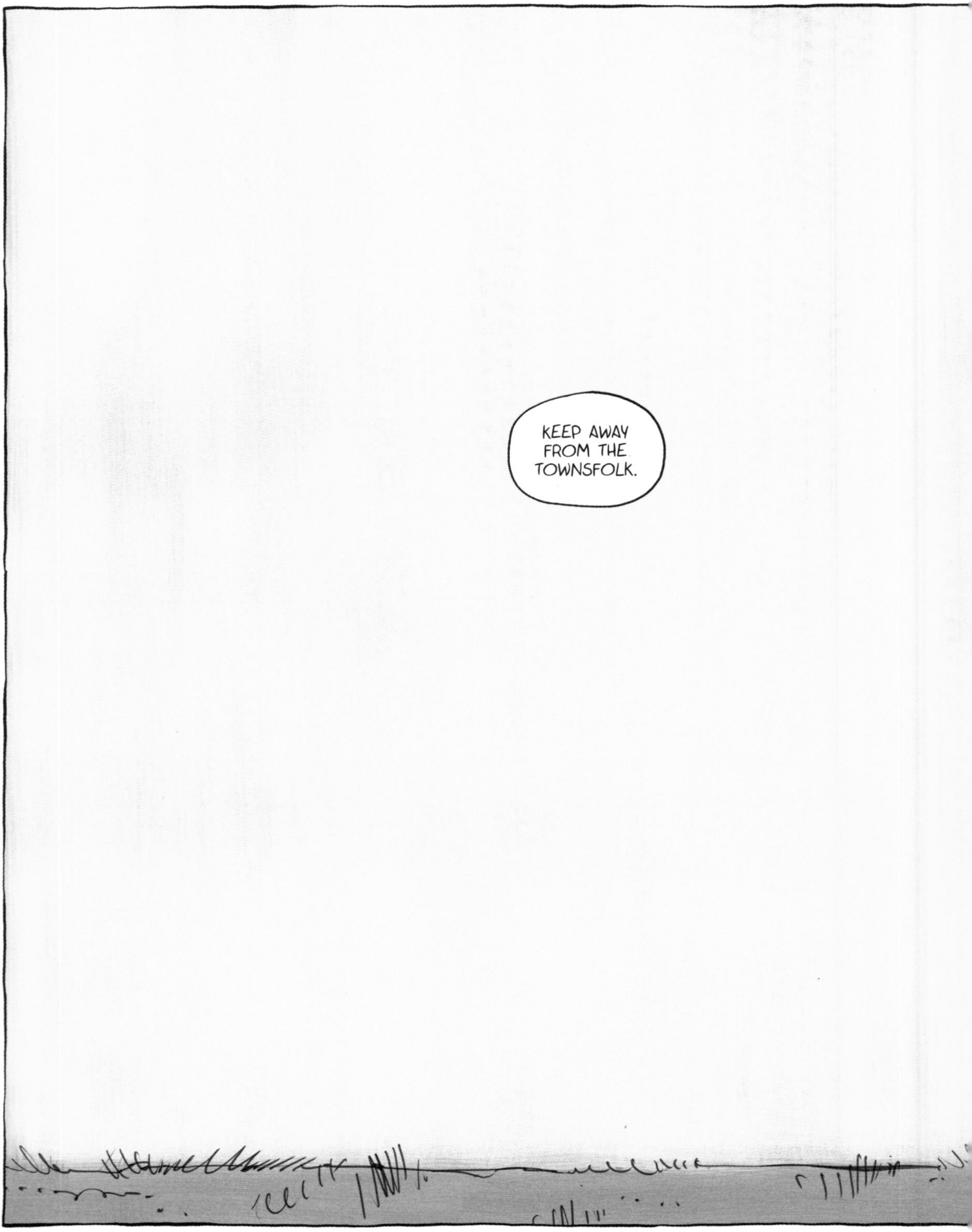
KEEP AWAY FROM THE TOWNSFOLK.

III

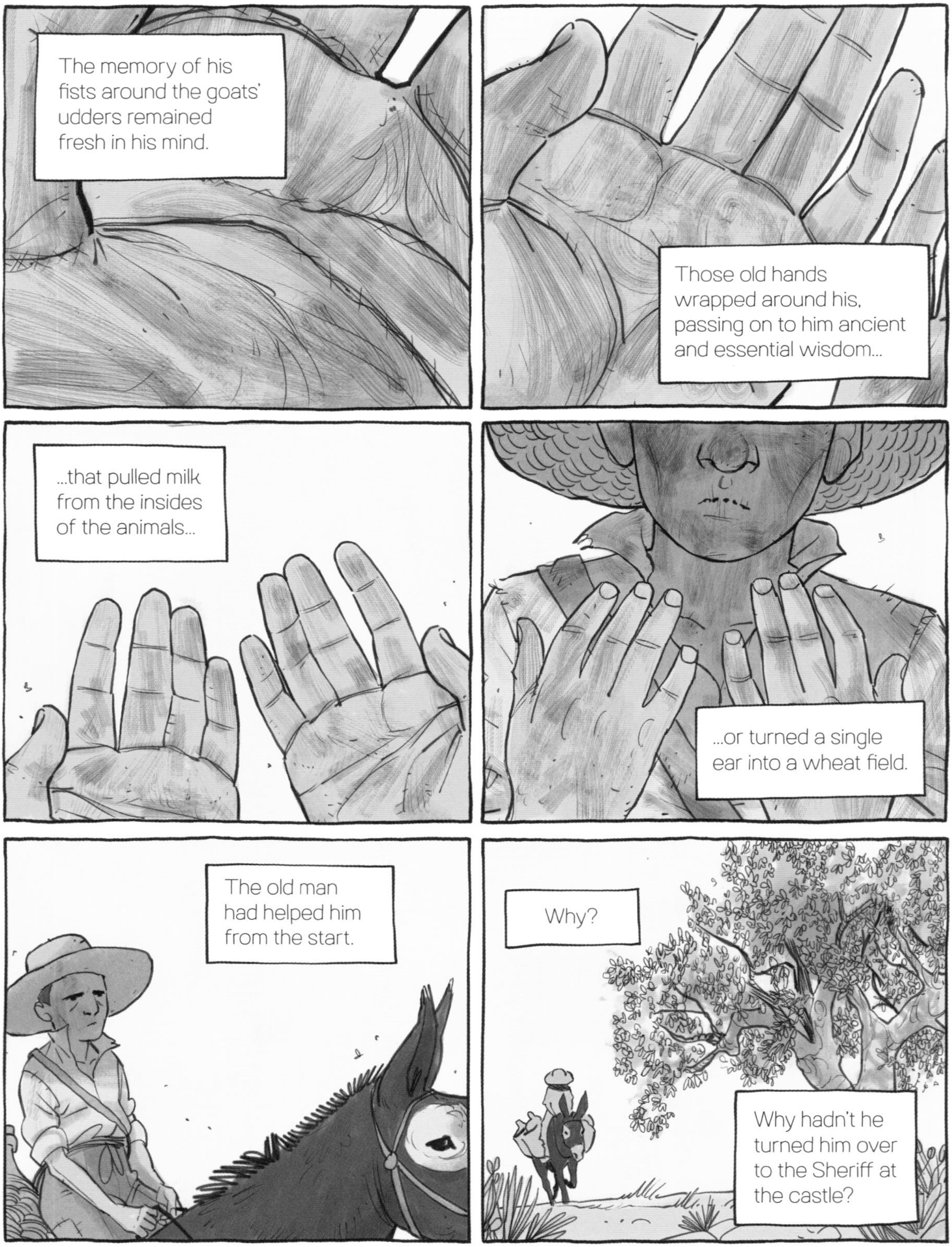
The memory of his fists around the goats' udders remained fresh in his mind.
Those old hands wrapped around his, passing on to him ancient and essential wisdom...
...that pulled milk from the insides of the animals...
...or turned a single ear into a wheat field.
The old man had helped him from the start.
Why?
Why hadn't he turned him over to the Sheriff at the castle?

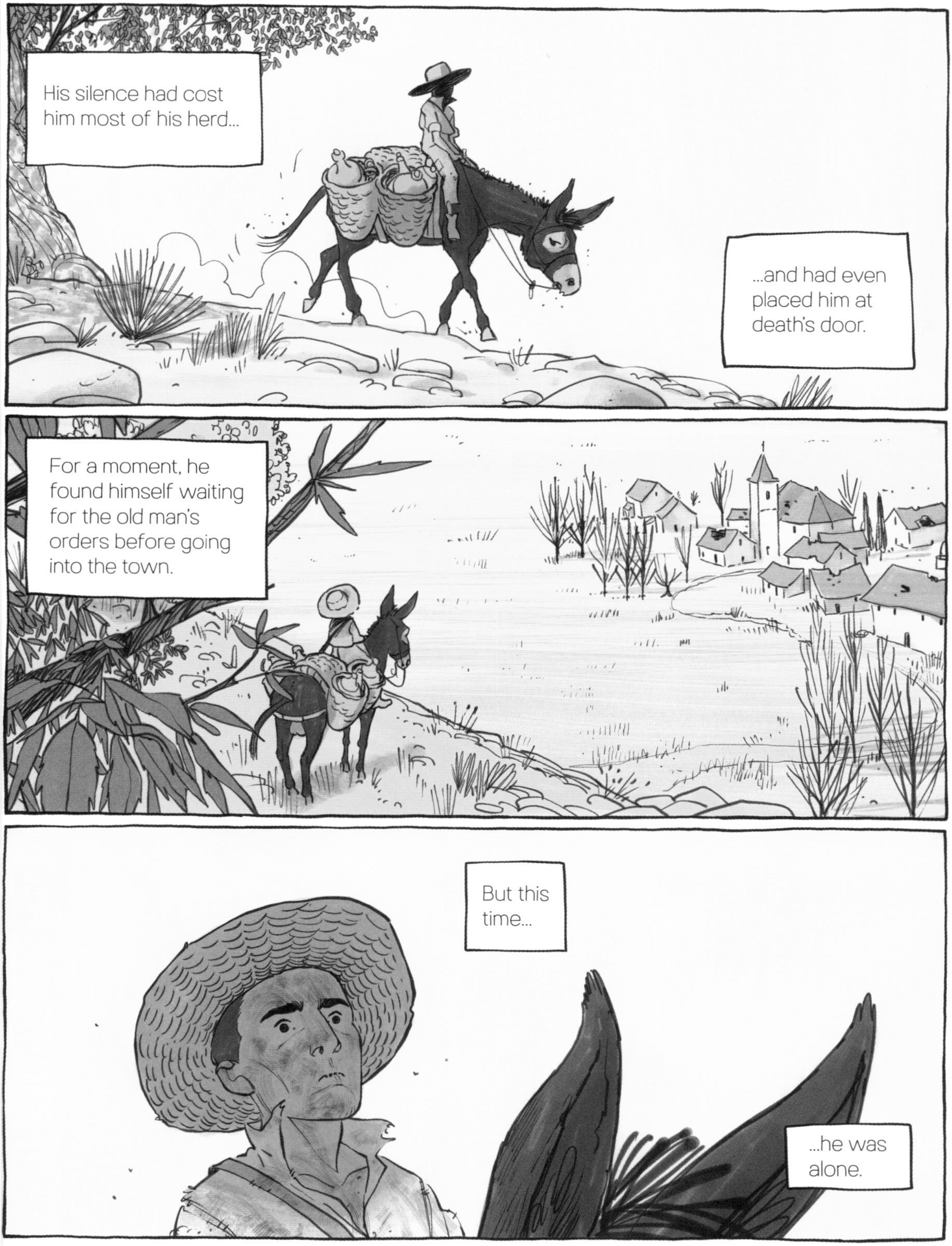
His silence had cost him most of his herd...
...and had even placed him at death's door.
For a moment, he found himself waiting for the old man's orders before going into the town.
But this time...
...he was alone.

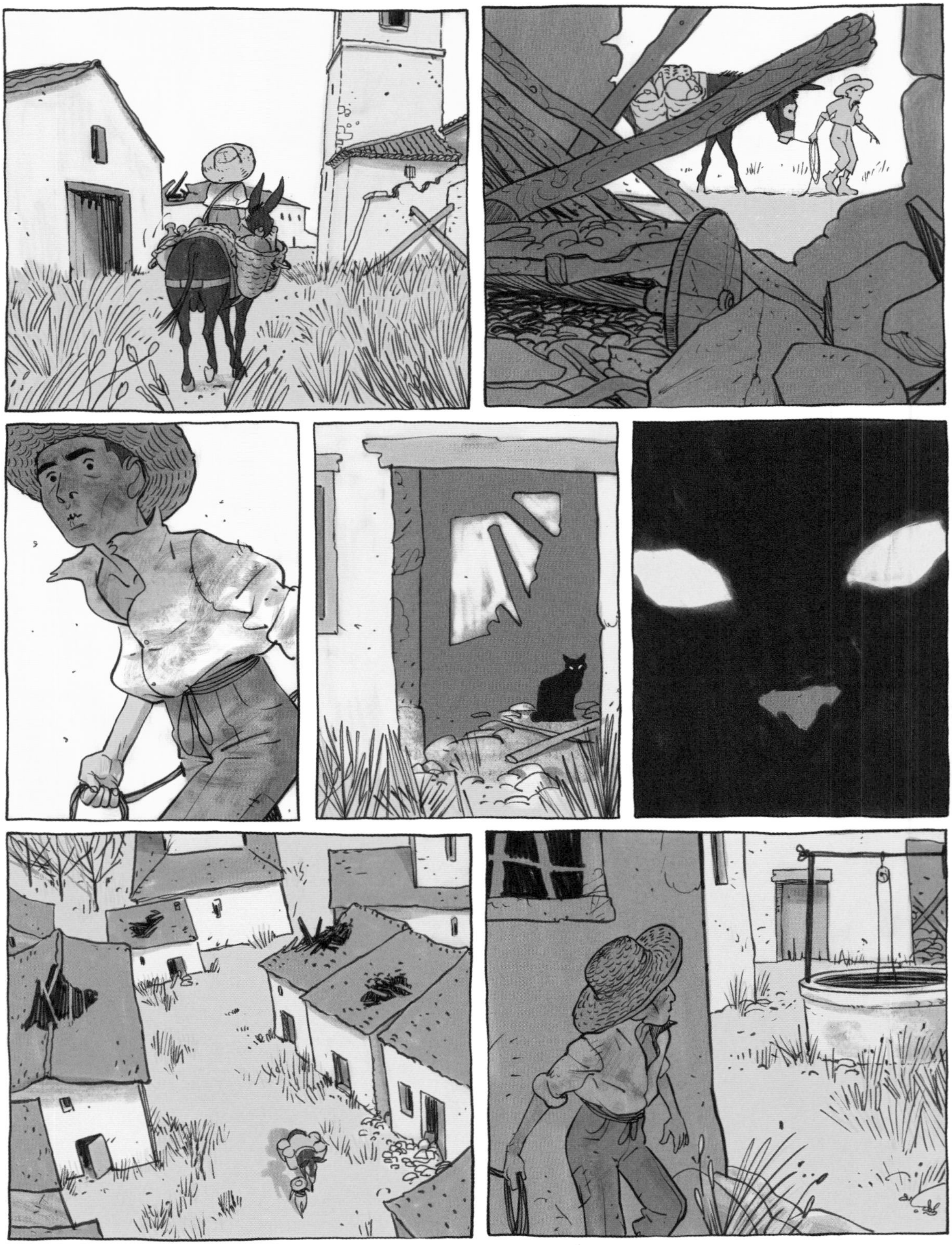

SSSSQUEEEEAK!

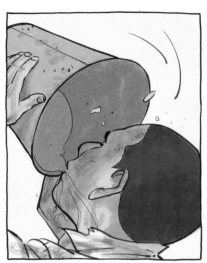

STAND STILL THERE AND GIVE ME SHADE.

ZZZZZZZ

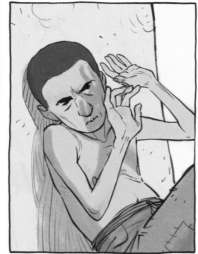

BLOODY STUPID DONKEY!

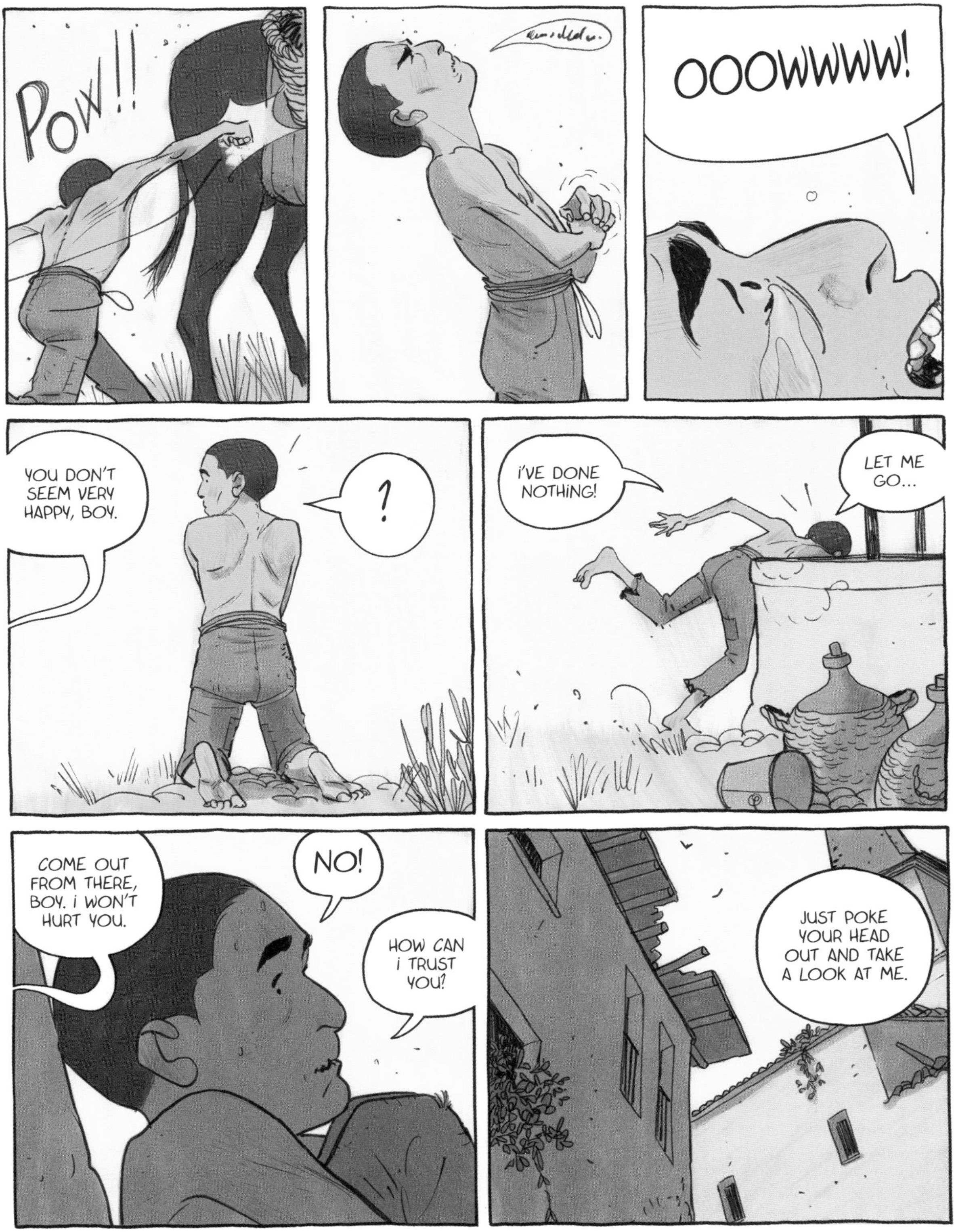
POW!!
OOOWWWW!
YOU DON'T SEEM VERY HAPPY, BOY.
?
i'VE DONE NOTHiNG!
LET ME GO...
COME OUT FROM THERE, BOY. i WON'T HURT YOU.
NO!
HOW CAN i TRUST YOU?
JUST POKE YOUR HEAD OUT AND TAKE A LOOK AT ME.

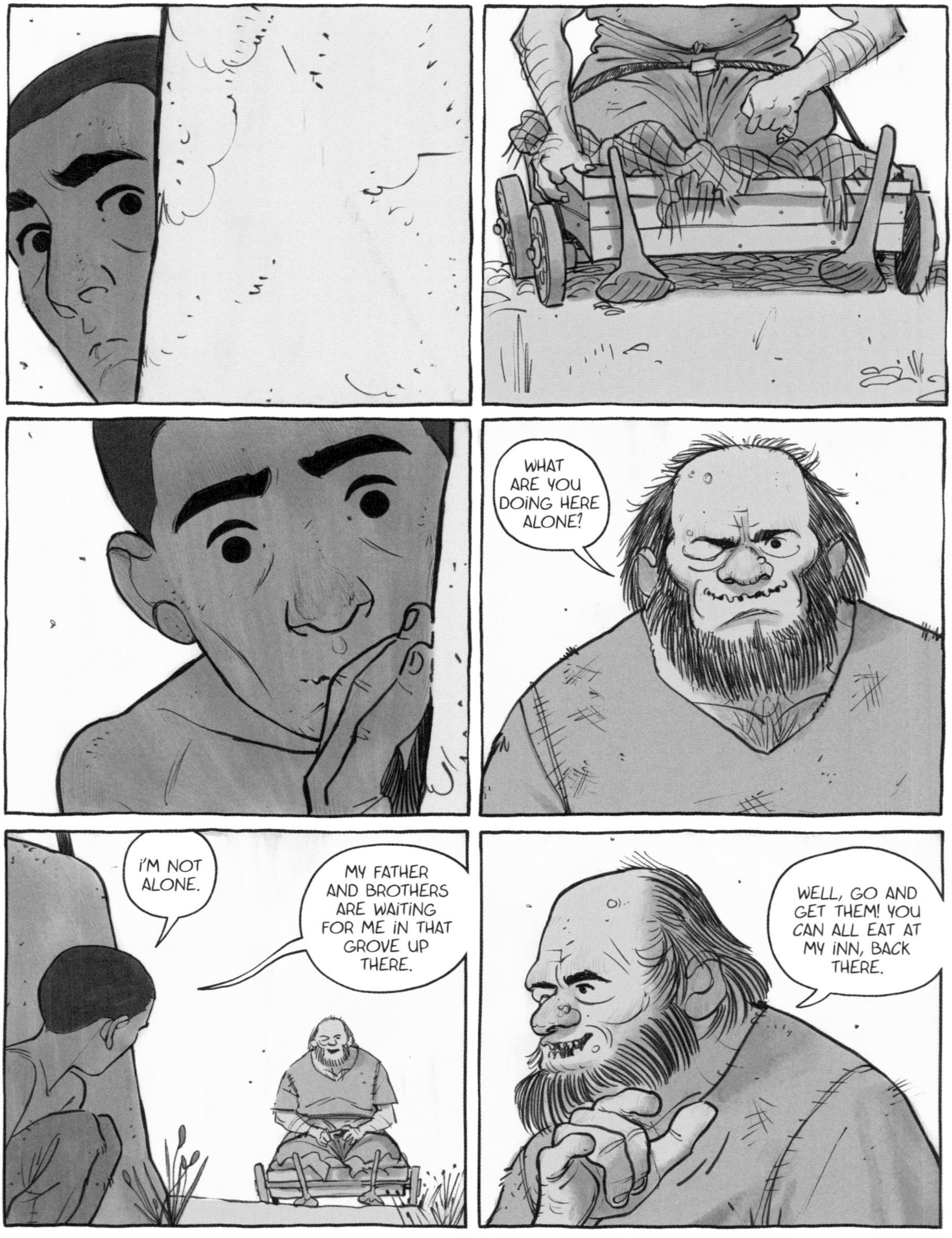
WHAT ARE YOU DOING HERE ALONE?
I'M NOT ALONE.
MY FATHER AND BROTHERS ARE WAITING FOR ME IN THAT GROVE UP THERE.
WELL, GO AND GET THEM! YOU CAN ALL EAT AT MY INN, BACK THERE.

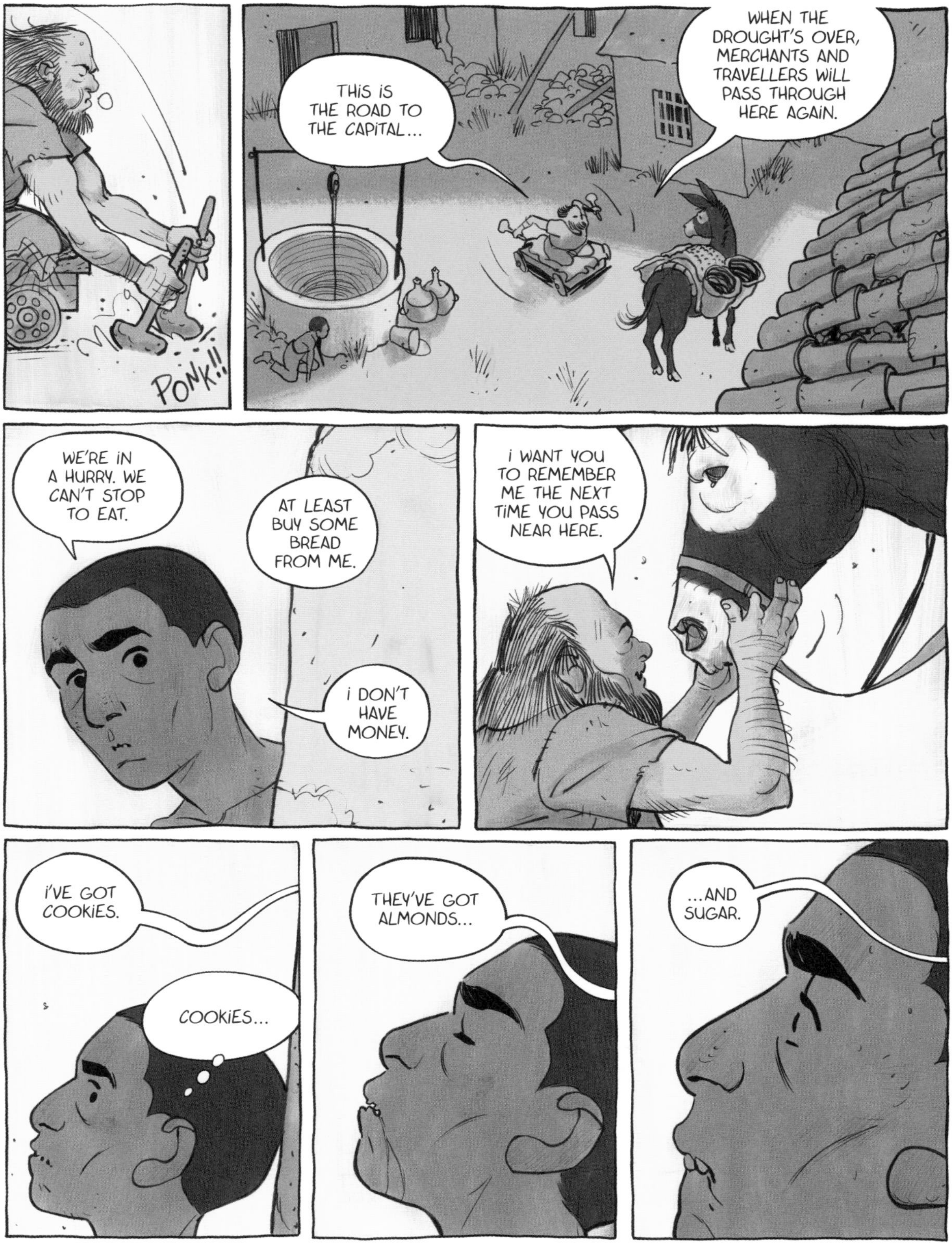
PONK!!
THiS iS THE ROAD TO THE CAPiTAL...
WHEN THE DROUGHT'S OVER, MERCHANTS AND TRAVELLERS WiLL PASS THROUGH HERE AGAiN.
WE'RE iN A HURRY. WE CAN'T STOP TO EAT.
AT LEAST BUY SOME BREAD FROM ME.
i DON'T HAVE MONEY.
i WANT YOU TO REMEMBER ME THE NEXT TiME YOU PASS NEAR HERE.
i'VE GOT COOKiES.
COOKiES...
THEY'VE GOT ALMONDS...
...AND SUGAR.

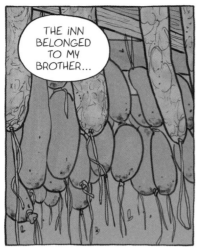

THE INN BELONGED TO MY BROTHER...

I LIVED HERE WITH HIM, MY SISTER-IN-LAW AND MY TWO NEPHEWS.

WHEN THE DROUGHT CAME, THEY WENT TO THE CITY TO LOOK FOR WORK.

THEY SAID THEY'D COME BACK FOR ME WITH A CART ONCE THEY WERE SETTLED.

OVER A YEAR AGO NOW.

BUT I'M CLEAR ABOUT ONE THING, LAD...

THE MULETEERS, THE WOOL MERCHANTS...

Glug Glug Glug

...THEY'LL ALL BE BACK.

NOLE SALT. JHEPCNTC DE LICTCA.

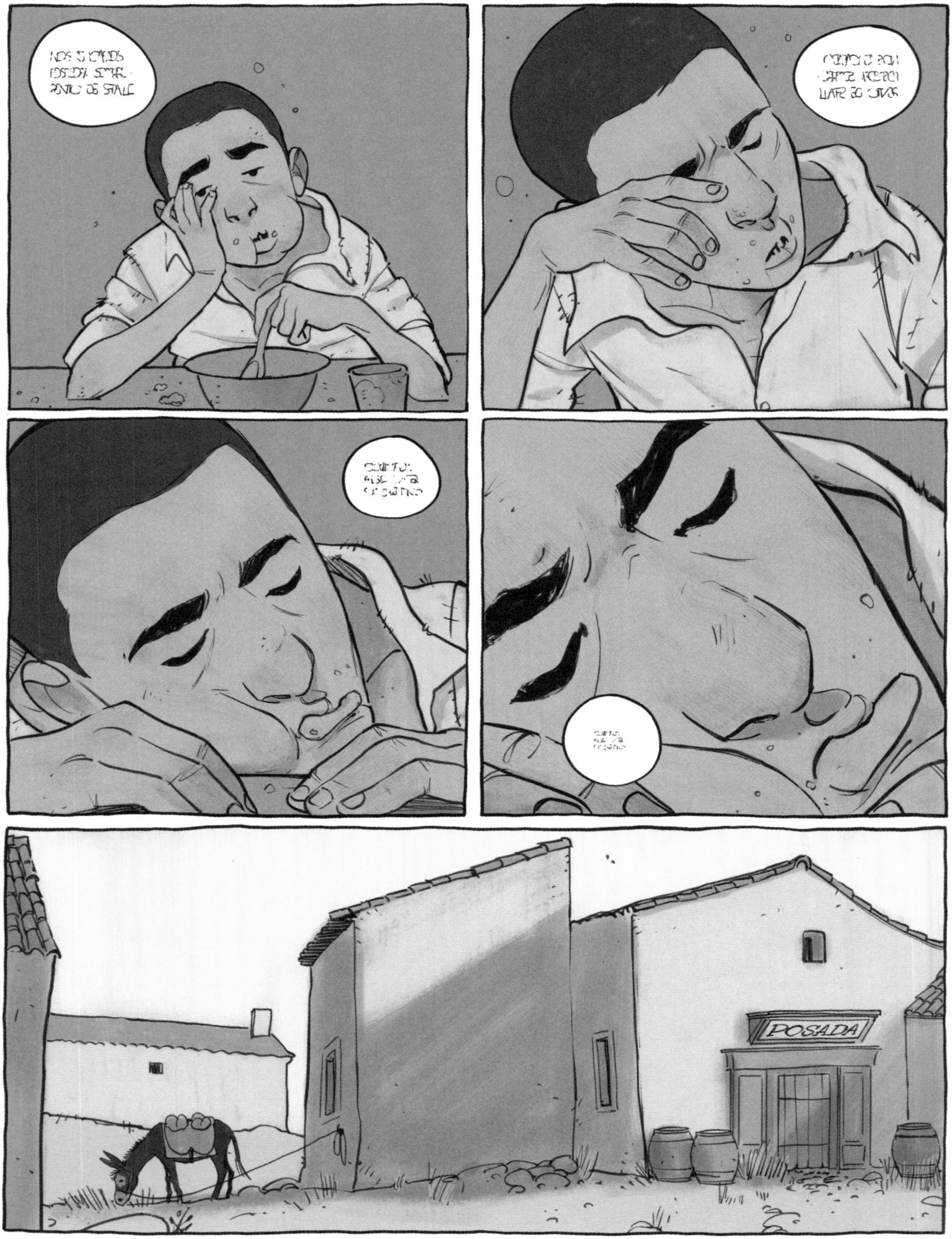
POSADA

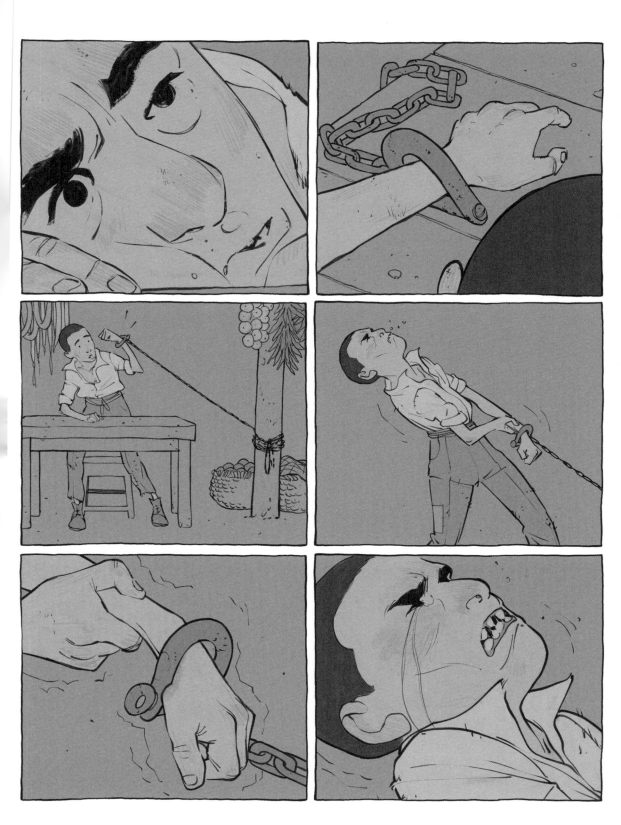

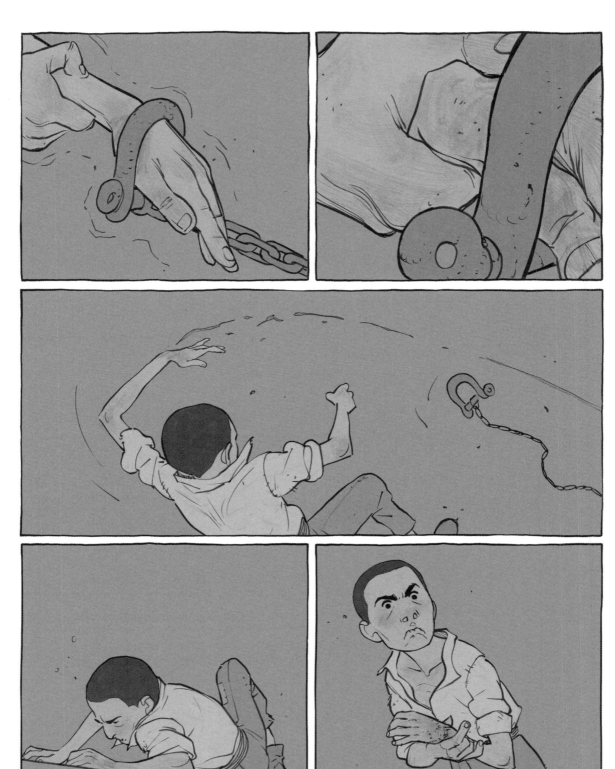

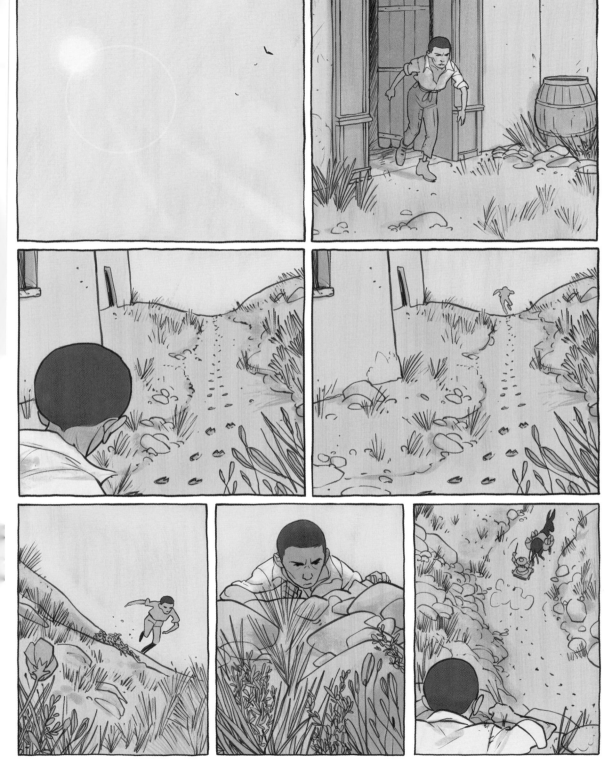

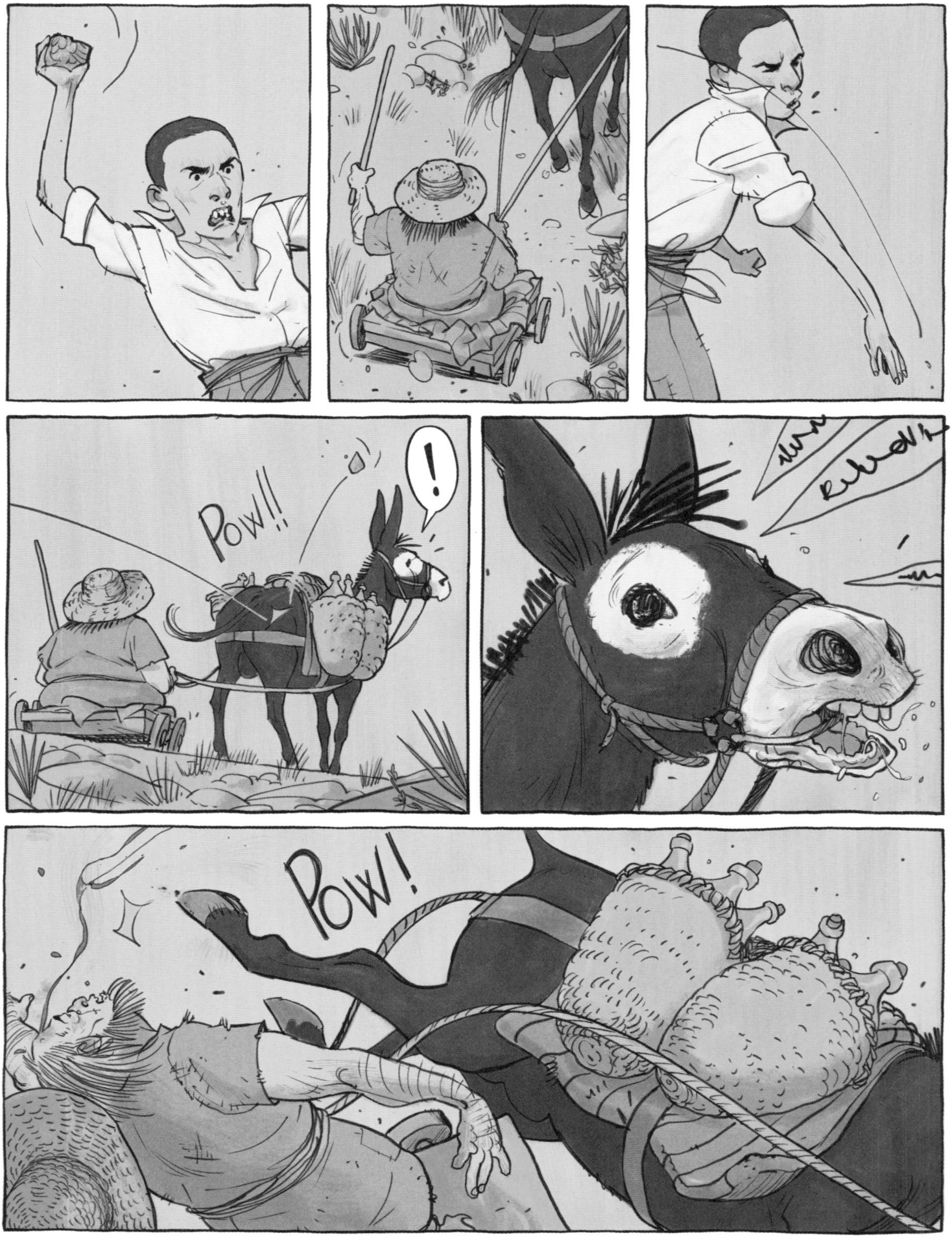
POW!!
!
POW!

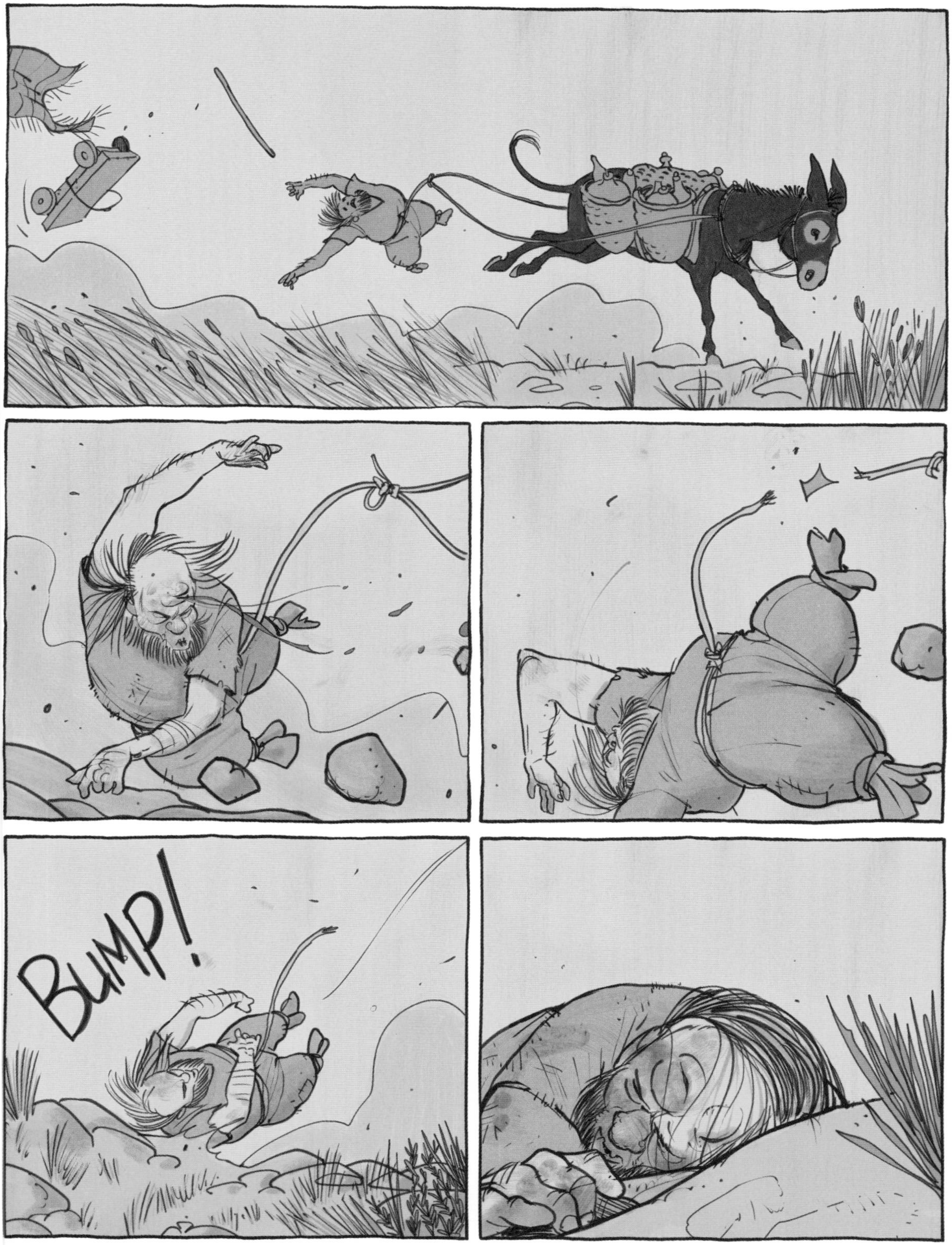
BUMP!

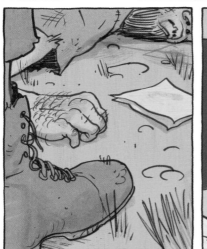

Let it be known:

Anyone providing information about his whereabouts will be repaid with:

twenty-five coins.

Sign

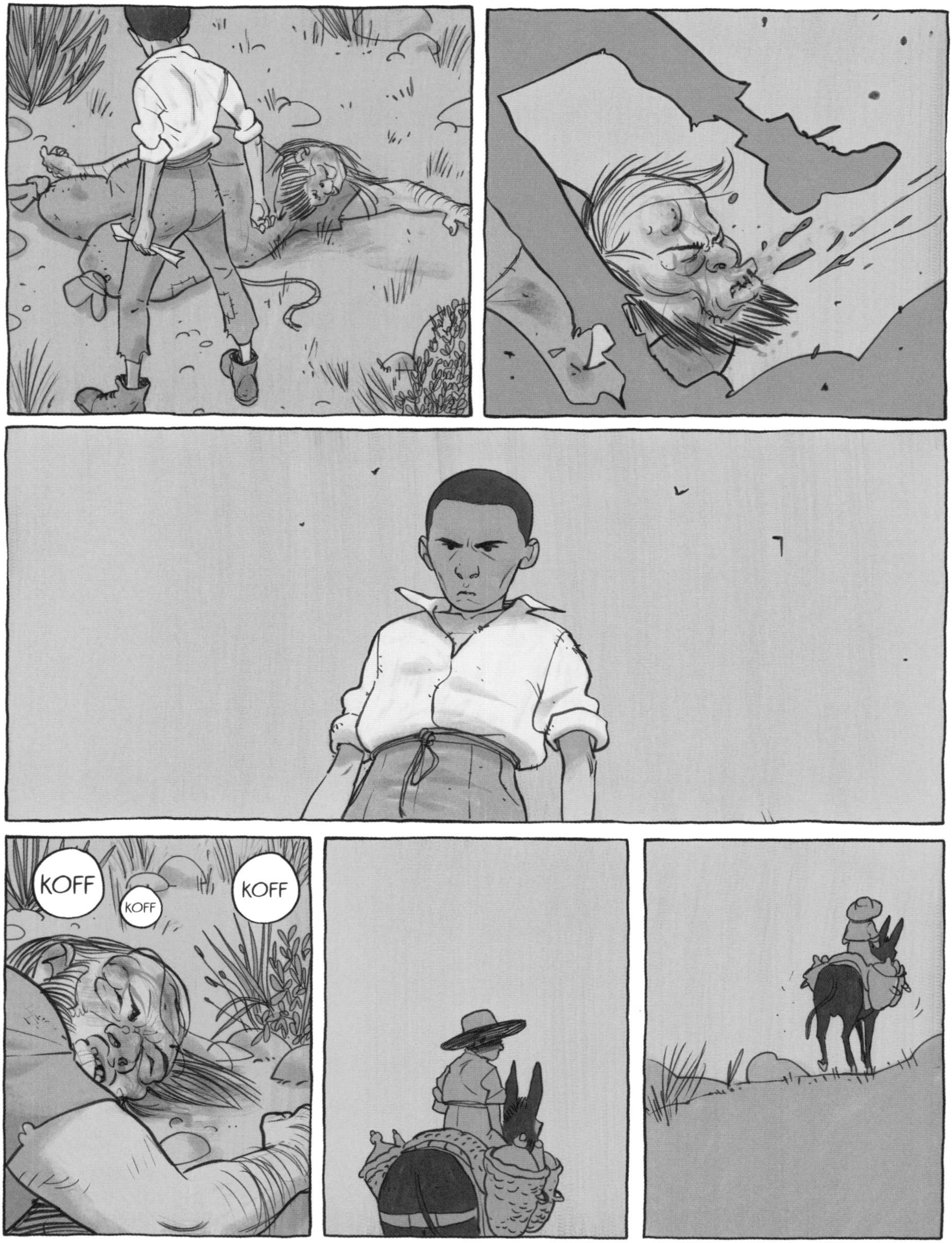
KOFF
KOFF
KOFF

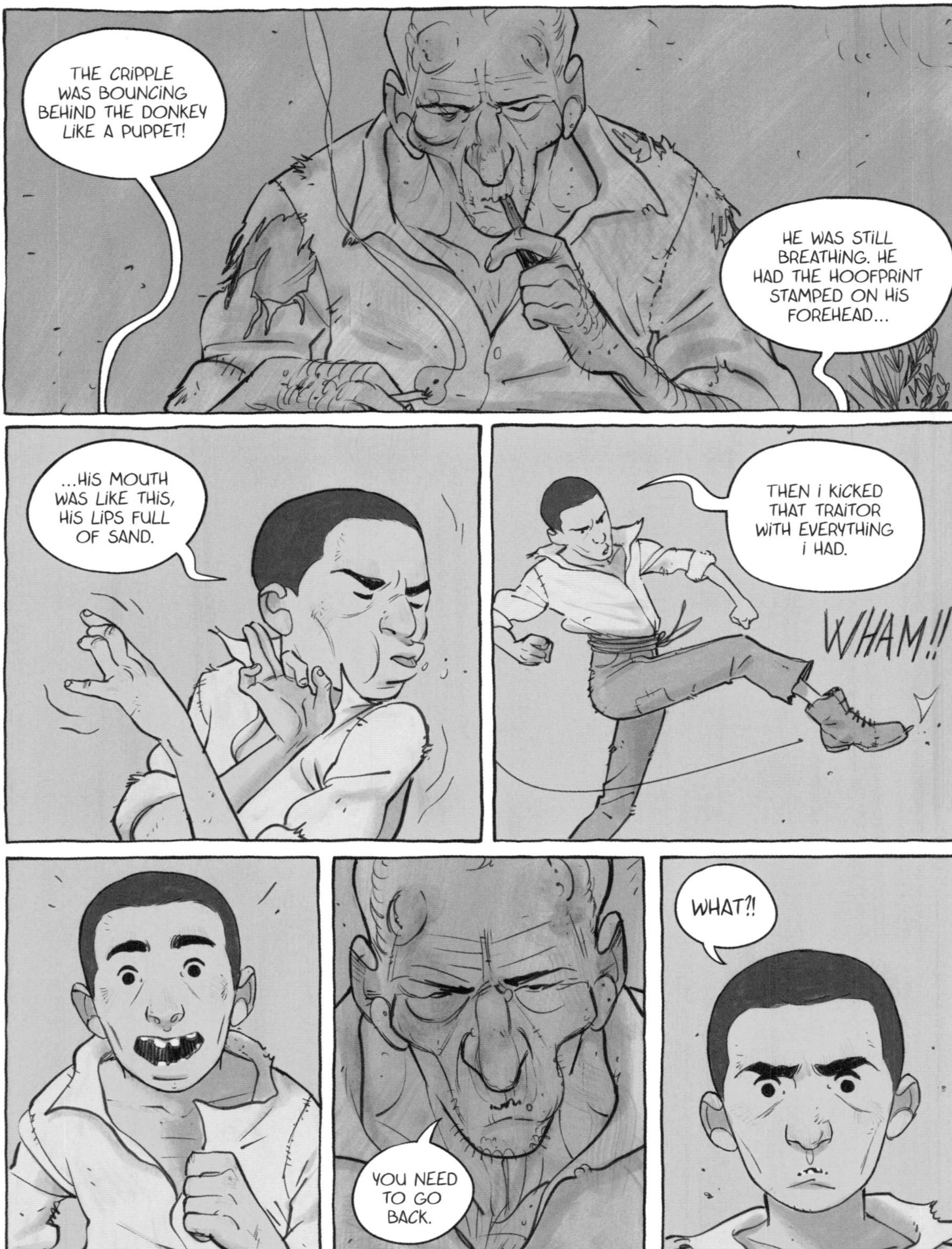
THE CRIPPLE WAS BOUNCING BEHIND THE DONKEY LIKE A PUPPET!
HE WAS STILL BREATHING. HE HAD THE HOOFPRINT STAMPED ON HIS FOREHEAD...
...HIS MOUTH WAS LIKE THIS, HIS LIPS FULL OF SAND.
THEN I KICKED THAT TRAITOR WITH EVERYTHING I HAD.
WHAM!!
YOU NEED TO GO BACK.
WHAT?!

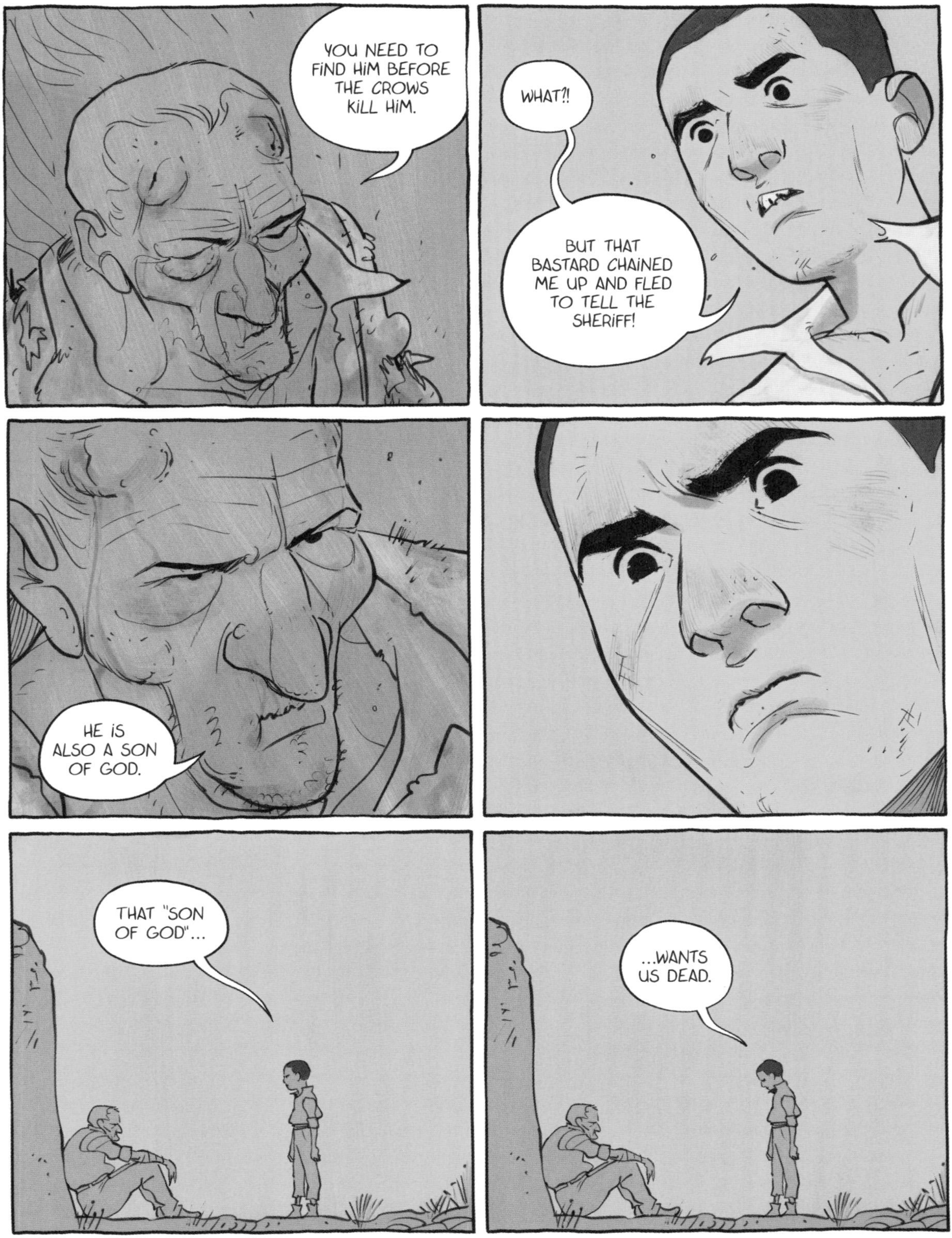
YOU NEED TO FIND HIM BEFORE THE CROWS KILL HIM.
WHAT?!
BUT THAT BASTARD CHAINED ME UP AND FLED TO TELL THE SHERIFF!
HE IS ALSO A SON OF GOD.
THAT "SON OF GOD"...
...WANTS US DEAD.

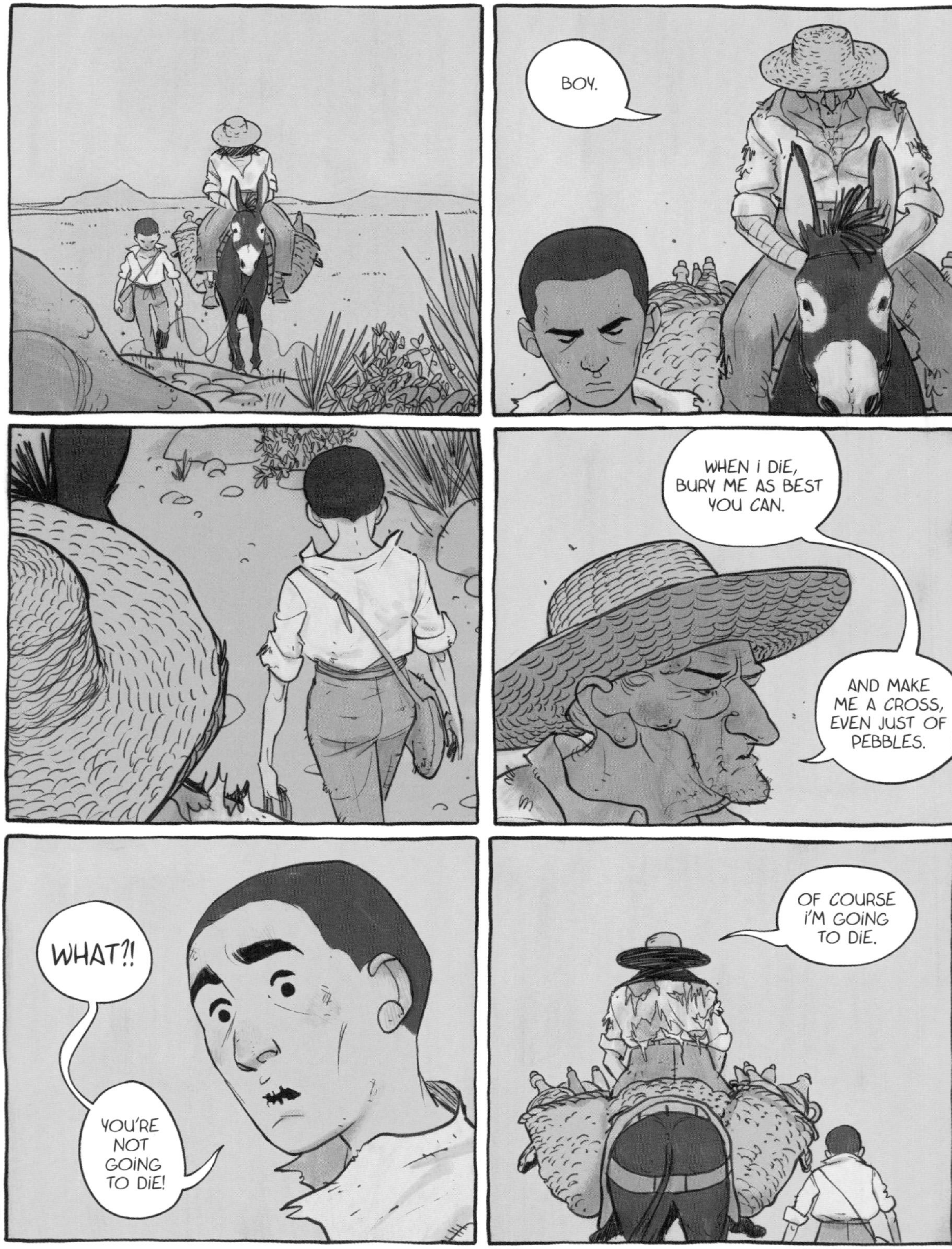
BOY.
WHEN i DiE, BURY ME AS BEST YOU CAN.
AND MAKE ME A CROSS, EVEN JUST OF PEBBLES.
WHAT?!
YOU'RE NOT GOiNG TO DiE!
OF COURSE i'M GOiNG TO DiE.

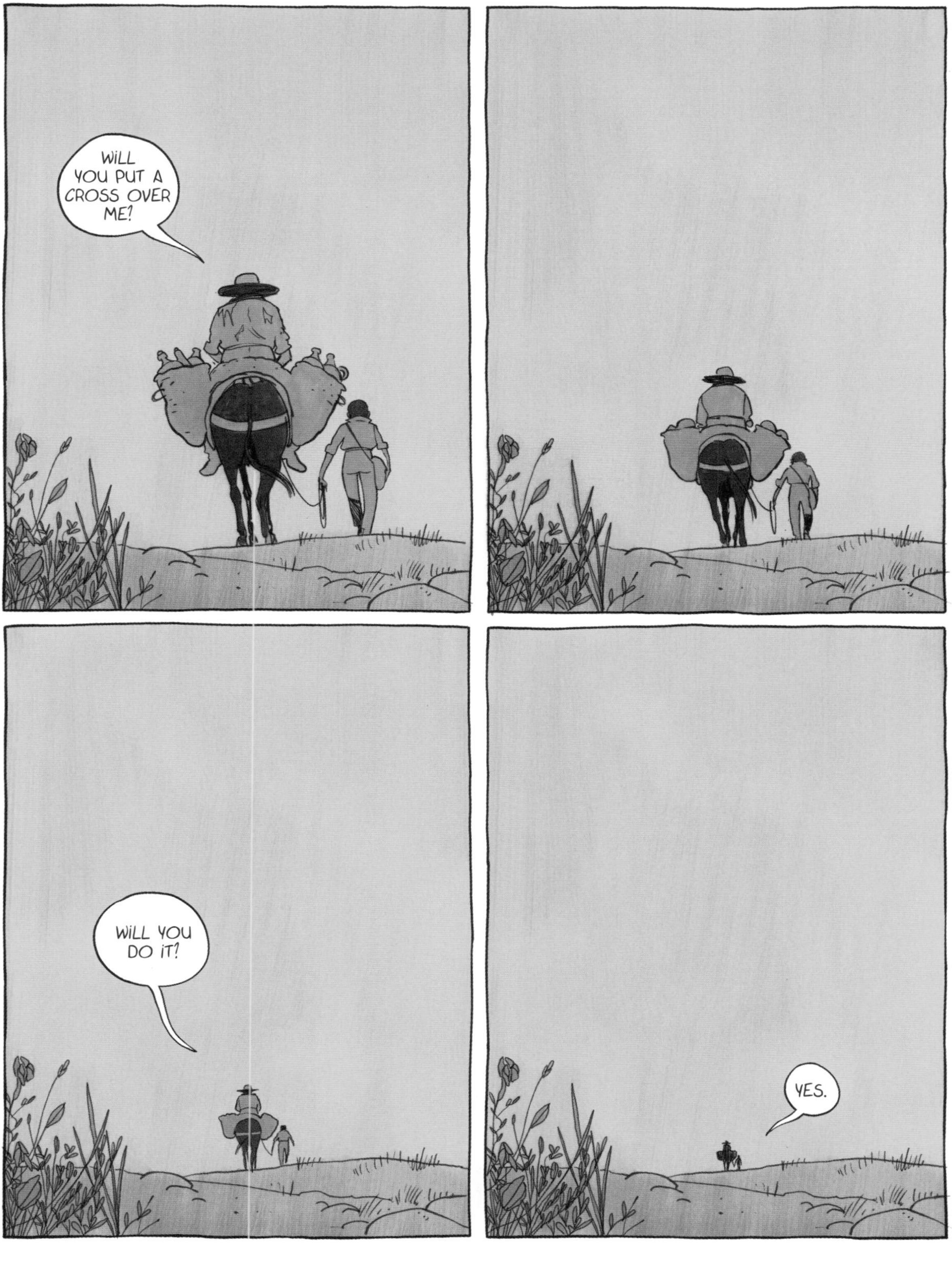
WiLL YOU PUT A CROSS OVER ME?
WiLL YOU DO iT?
YES.

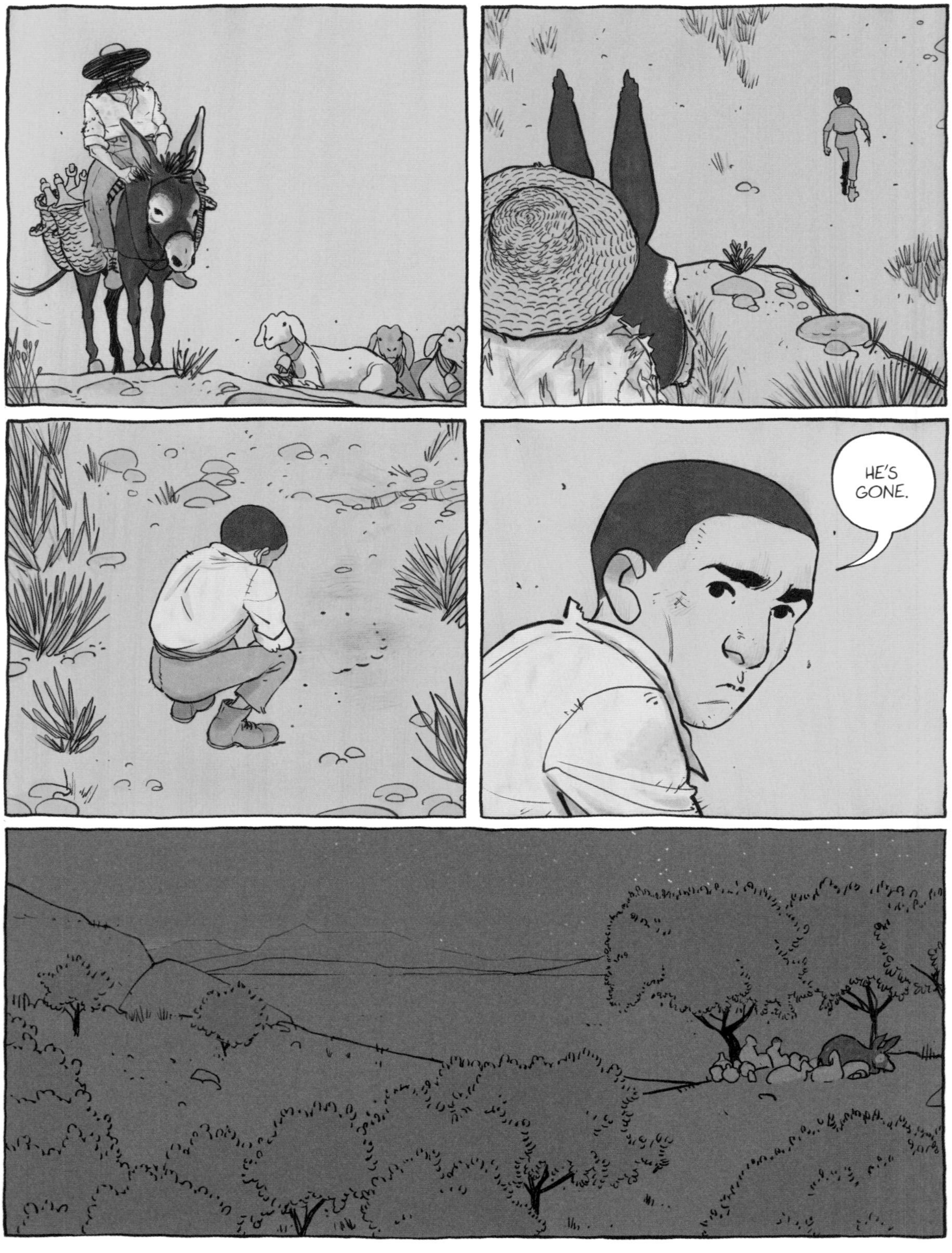
HE'S GONE.

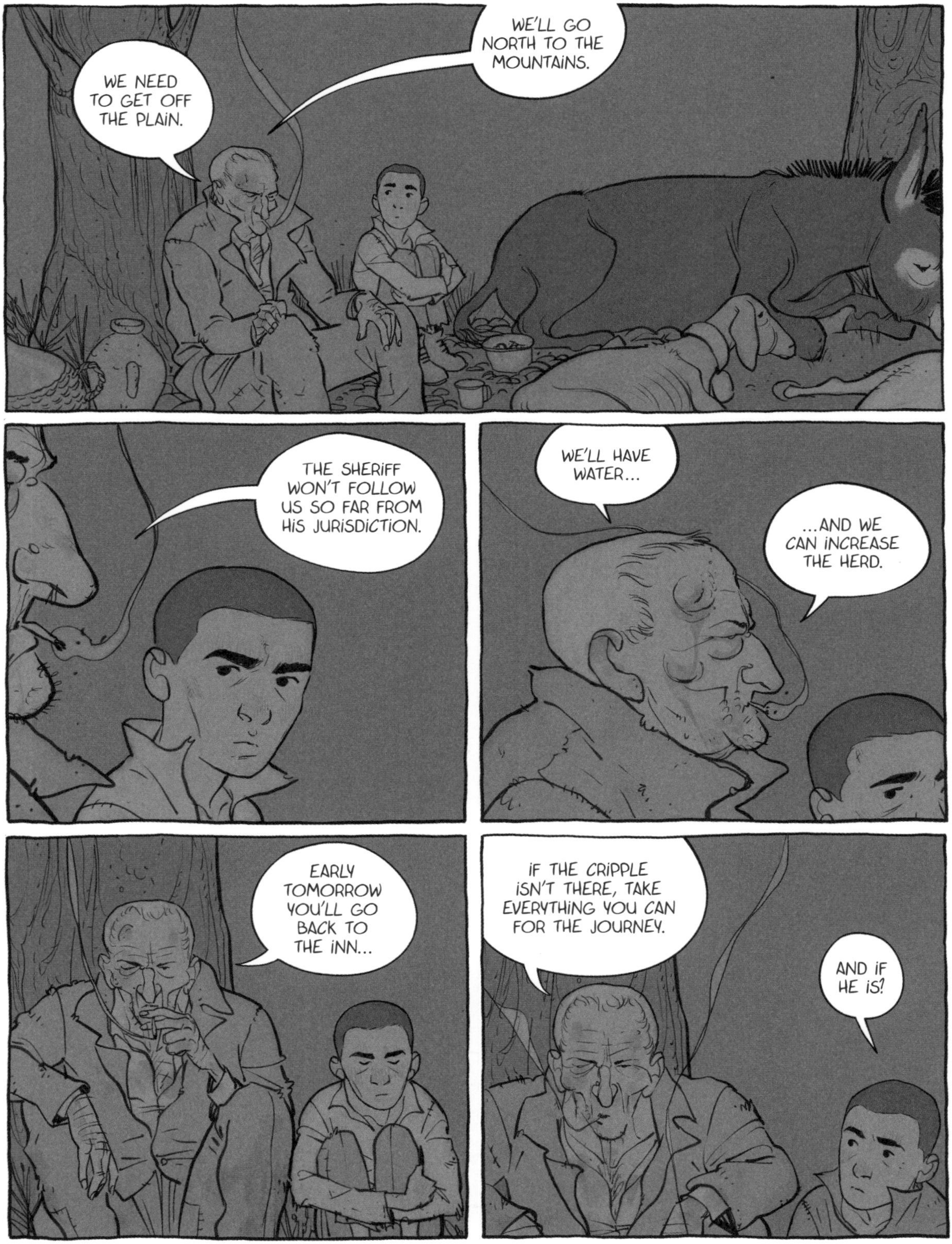
WE NEED TO GET OFF THE PLAIN.
WE'LL GO NORTH TO THE MOUNTAINS.
THE SHERIFF WON'T FOLLOW US SO FAR FROM HIS JURISDICTION.
WE'LL HAVE WATER...
...AND WE CAN INCREASE THE HERD.
EARLY TOMORROW YOU'LL GO BACK TO THE INN...
IF THE CRIPPLE ISN'T THERE, TAKE EVERYTHING YOU CAN FOR THE JOURNEY.
AND IF HE IS?

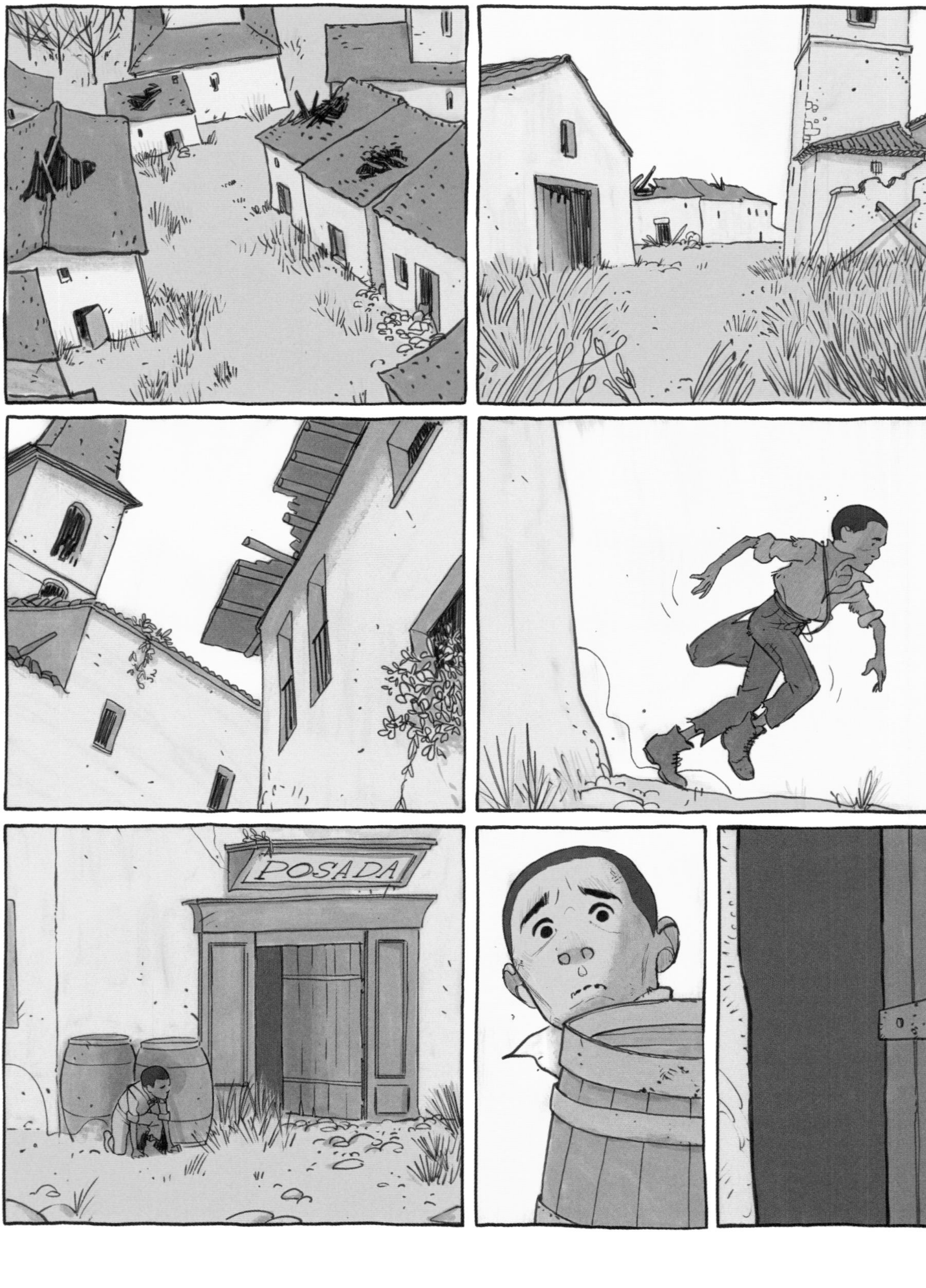
POSADA

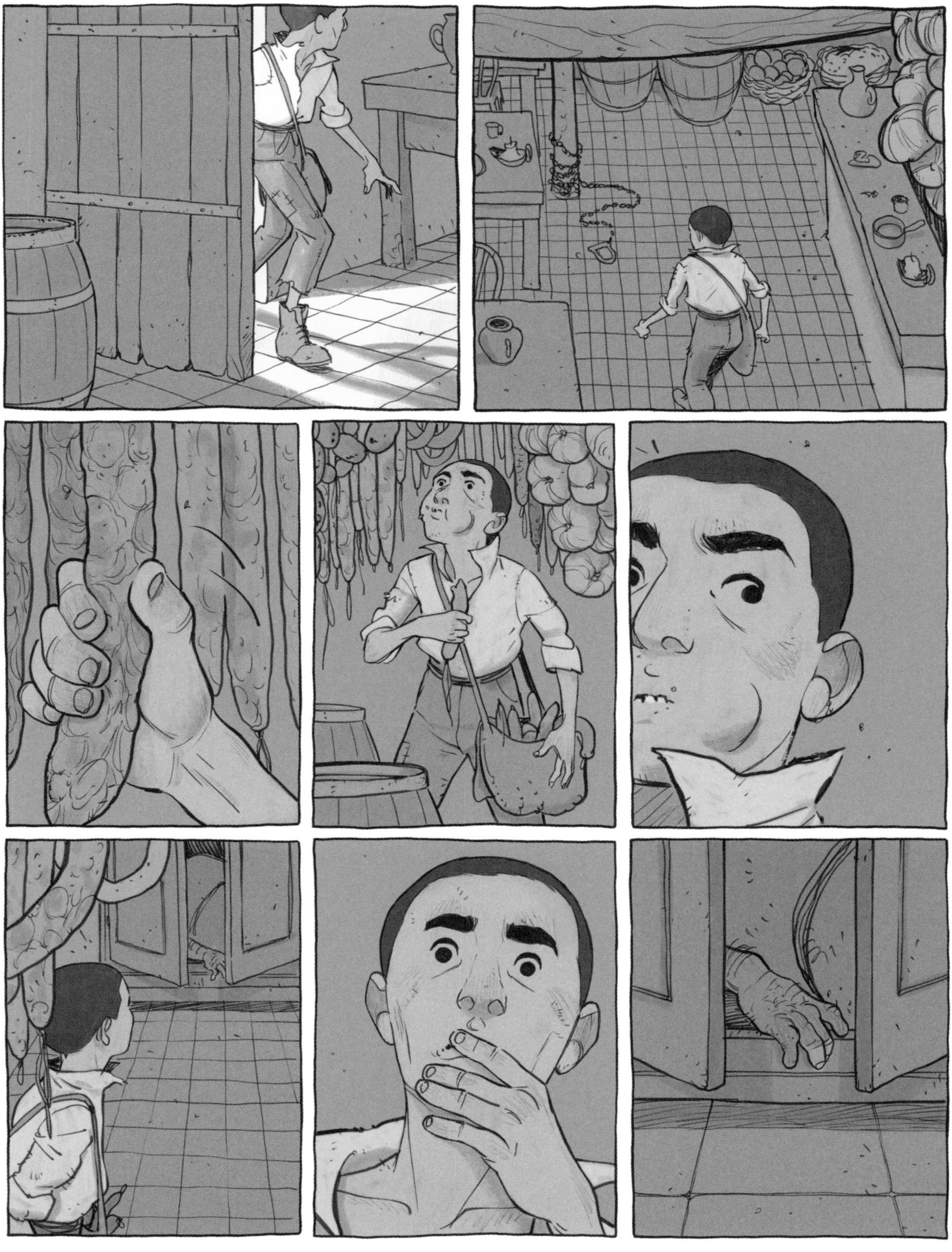

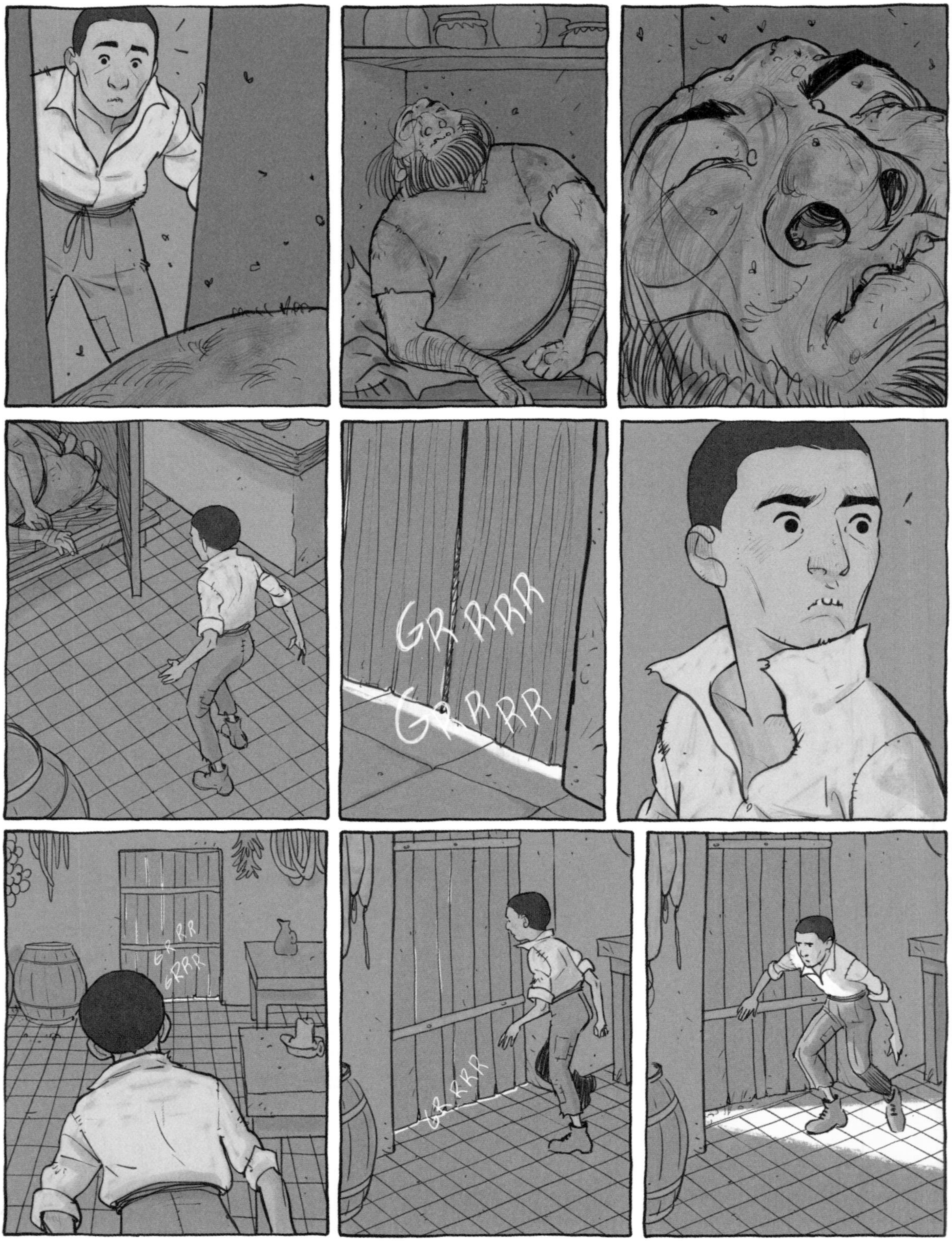
GRRRR
GRRRR
GRRR
GRRR
GRRRR

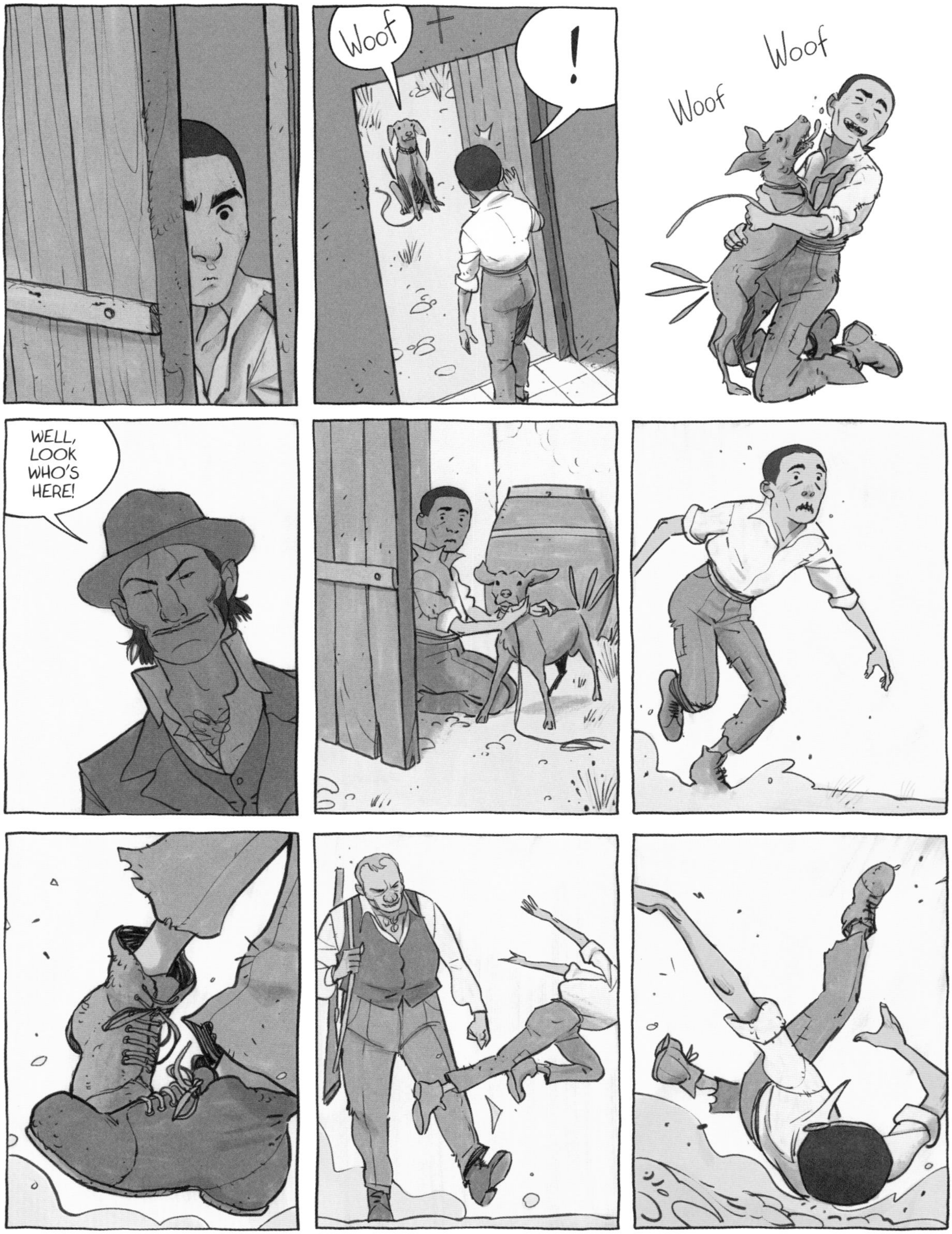
Woof
!
Woof
Woof
WELL, LOOK WHO'S HERE!

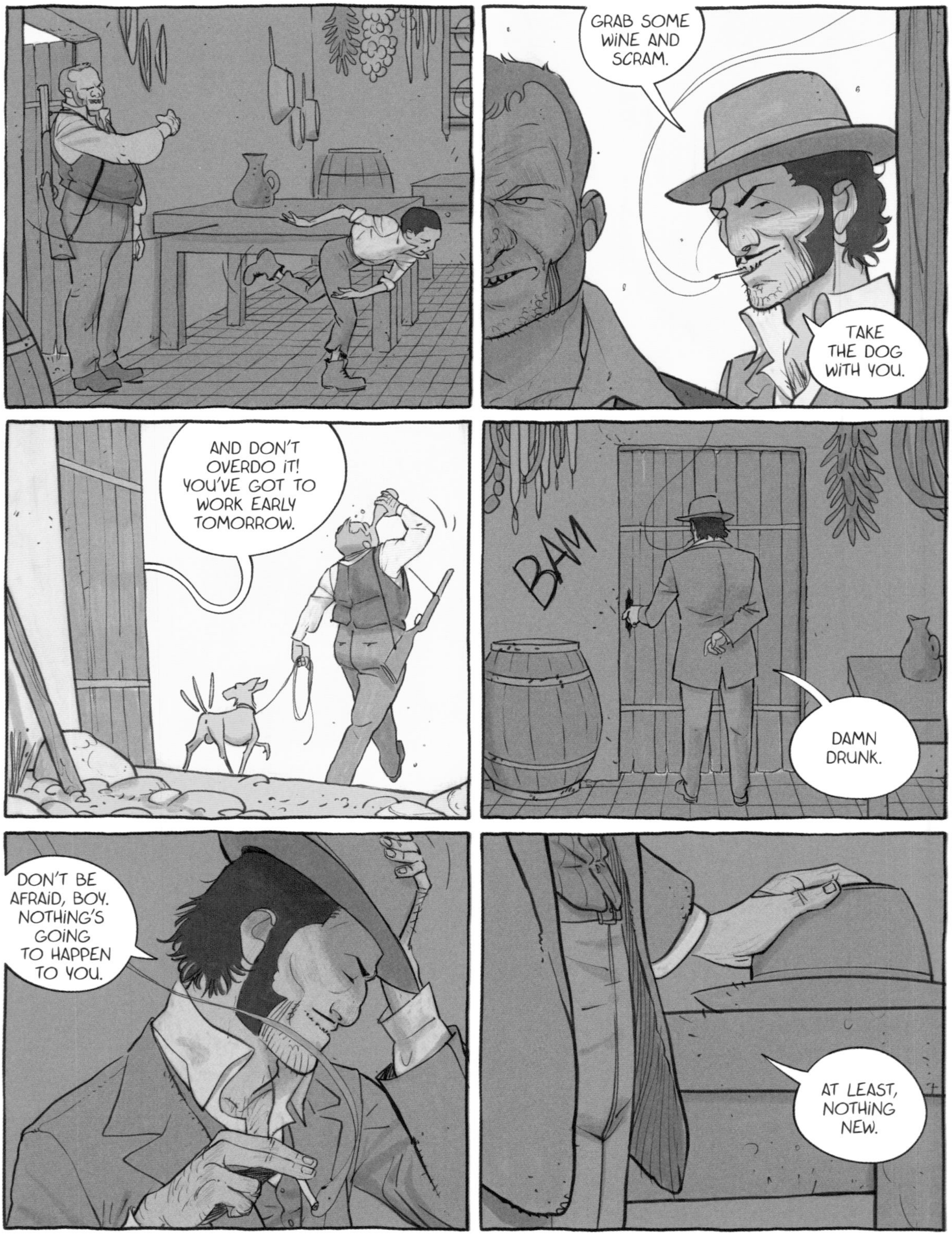
GRAB SOME WINE AND SCRAM.
TAKE THE DOG WITH YOU.
AND DON'T OVERDO IT! YOU'VE GOT TO WORK EARLY TOMORROW.
BAM
DAMN DRUNK.
DON'T BE AFRAID, BOY. NOTHING'S GOING TO HAPPEN TO YOU.
AT LEAST, NOTHING NEW.

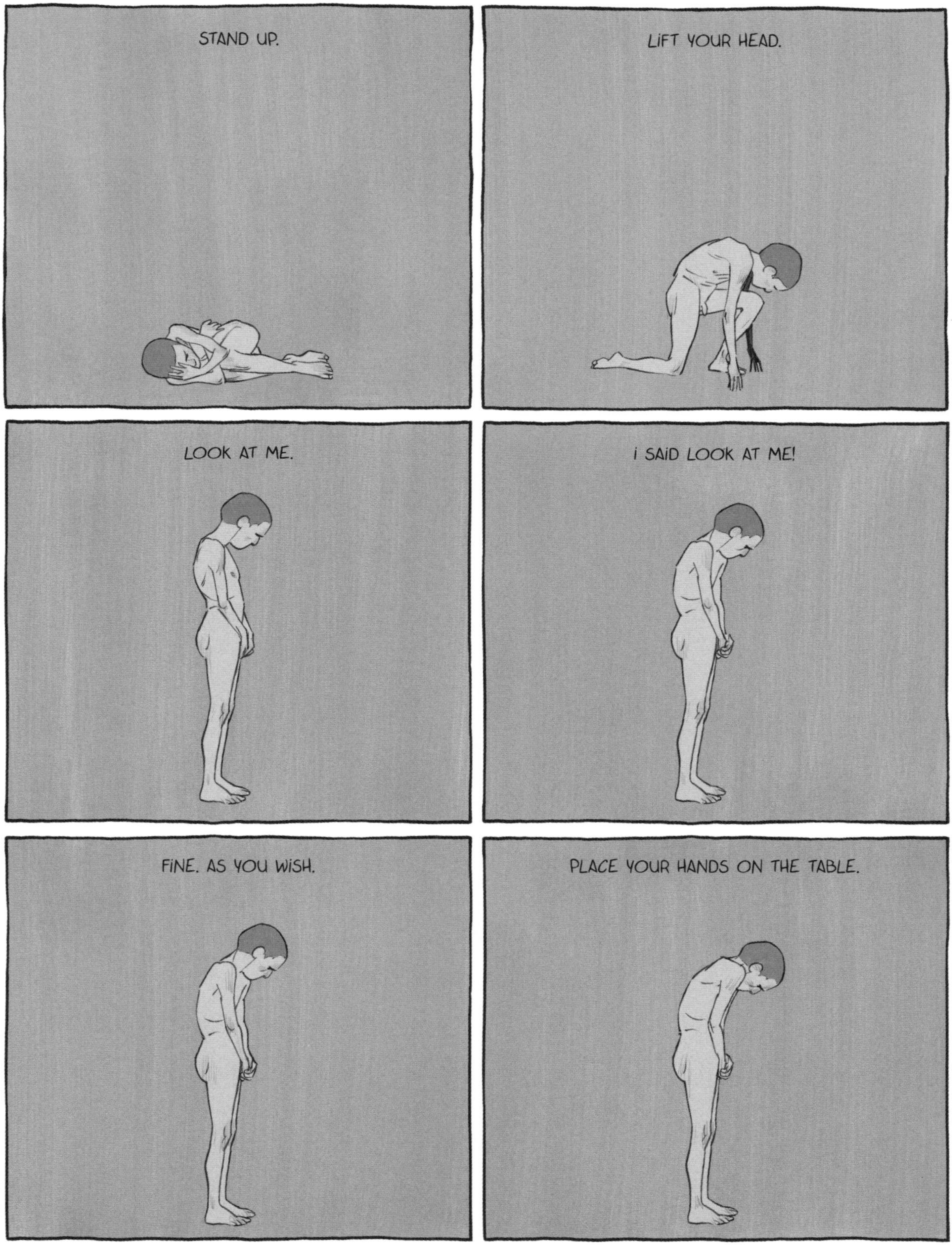
STAND UP.
LIFT YOUR HEAD.
LOOK AT ME.
I SAID LOOK AT ME!
FINE. AS YOU WISH.
PLACE YOUR HANDS ON THE TABLE.

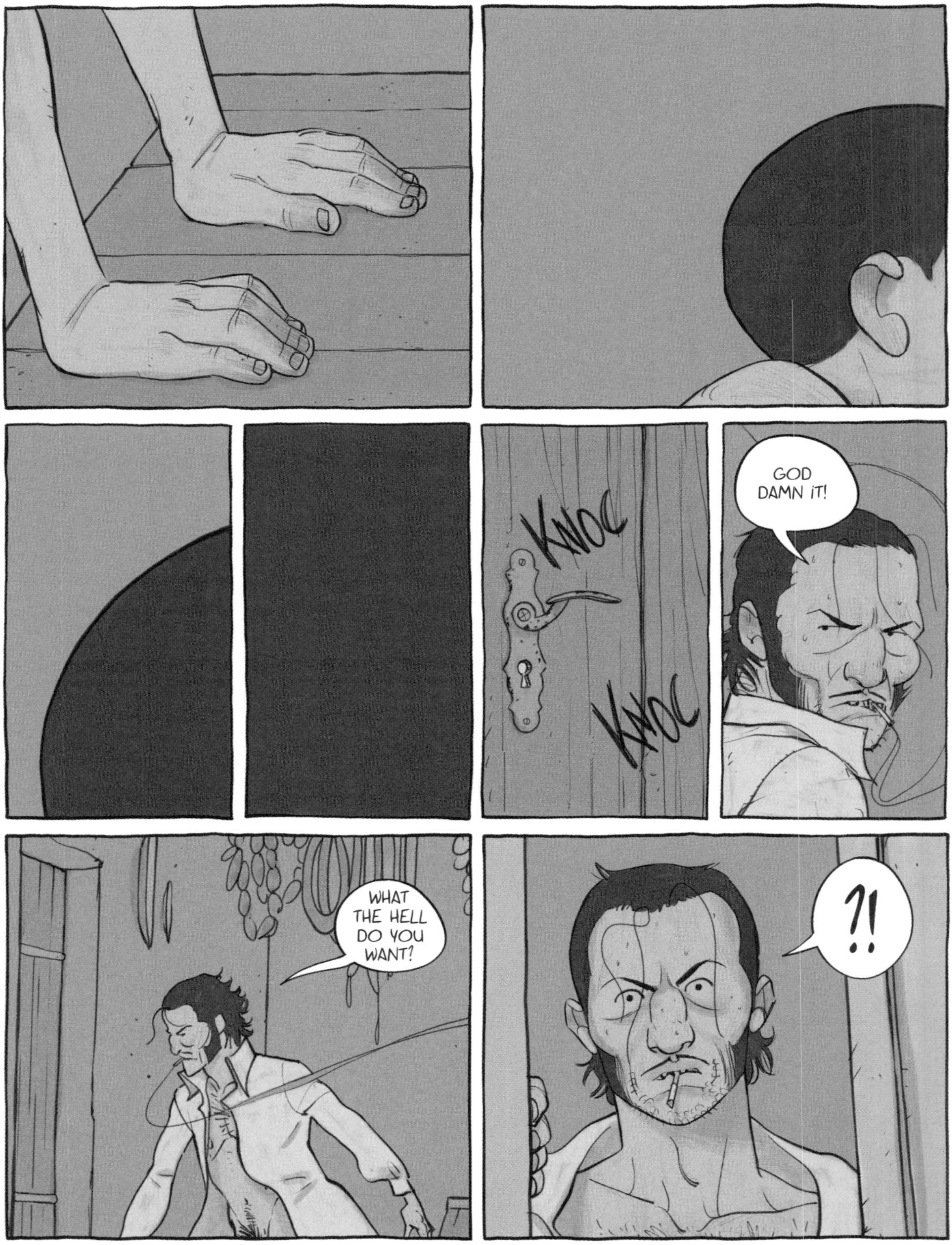
KNOC
KNOC
GOD DAMN IT!
WHAT THE HELL DO YOU WANT?
?!

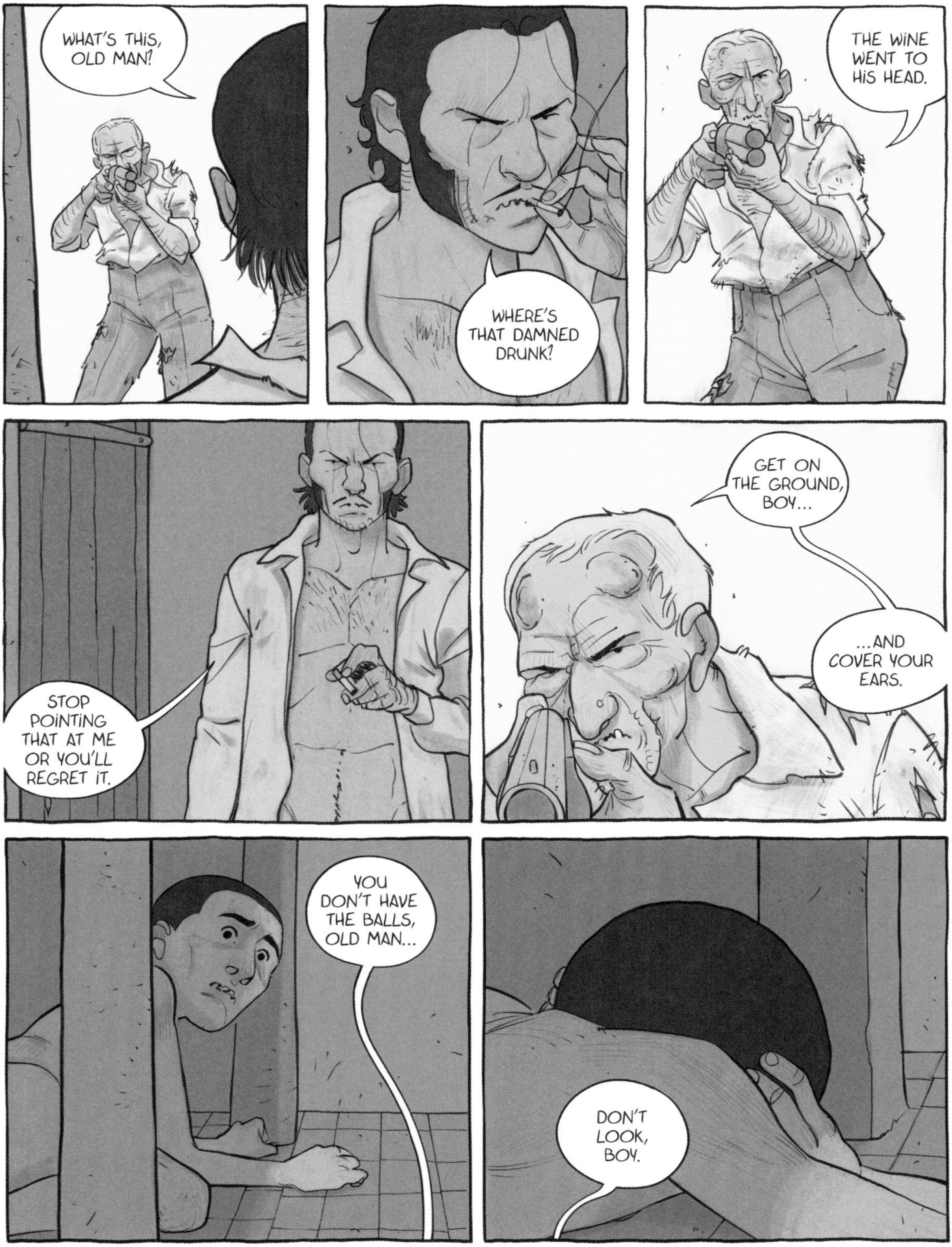
WHAT'S THIS, OLD MAN?
WHERE'S THAT DAMNED DRUNK?
THE WINE WENT TO HIS HEAD.
STOP POINTING THAT AT ME OR YOU'LL REGRET IT.
GET ON THE GROUND, BOY...
...AND COVER YOUR EARS.
YOU DON'T HAVE THE BALLS, OLD MAN...
DON'T LOOK, BOY.

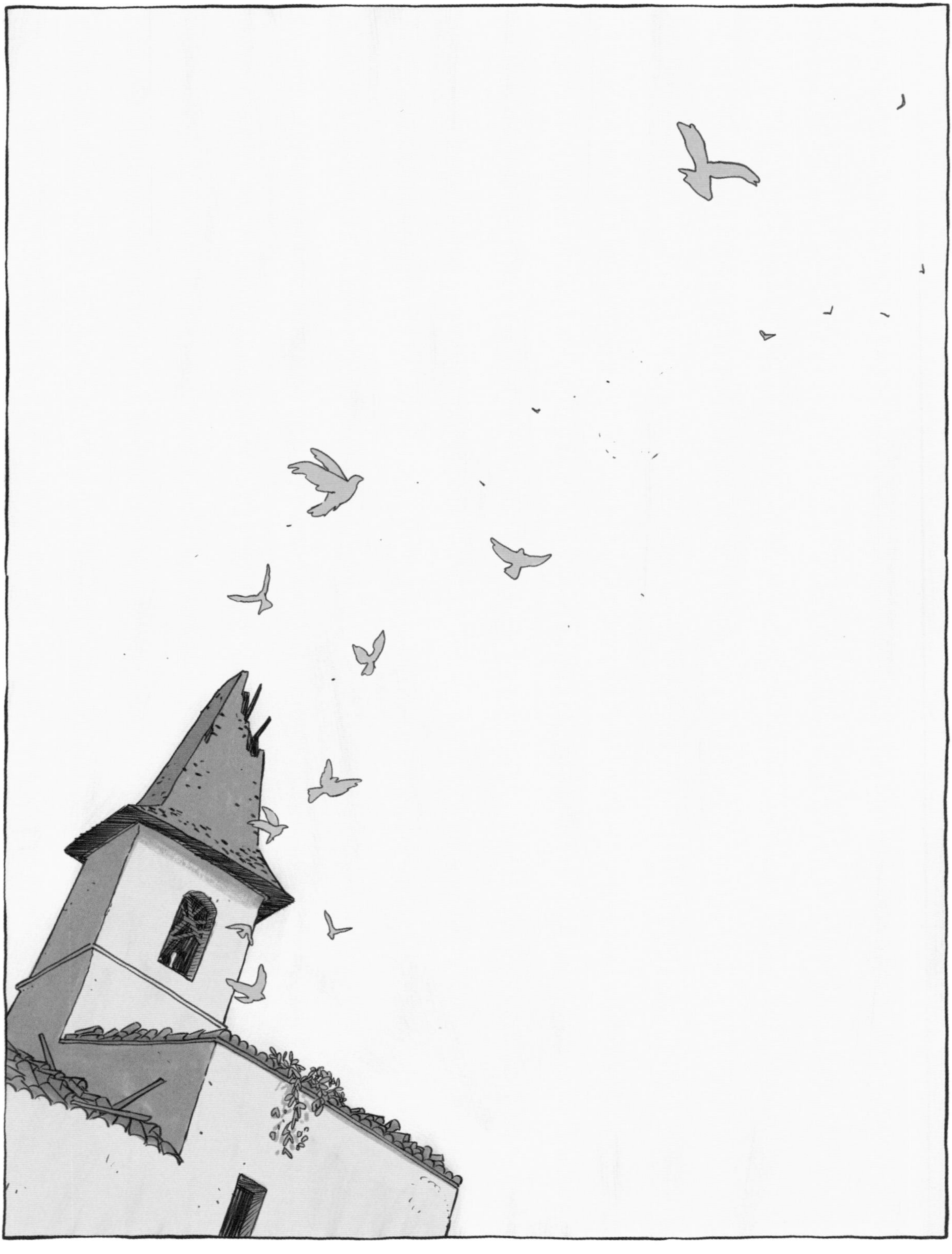

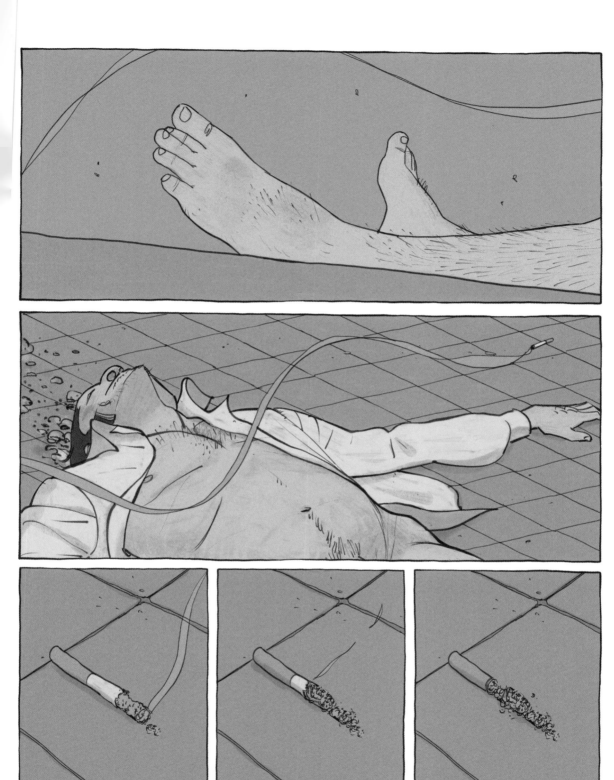

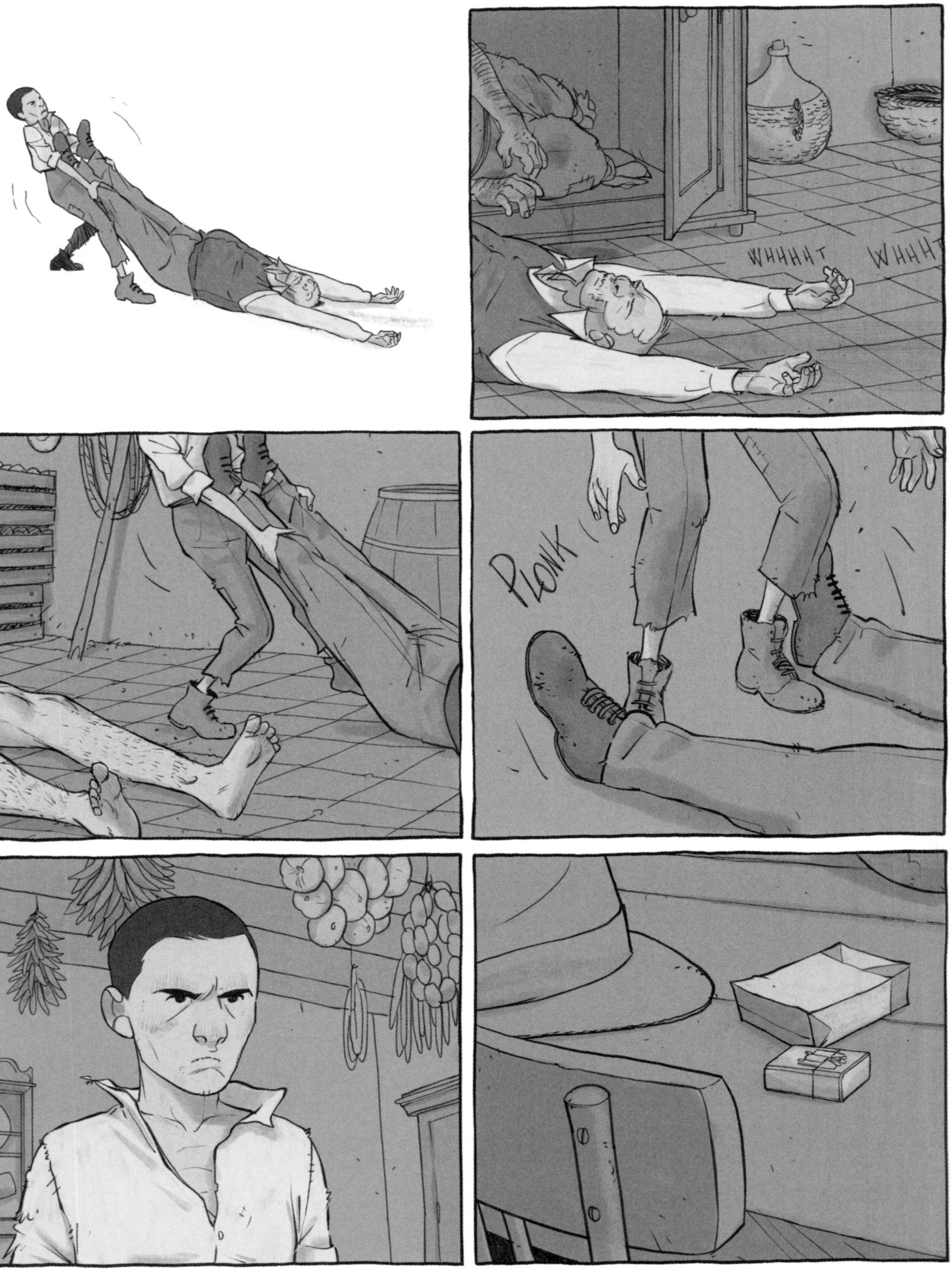
WHHHHT
WHHHT
PLONK

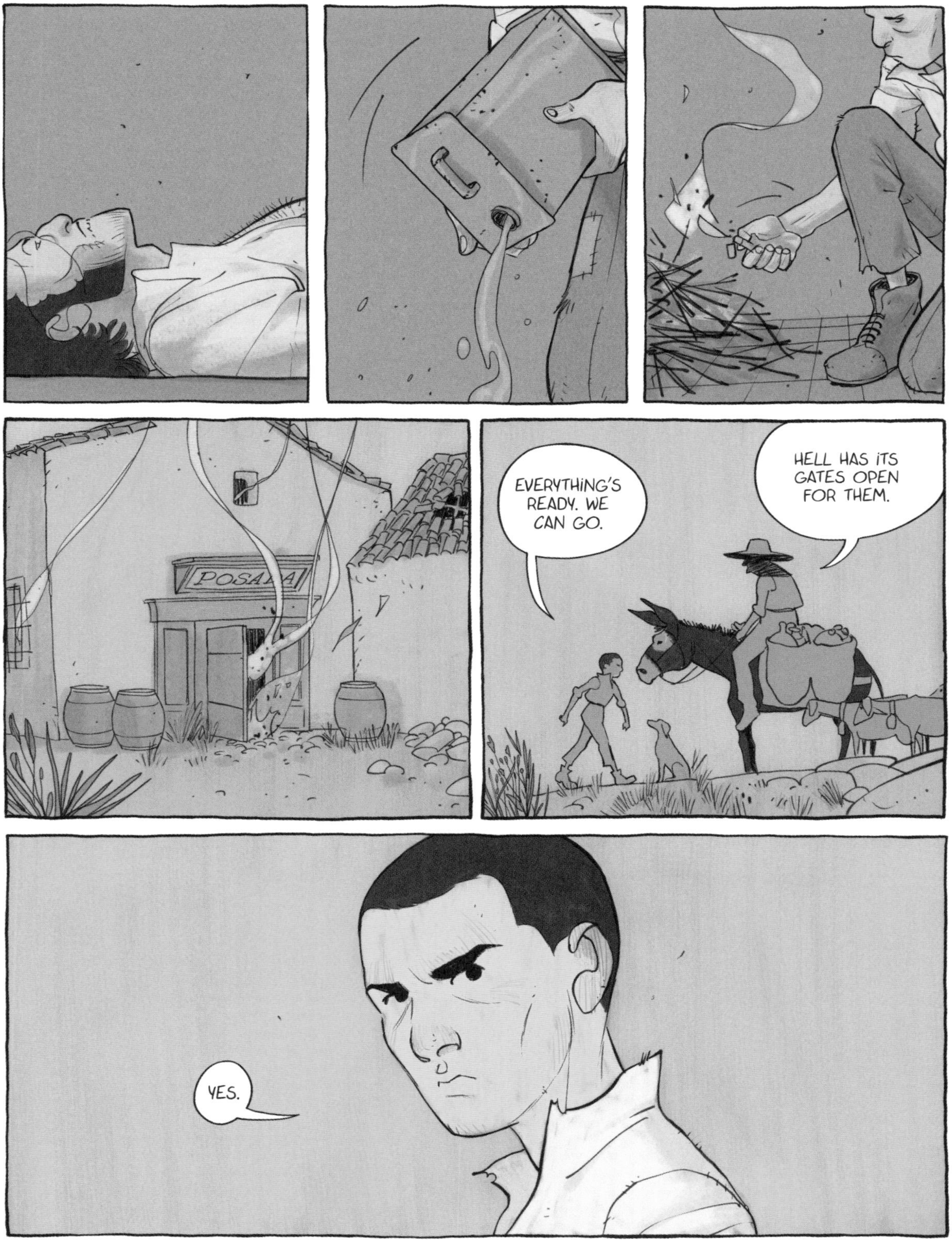
POSADA
EVERYTHING'S READY. WE CAN GO.
HELL HAS ITS GATES OPEN FOR THEM.
YES.

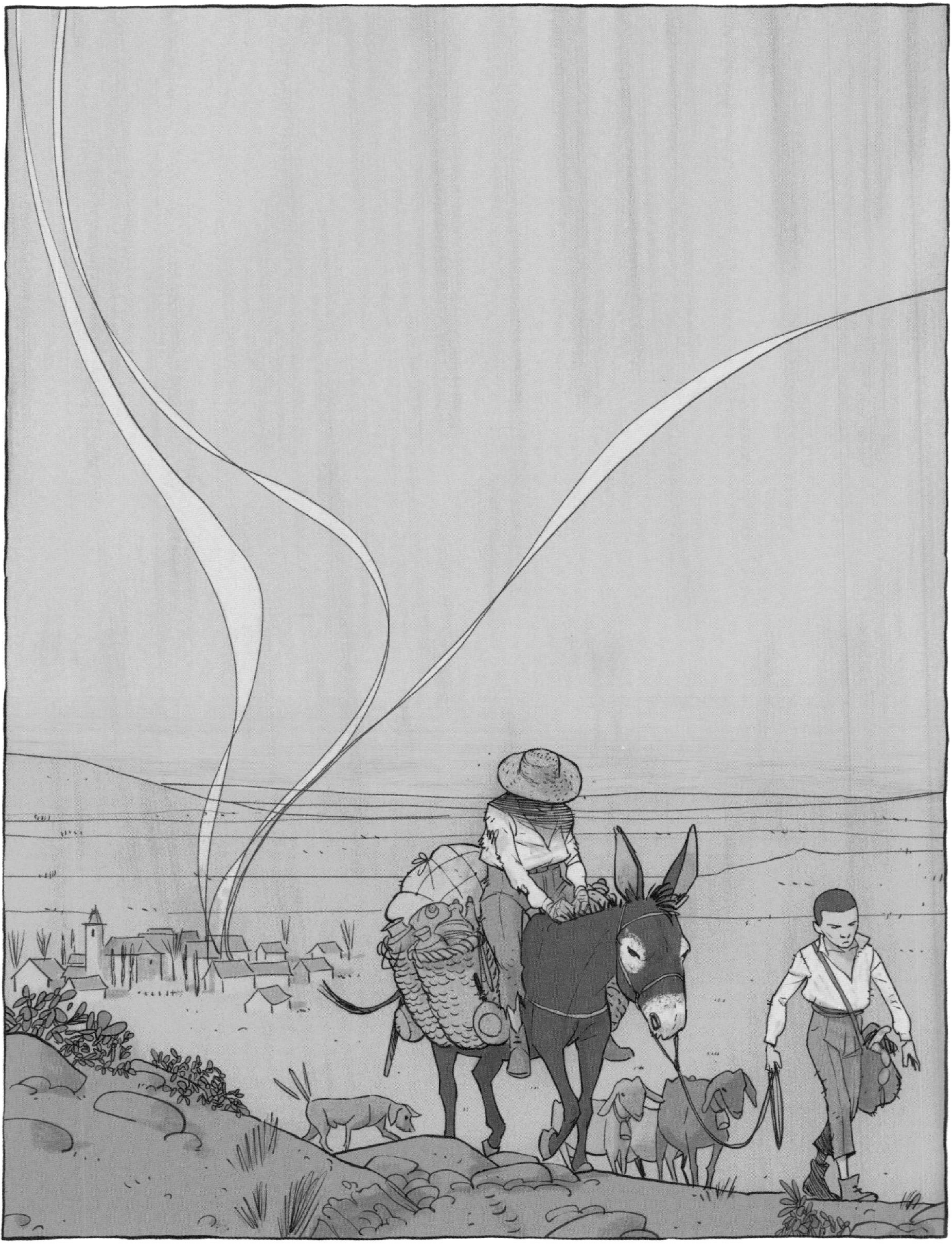

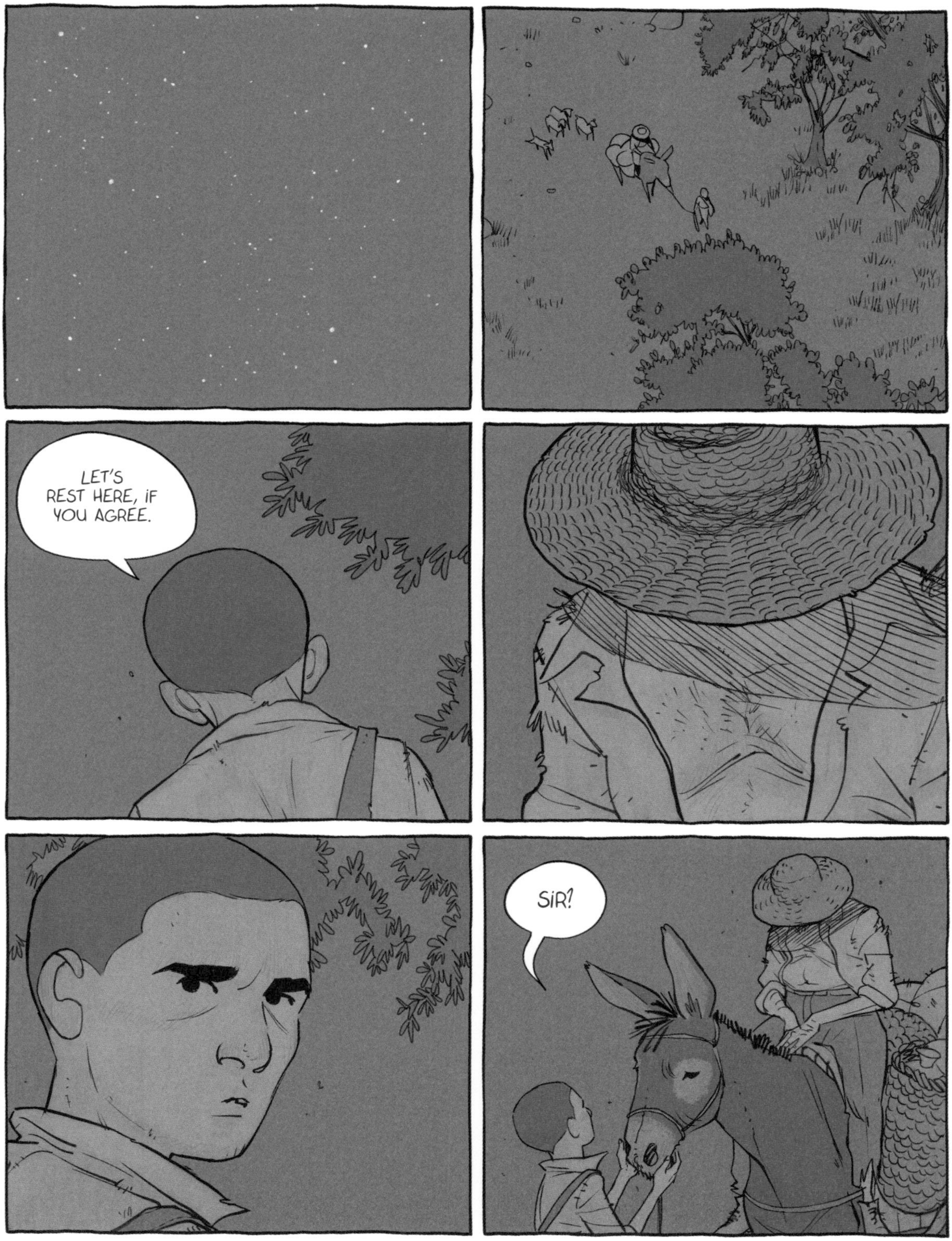
LET'S REST HERE, IF YOU AGREE.
SIR?

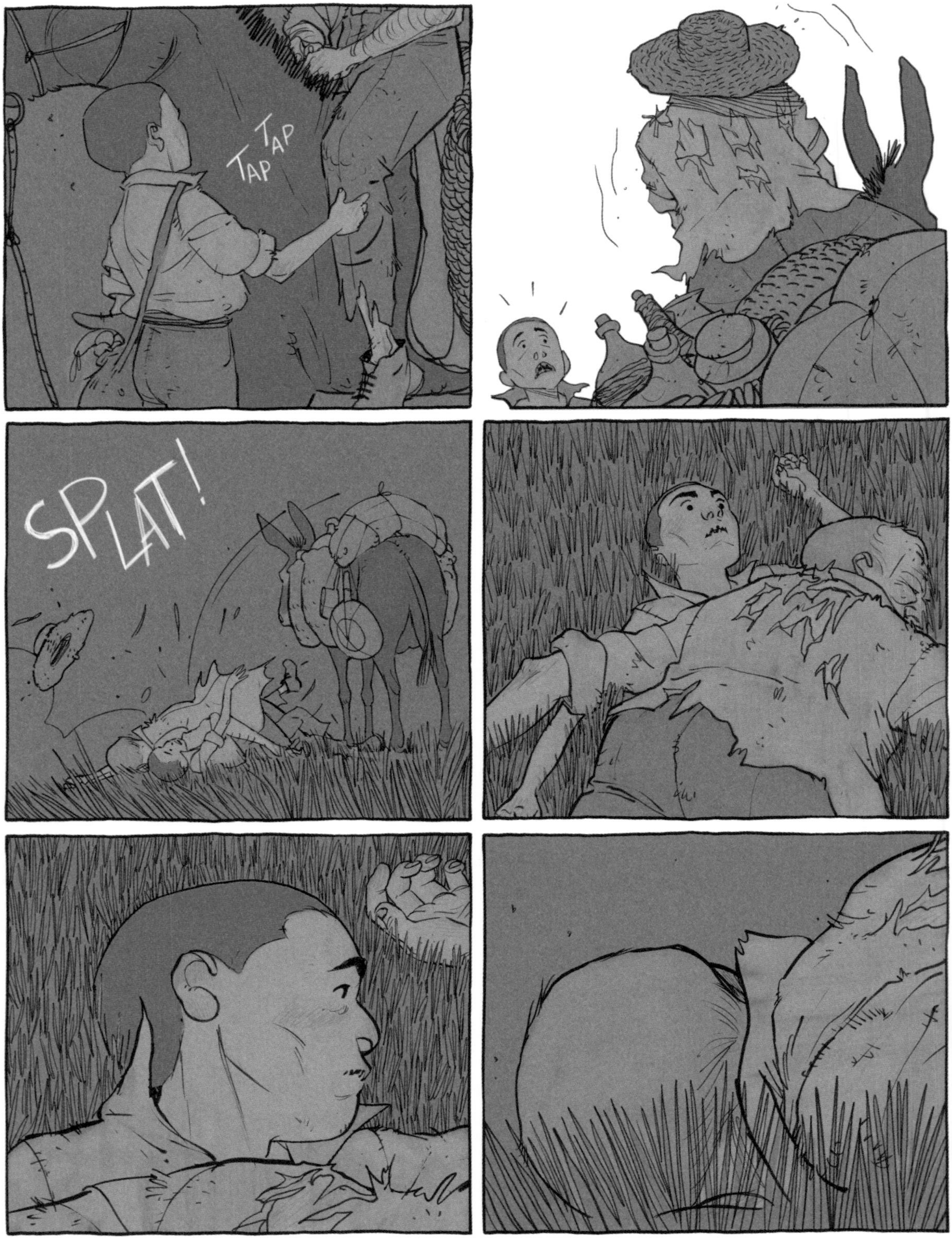
TAP
TAP
SPLAT!

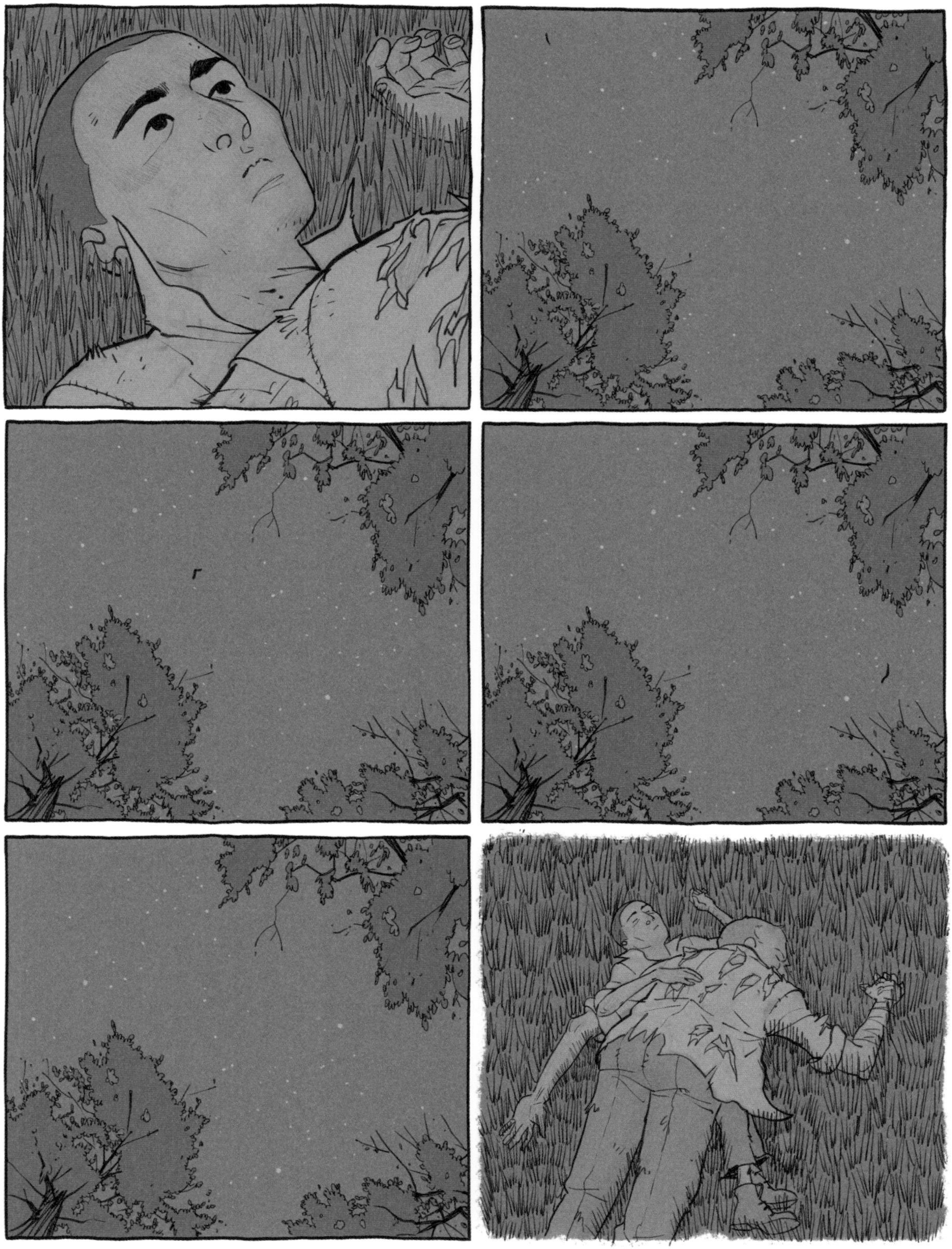

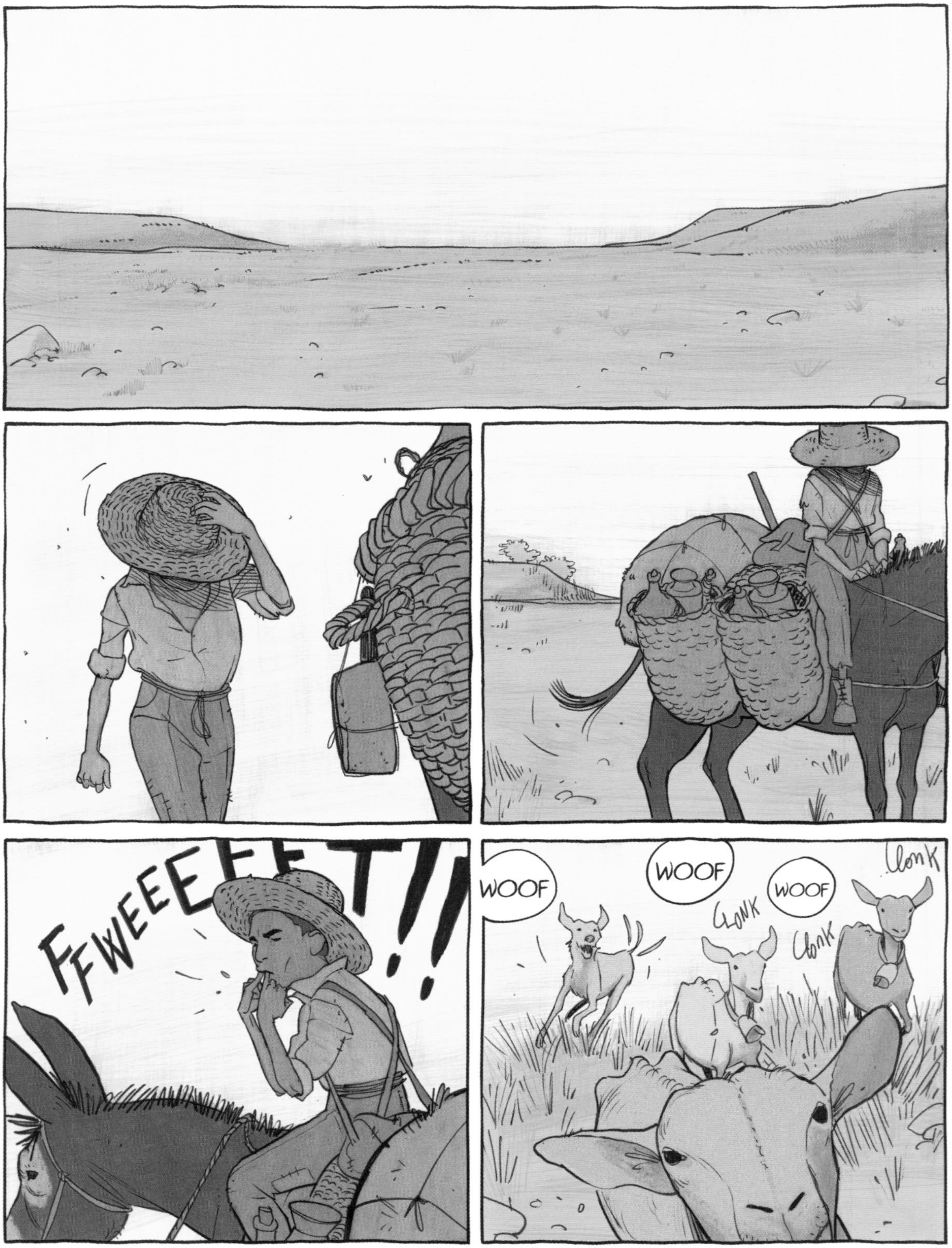
FFWEEEEET!!
WOOF
WOOF
WOOF
CLONK
CLONK
CLONK

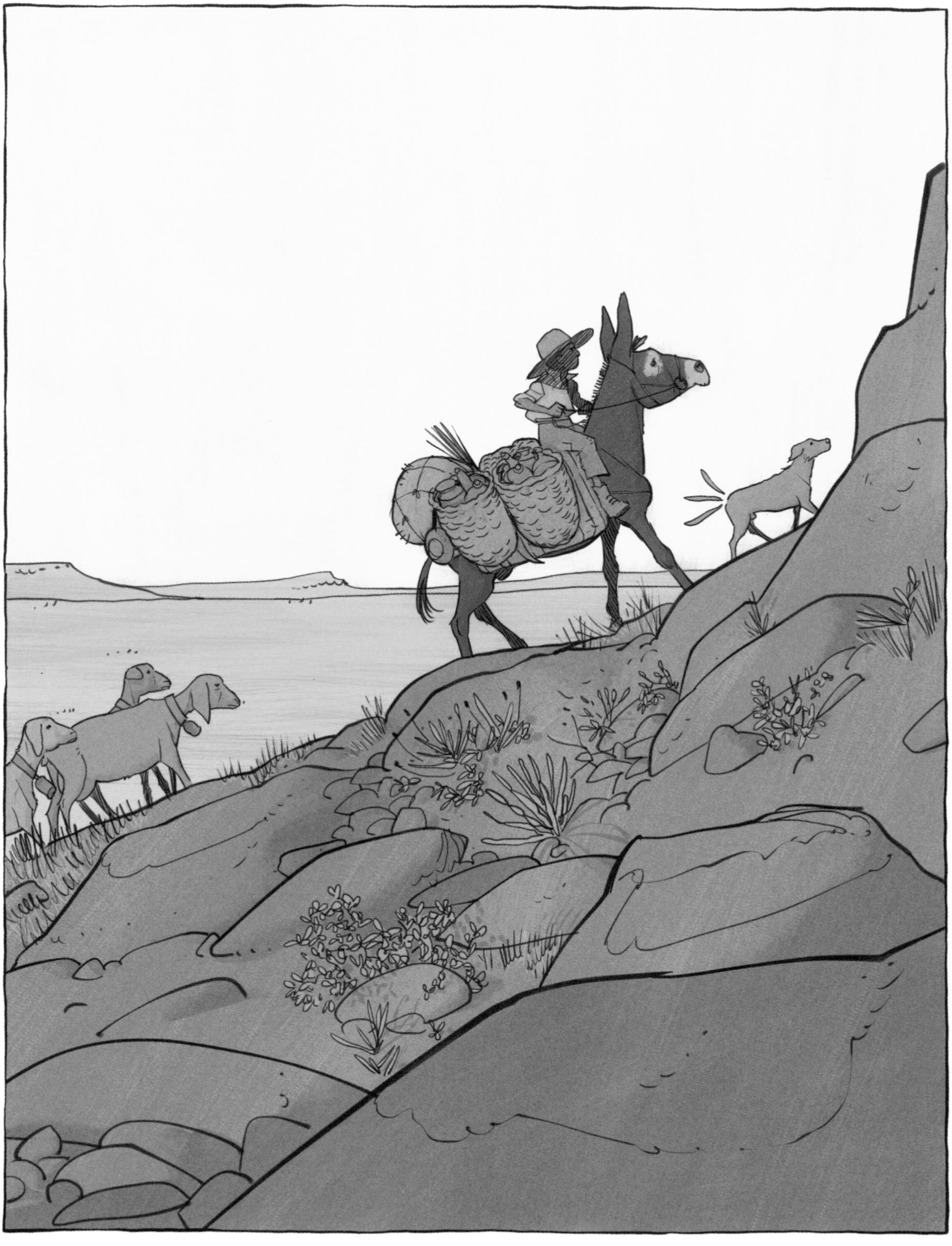

Epilogue

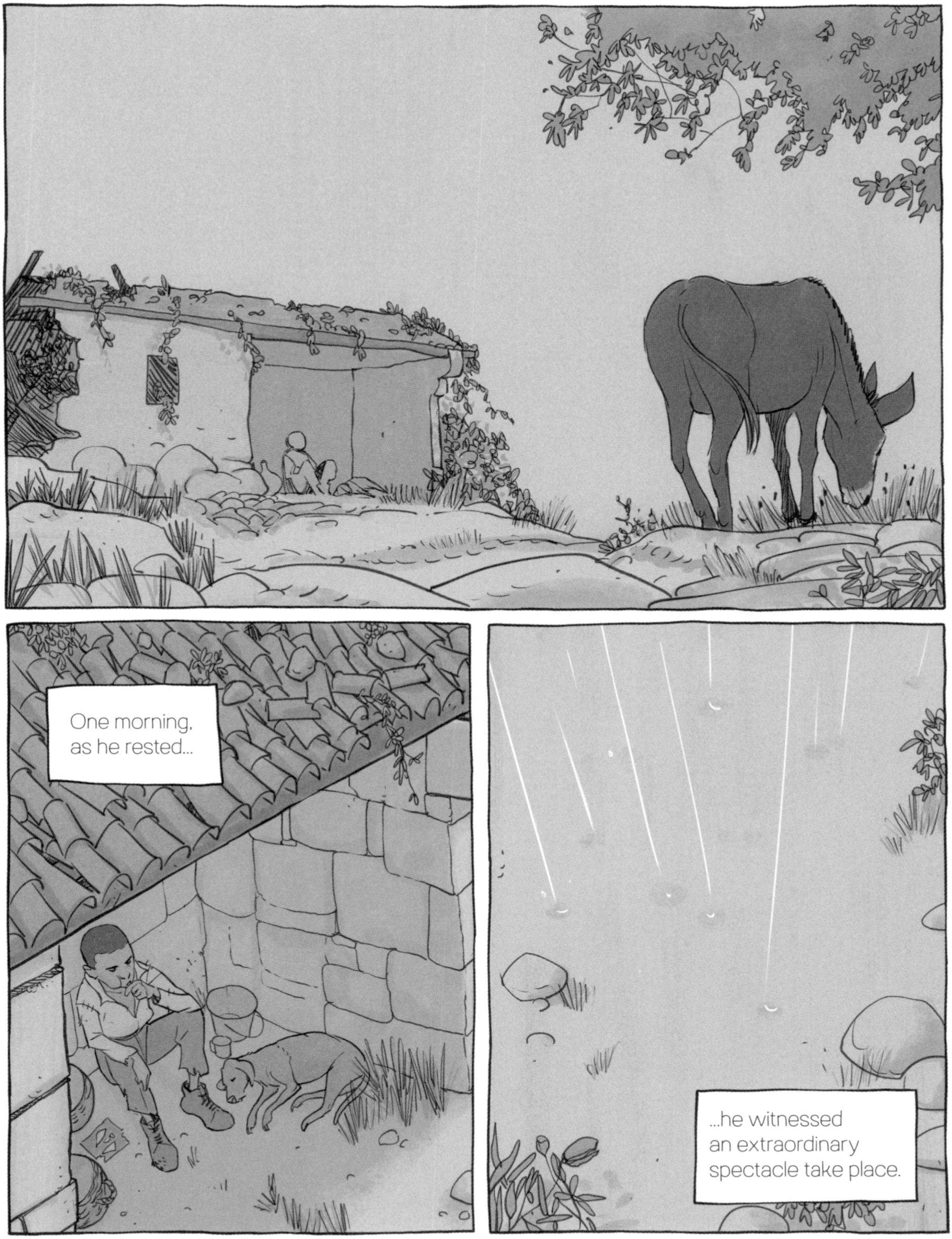
One morning, as he rested...
...he witnessed an extraordinary spectacle take place.

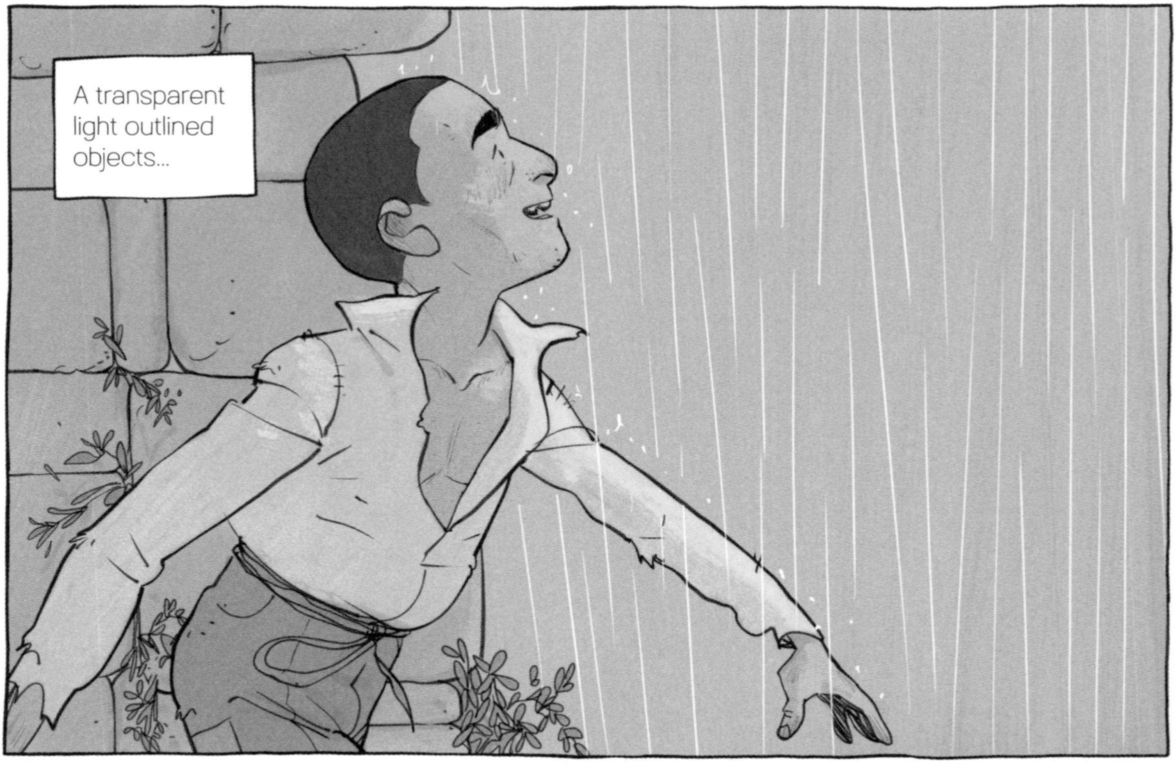
A transparent light outlined objects...

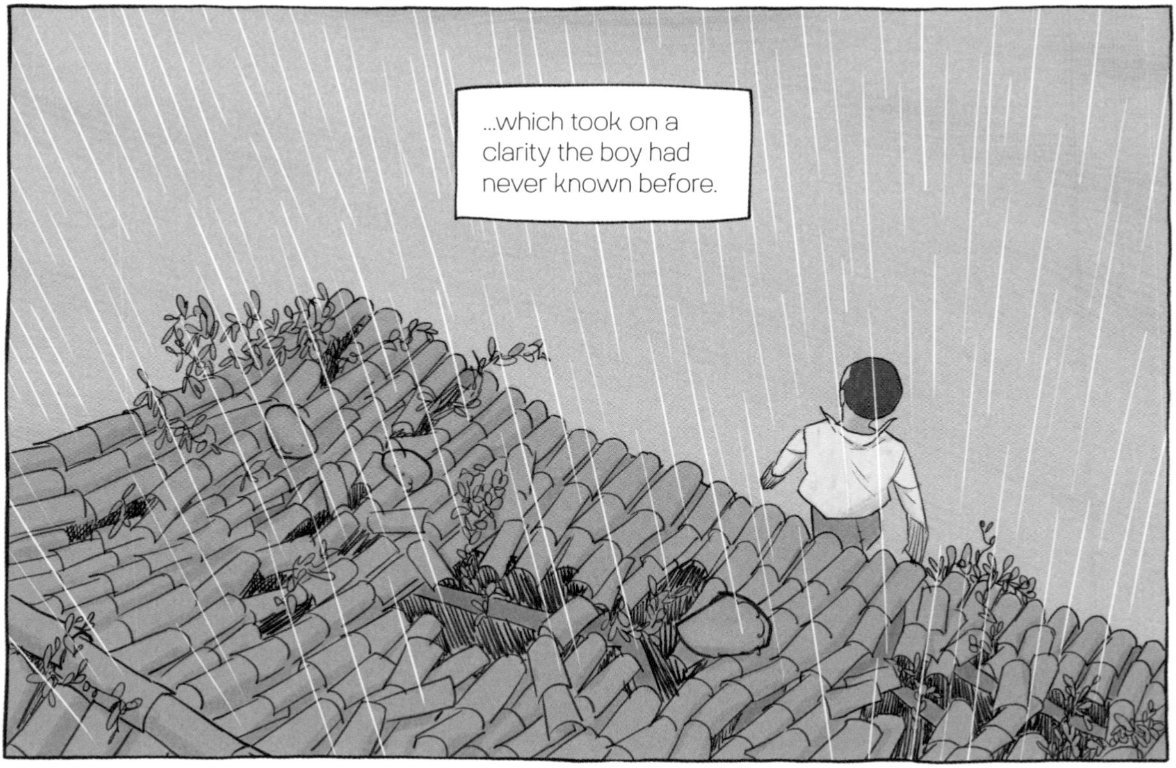
...which took on a clarity the boy had never known before.

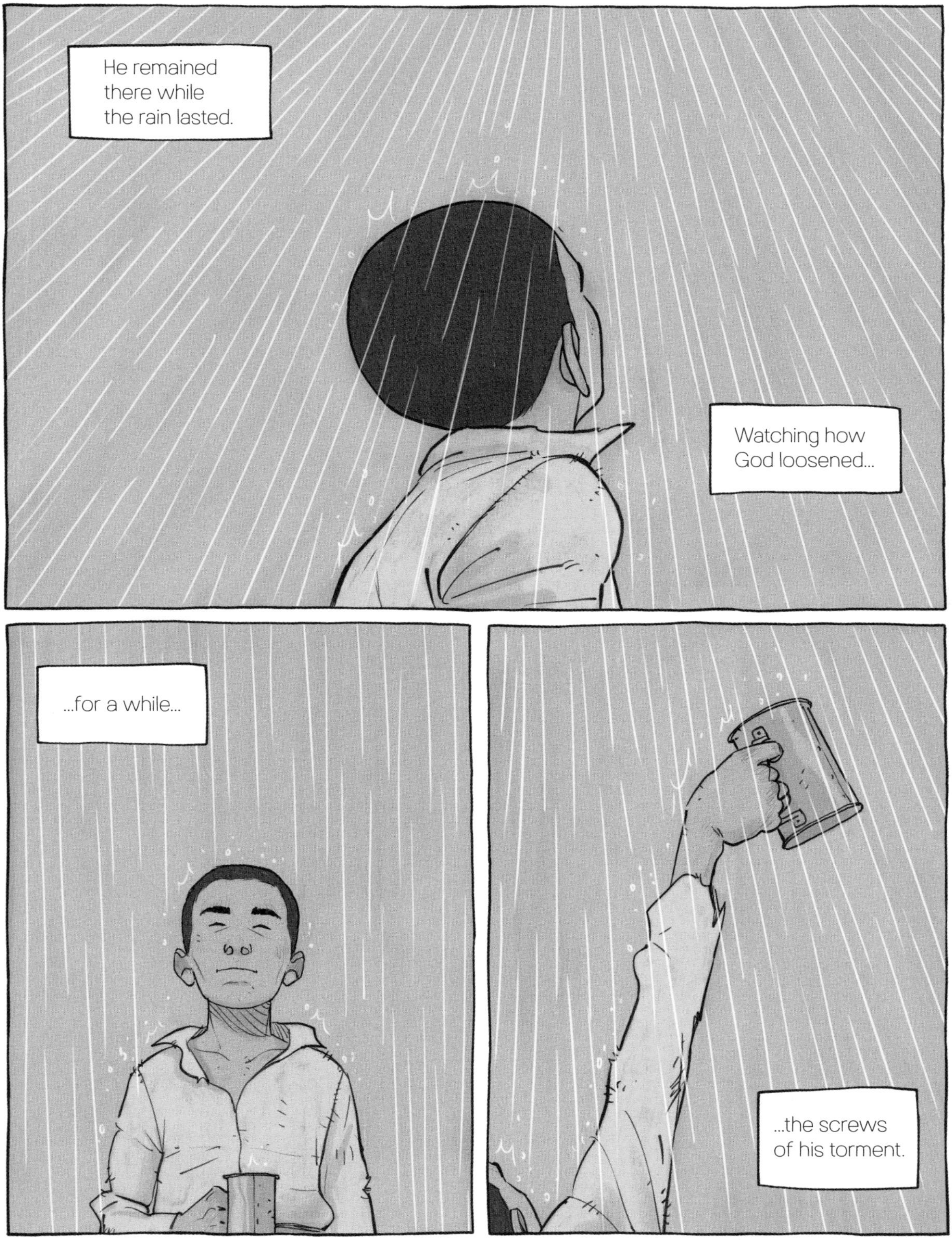
He remained there while the rain lasted.
Watching how God loosened...
...for a while...
...the screws of his torment.

END